WHITE THUNDER

Books by Aimée and David Thurlo

Ella Clah Novels

Blackening Song
Death Walker
Bad Medicine
Enemy Way
Shooting Chant
Red Mesa
Changing Woman
Tracking Bear
Wind Spirit
White Thunder

Lee Nez Novels

Second Sunrise
Blood Retribution

Sister Agatha Novels

Bad Faith
Thief in Retreat

Plant Them Deep
The Spirit Line

WHITE THUNDER

✕ ✕ ✕ ✕ ✕

AN ELLA CLAH NOVEL

AIMÉE & DAVID THURLO

A Tom Doherty Associates Book
New York

WHITE THUNDER

Copyright © 2005 by Aimée and David Thurlo

This book is printed on acid-free paper.

A Forge Book
Published by Tom Doherty Associates, LLC
175 Fifth Avenue
New York, NY 10010

www.tor.com

Forge® is a registered trademark of Tom Doherty Associates, LLC.

Library of Congress Cataloging-in-Publication Data

Thurlo, Aimée.
    White thunder : an Ella Clah novel / Aimée & David Thurlo.—1st ed.
      p. cm.
    "A Tom Doherty Associates book."
    ISBN 0-765-31174-7 (alk. paper)
    EAN 978-0765-31174-0
    1. Clah, Ella (Fictitious character)—Fiction. 2. Government investigators—Fiction. 3. Police—New Mexico—Fiction. 4. Missing persons—Fiction. 5. Navajo Indians—Fiction. 6. Navajo women—Fiction. 7. Policewomen—Fiction. 8. New Mexico—Fiction. I. Thurlo, David. II. Title.
    PS3570.H82W47 2005
    813'.54—dc22

                                2004056449

First Edition: April 2005

Printed in the United States of America

0 9 8 7 6 5 4 3 2 1

To M. N.
for all your help and support

ACKNOWLEDGMENTS

Special thanks to our Bureau and Tribal sources who prefer to remain anonymous, but never fail to answer our questions.

Also, a heartfelt thanks to everyone who helped make the Crime Stoppers Raffle such a success, particularly Page One Books, Destination Southwest, and our terrific publisher, Forge.

WHITE THUNDER

ONE

Day one

Special Investigator Ella Clah could feel the promise of rain in the cool breeze coming in her open driver's side window. The wind had a fresh and clean scent, as if it had just passed through a cloud.

It was September and New Mexico's rainy season was tapering off. A three-year drought had plagued the land and most of the storms had amounted to nothing more than howling wind, blowing dust, and darkened skies. Mother Earth was parched, and animals had gone hungry as they'd searched for something other than cheat grass and snakeweed to graze on. Some kinds of snakeweed could poison livestock, and cheat grass would cut their mouths. But in a drought year, pickings were slim and their choices few.

Yet, today, there was a good change in the air. Dark gray clouds had formed over the mountains and the slanted streaks in the sky above Ute Mountain were more than just virga, or what her mother called false rain, that evaporated before it reached the ground. With luck, they'd have a downpour that would fill the smaller arroyos.

At thirty-four, Ella had seen droughts come and go many times, but she couldn't remember it ever being this bad. She could feel the hopelessness of the older Navajos who sometimes stood by their barren fields, wondering when the rains would return.

At one time, the People had used ceremonies to ease a drought, but most of the *hataaliis* these days didn't know the right Sings. Not that it mattered now. Truth was, when crops failed and food was scarce, no one had the money to pay for ceremonies anyway. Still, many prayed on their own for relief.

These were hard times even for the long-suffering Dineh, the People, but Ella was glad to be here on the reservation with her family. She'd faced death in an abandoned uranium mine shaft after a cave-in several months ago and, as a result of that experience, was grateful for each day, for the chance to see her daughter, Dawn, grow up, and for work that allowed her to help restore the balance between good and evil.

For Ella, it was a daily struggle to walk in beauty—to be in harmony with everything that surrounded her. Police work could be demanding and, at times, overwhelming. For years it had dominated everything she'd done. She'd been the servant, and her career the master. But things would be different now. Although she still loved her chosen profession, serving as a special investigator for the Navajo tribal police, she wouldn't let it rule her life anymore.

At least that was her new goal. One thing that deadly experience at the mine had taught her was that it didn't pay to plan things too carefully. Life always had the final say, and it seemed to take almost perverse pleasure in muddling everything up.

Ella thought of her daughter, Dawn. After the accident, aware of how quickly time passed, Ella had been determined to become an even greater part of her daughter's life. She'd wanted to start spending more quality time with her daughter, who was now nearly six and a half and in the second grade, but Dawn, an independent kid with a mind of her own, hadn't been interested in that prospect.

Undaunted at first, and knowing how much Dawn loved riding her pony, Ella had bought a horse so they could ride together. She'd envisioned long, heartwarming talks during trail rides that would become nothing less than bonding sessions. But the reality had turned out differently. Her daughter invariably spent the time they were out together chattering nonstop about her plans to compete in barrel racing someday.

Ella had made it clear that it wasn't a matter of age or size exclusively. She'd never give her permission to race on a horse until Dawn could demonstrate the required coordination and control needed, because it was dangerous. Yet Dawn still took every available opportunity to lobby for it, and Ella had to remind her to remain patient and continue building her skills.

Ella was just five minutes from the police station when a call came over the radio. She focused on the message, grateful for the interruption. Police work was infinitely easier to deal with than raising a child—she'd been trained in the former, after all. Parenting seemed more like trial-and-error learning these days.

"We have a probable burglary in progress," Dispatch told her, giving her an address on the south side of Shiprock across the bridge in the opposite direction. "May John, the neighbor, made the call. She says the home owner, Herbert Tapaha, is inside the residence. Tapaha's bedridden."

Ella recognized the name. The man had to be at least ninety by now. "I know the neighborhood. I'm ten minutes away—make that five."

"Backup should arrive in eight. Ten-four?"

"Ten-four."

Ella switched on the emergency lights, checked for traffic, then pulled over to her left, making a one-eighty across the median into the west-bound lanes.

They'd had problems with gangs again lately. Maybe it was just another kid searching for something to steal. But the elderly man would be easy prey and young gang-bangers, by and large, didn't care much about mercy or compassion.

Knowing sirens would warn the perps and set up a possible hostage situation, she opted for a silent approach. As she headed across the narrow steel trestle bridge fording the San Juan River, experience told her that this was the type of call that could end up going sour in an instant, particularly if the thief encountered the owner.

Ella switched off her emergency lights as she approached the residential area, which was just to the right of old Highway 666, now renamed Highway 491 thanks to pressure from those who feared its old nickname, the Devil's Highway. Most of the houses in the low-income neighborhood were small wood-framed stucco and had been constructed forty or more years ago. Vehicles in various states of repair, mostly pickups or inexpensive sedans, were scattered along the street.

Her vehicle was unmarked but well-known in the community, so, watching the numbers on the street side mailboxes, Ella parked three houses down from Tapaha's home. The lack of curbs in the poorly developed area allowed residents to park almost anywhere and Ella spotted an old white compact sedan twenty feet from the front door of the pale green house. Farther back, along the side of the house, a weathered blue van with gray primer showing through was adjacent to an open window. No doubt this was the perp's vehicle.

Ella called the information in, then slipped out of her unit. She'd barely taken a step when a Navajo woman came rushing up to her. The neighbor was dressed in jeans and a maroon and gray football jersey, the local team's current colors. Her dark hair was peppered liberally with silver and her eyes were round and wide with excitement. Her arms were in constant motion as her words came tumbling out in a rush.

"I'm May John. You're Officer Clah, right? Herbert, the owner, is in that house, I'm sure of it because his car's there. I watched from my house while that kid parked his van by the side window and crawled inside. Well, the window was already open so maybe he didn't really break in. But he wasn't invited into the house, that's for sure."

"Did you recognize the kid?" Ella asked. She knew which gang members were likely to present major trouble, and an ID would let her know roughly what to expect.

"No, I don't know who it was, but I did catch a glimpse of him," May said, her eyes narrowing as she tried to remember the details. "He's Navajo, or at least Indian, and tall and thin, wearing a dark T-shirt and tan, baggy pants."

That was the general "uniform" of several reservation gangs these days. Once she saw the kid up close, identified the exact colors, plus any tattoos, she'd know for sure. "Was he carrying a weapon?"

"I don't know. . . ." Her eyes widened even more. "Do you think he had one?"

Ella raised her eyebrows. "I have no idea. *You're* the one who saw him."

"Yeah, right. This whole thing just got me so upset! In my day, we never had this kind of problem on the reservation."

Ella grabbed her handheld radio and updated Dispatch. "I'm going to check out the residence."

Ella unsnapped the safety strap that kept her pistol in place and started toward the house. She angled toward the side so she could see between the van and the building in case the perp came back out through the window.

She'd expected May to hang back, but hearing footsteps, she turned her head and saw that the woman was following along behind her. Ella glared at her. "Please go back inside your house and shut the door."

"Oh, okay. Yeah." May turned and ran back across the street.

By the time Ella reached the front corner of Tapaha's house, the woman had already disappeared. Ella stepped along the wall, watching the front door, van, and side window by glancing back and forth. Stopping beside the van's driver's side door, she peered into the unoccupied vehicle. The keys were still in the ignition, so she reached inside through the rolled-down window and pulled them out.

Ella placed them into her jacket pocket and continued around the house with her back against the house wall, listening as she moved. The faint opening of drawers and light footsteps indicated someone was inside but had already gone past the room adjacent to the window as he worked the interior of the home.

Moving with the practiced grace of a hunter, she crept lightly to the back door and tried the handle. It wasn't locked. Times had changed, but people hadn't. The older ones seldom locked their doors. If the kid had tried this entry, he would have probably gotten in undetected, providing he'd parked around the back.

Ella slipped inside the small kitchen, grateful that the hinges didn't creak. The house smelled of bacon grease and cigarettes, but was otherwise clean and cozy. Two old-style dinette chairs were pushed against a matching shiny chrome table with a white top. Several cigarette burns suggested the old man was careless with his smokes and lucky so far not to have burned down his house. Through the next doorway Ella could see what looked like the living room, then a short hall that led farther back into the interior.

Someone inside one of the bedrooms cursed, then something heavy crashed to the floor. Ella heard the sound of hurried footsteps and, gripping her pistol tightly, crouched and pressed against the side of the refrigerator, watching as she made herself as small a target as possible. Suddenly a Navajo boy nearly her height came racing down the hall. His hair was cut short and styled in multicolored spikes, and his ears and nose were pierced with small gold rings. He seemed to be in a panic and going so fast that he failed to make the turn into the living room. He skidded, and bounced off the trim of the doorway.

As he recaptured his balance, he saw her standing there. "Stay away from me!" he yelled, raising a small, shiny pistol. His finger jerked the trigger and there was a loud pop and a thud in the living room wall. He'd missed her by at least ten feet.

Obviously, he hadn't meant to hit her. No one was *that* bad a shot. Knowing that, she gambled and chose not to return fire.

"Police officer! Put down the gun and drop to the floor, kid. You're trapped."

"Keep the gun, but I'm getting out of here *now!*" he shouted back, tossing the pistol toward a worn-looking green sofa. In a flash, he dove to the left and out of her line of sight, scrambling, she supposed, either toward a window or the front door.

Ella moved out from behind cover cautiously and saw him crawling out the window into his van. Knowing he was in for a big surprise, she chuckled softly. She had his keys. Turning, she ran through the kitchen and out the back door. As she went around the corner, she heard him cursing and knew he'd just realized that he wasn't going anywhere in his vehicle.

Ella ran up to the van and, as he poked his head out the driver's window, raised her hand and showed him the keys. "Give it up," she ordered.

In a flash, he jumped across the front seat and leaped out the passenger's door. The burglar sprinted out of the yard and onto the street as if his shoes were on fire. As the boy ran away, Ella followed, jamming her pistol back into the pancake holster at her belt, then picking up the pace as the teen raced up the street. She wasn't a sprinter, but she could go for miles across country, so unless he was a long-distance runner, or managed to hide somehow, she'd catch up to him sooner or later.

The kid took a right at the intersection, heading west down a dirt road that paralleled Highway 64. Hopefully he wasn't really trying to make it to Arizona, but he was moving as though he had a pit bull at his heels. And, in a way, he did. Ella knew she'd never quit until the punk ran out of gas.

There were a few houses to the right, but cutting across yards and dodging cars and clotheslines would make the going slow, and the kid apparently realized that. Ella stayed with him, not losing any more ground, and, before long, about a half mile past the old farm training turnoff, he left the road and began to angle across an alfalfa field toward the distant river. It was then that she pressed herself for more speed and quickly closed in.

Finally, a hundred yards before reaching an arroyo, she caught up to him and dove, tackling him to the ground. She rolled him over, ready to punch his lights out, but he held out his arms and lay flat on his back, gasping for air.

"Okay, okay, you caught me. I give up!"

Ella rolled him onto his belly easily, and he offered no resistance as she handcuffed his wrists behind his back.

"I really wasn't running away from *you*," he said.

"You could have fooled me." As Ella helped him to his feet, she glanced back down the highway and saw a tribal police unit heading her direction, lights flashing.

"I just wanted to get as far away from that place as I could," he said with a grimace.

"What's your name?"

"Elroy Begay."

Ella read him his rights and saw from the expression on his face that he was very familiar with the routine. "Where's Mr. Tapaha?" she demanded.

"Who?"

"The man who lives in the house you broke into," she answered, nudging him into motion toward the highway.

"Don't say his name," he said quickly, cringing.

Ella heard the fear in his tone and pressed him instantly for more of an answer. "Why not? What did you do to him?"

"Nothing, not a thing. Nada. I *never* touched that old man. Okay, I admit to unlawful entry, even attempted burglary. But that's it."

He was obviously acquainted with the legal system. "Then what's got you so spooked? Is the old man okay?"

"Hey, I'm not saying another word. Not without my lawyer."

Ella hurried back with Elroy in tow to the road where Officer Justine Goodluck, her second cousin and partner, was waiting. Justine was smaller than Ella, and her hair, when it wasn't tied in a bun, was well past her waist. Justine could pass for a teenager, but was as tough as the best cop, and could handle herself in a confrontation with both skill and courage.

"What've you got?" Justine asked, sizing up the prisoner at a glance. "Nice hair," she chuckled, noting leaves on some of the spikes, but the boy barely glanced at her.

"Take him," Ella said, gesturing to Elroy, then opening the back door to Justine's unit. "I need to return to the house he was burglarizing and look for the owner."

"I wouldn't go back in there if I were you," Elroy said as Ella maneuvered him into the vehicle. His tone was deceptively flat and in sharp contrast with the vivid spark of fear in his eyes.

"Let's roll, partner," Ella said, now really worried about the old man. She scrambled into the passenger side as Justine ran around the vehicle.

Two minutes later they were in front of Tapaha's house. Ella had tried to get Elroy to talk again, but he'd only shake his head in response to her questions and refused to make eye contact. Instinct and experience told her to expect major trouble in the man's home.

Ella hurried inside via the unlocked front door. "Mr. Tapaha? It's okay to come out now. I'm a police officer."

There was no answer. An unnatural total silence permeated the house. Afraid that she'd wasted too much time already, Ella looked inside the first bedroom, then the bathroom, but found nothing except open drawers and a closet. As she headed down the hall, a familiar, repulsive scent, reminiscent of a meat locker, led Ella to the last bedroom. As she stepped around the smashed TV Elroy had probably dropped, she found Mr. Tapaha, his pajama-clad body sprawled on the bed, one arm dangling over the edge. An open, empty, pill bottle lay just beyond his fingers. Tapaha's eyes were open, blank, and glazed over with a cloudy film. They seemed to stare at nothing and everything at the same time.

The smell of decaying flesh was strong here and she didn't need to touch the body to know that he'd been dead for some time. Ella studied the label on the prescription bottle. It had been refilled recently but it was empty now. She recognized the brand of painkillers as a common but powerful drug. She'd been given some after a dental visit and cautioned against overdosing. The counterindications had disturbed her so much she'd decided not to take any at all. Sometimes pain was preferable to the alternative.

"What have we got?" Justine asked, having followed her in. She stopped by the doorway, lifted a hand to cover her nose, and stepped back. "Never mind. Suicide?"

"Looks like it, though that's kind of rare for old Navajos," Ella said, backing out of the room. "At least this is a modernist area so maybe his death won't impact too badly on the neighborhood."

Fear of the *chindi*—the evil side of a person that remained earthbound after death—was still strong on the reservation, but not with the modernists. Relatives or neighbors still wouldn't line up to move into this house once it became available, but even in the Anglo world few people wanted a house where a tragedy had occurred.

"Now I know why the boy ran off like he did," Ella commented.

Justine nodded. "He's sitting in my unit now, and he won't even look at the house."

Another cruiser pulled up outside and Ella saw Joseph Neskahi, a sergeant in the department, climb out of his unit. Joseph was a sturdy Navajo, with a barrel chest and powerful arms. His dark eyes were flat—the look of a cop who'd long lost any hope that human nature could surprise him.

Neskahi came in, caught the smell in the air, then stopped without moving any farther into the room. "I heard the call and wanted to check it out. I know . . . knew Mr. H," he said, avoiding mentioning the deceased's first name out loud out of respect for tradition. The Navajo Way taught that using the name of a dead person would call their *chindi*. "He was a friend of my dad's and I knew he'd been sick for a long, long time—the big C—and things were getting worse. A week or so ago my dad mentioned that Mr. H had left the hospital, telling everyone that he didn't want to die there. There was no hogan for him to go to anymore, and even if there had been, he couldn't have made it far into the desert. So, since he had no family to speak of, he decided that he'd go on his own terms in the comfort of his home. He told my father that his modernist neighbors wouldn't give a rip if he died here."

"It's a sad way to go . . . with no way out and no friends around to comfort you," Ella said, remembering being alone in the mine, facing hopelessness and the certainty of death.

"He'd already said good-bye to the few friends he had," Neskahi said. "The only thing his future held out to him was the certainty of more pain. He didn't have many options."

"I've always wondered if I'd make that same choice if I were faced with a long, painful illness I knew I couldn't beat," Justine said. "What about you?" she asked Ella.

"I don't dwell on things like that," Ella replied honestly. "I figure I'll cross each bridge as I get to it."

"At least he controlled the way he went," Neskahi said. "That's a win in my book."

Joseph's answer didn't surprise Ella. Almost everyone she knew in law enforcement prized control. It was a survival skill so ingrained that it became a part of who they were. But her own perspective about Tapaha's death was different.

From personal experience she was convinced that the end of this life wasn't the End. Would Tapaha get to the other side and regret speeding up the clock? Would he miss all the little things that he'd taken for granted, or just be happy the ride was over? She hoped for his sake that he'd find peace in the hereafter.

"Call the funeral home that the tribe uses to take care of unclaimed bodies," Ella instructed Neskahi. "You've got the name and number?" When he nodded, Ella continued. "It's not a suspicious death, so our role is over except for documenting the burglary attempt—just the TV, probably. The tribe's ME gets a pass on this one."

"I'll handle it," Neskahi said, then glanced around the room. "I don't see a phone, so I'll just relay the message through Dispatch."

"Use my cell." Ella tossed him the phone. She and Justine had cell phones, courtesy of a community program, but routine patrol officers, as Neskahi was at the moment, had to rely on regular equipment unless they were called in for emergency duty, or carried one at their own expense.

Ella looked at Justine. "Take the kid back to the station and book him. Neskahi will process the break-in, and I'll be in shortly. I want to talk to the dead man's neighbors and make sure that there's no family that should be notified. After that, I'll head to the station."

Leaving Justine, Ella went across the street. May opened the door before Ella had the chance to knock. "Is he all right? Herbert, I mean. I haven't seen him for several days, so I was wondering. . . ."

"I'm afraid he passed away," Ella said, deciding that May didn't need to know it had been a suicide.

May crossed herself, which marked her as a Catholic as well as a modernist.

"Do you know if he had family on the Rez?" Ella asked.

"No, I don't think there's anyone left now. I'd go over just to talk to him sometimes—to give him a little company, you know—and he told me once that he'd outlived all of them." She sighed softly. "I tried to help him out whenever I could, but he wasn't easy to get along with. He never came right out and said so, but I got the distinct impression that he didn't want me to come over too often. He said that he'd made peace with himself a long time ago and he preferred being alone. He even ran off his caregiver last time he came back from the hospital."

Thanking her, Ella returned to Tapaha's house and retrieved her cell phone from Sergeant Neskahi, who was already busy taking photos of the interior of the house. Leaving him to his work, Ella headed down the street toward her unit. The run had left her sweaty and she absently lifted her long black hair off the back of her neck for a moment with her fingertips, enjoying the cool air that touched her skin.

Ella thought about Mr. Tapaha trapped inside a body that had turned traitor, with no way to escape the disease that had been consuming him. Life without hope soon became unbearable. Without hope, you stopped moving forward and reaching toward the next goal, and you died inside long before you took your last breath.

Ella took one more look around the neighborhood as she opened the door to her unit. Here in this area of essentially modern housing filled with amenities, hope had a chance of being more than a fading dream shadow. But there were other places deep on the Rez that hope had deserted, where the land lay wounded with little chance of full recovery. Those places, ravaged by greed, stood empty and seemed as soulless as the gaze in Tapaha's eyes. And that hopelessness, in turn, touched everyone because the land and the Navajo were one. Mother Earth provided the food they ate and nourished their spirits, and, eventually, all living things went back to her, completing the endless circle.

Ella drove back to the station in a dark mood, unable to get the image of the old man out of her mind. With any luck this morning wouldn't be an indication of how the rest of the week would go.

Ella had just pulled into a parking spot at the station when her call number came over the radio. She answered Dispatch quickly. "I just pulled up at the station."

"That explains the strong signal. Big Ed wants to see you right now, Investigator Clah."

Before leaving her unit, Ella cracked the window open just a bit so the heat wouldn't build up inside. Venting was the only way to avoid returning to a vehicle that would feel like a cross between a pressure cooker and an oven in a very short time. It was nearly eleven-thirty now, and the cool air was quickly being replaced by high desert temperatures that only the long-awaited afternoon downpour would abate.

She'd just stepped into the station lobby when Big Ed spotted her from down the hall. Their chief of police was a large man. If Neskahi was a barrel of a man, Big Ed Atcitty was a refrigerator with arms and legs. His hair was turning gray these days but to assume that he'd passed his prime was a huge mistake. As it always was on the reservation, appearances were deceiving. Big Ed could not only keep up with his officers, he qualified with them every year.

"Chief," she said with a nod.

"You're back. Good. In my office," he said, cocking his head down the hall.

The lack of inflection in his tone caught her attention and made her skin prickle with discomfort. He was trying too hard to act casual, and whenever that happened major-league trouble was at hand.

Ella took a seat in the chair across from his cluttered desk and waited as he closed the door and walked toward her.

"We have a situation," he said, as he slowly lowered himself into his old vinyl-covered swivel chair.

His words let her know without a doubt that something was brewing. Another bad sign was that the light on his phone was blinking, indicating he had someone on the line, holding. As silence stretched out between them, she waited, noting that her boss was rocking back and forth in his chair, an unspoken signal that he was thinking and didn't want to be interrupted. The chair squeaked slightly, but he apparently hadn't noticed, and she wasn't about to point it out or dare crack a smile.

Although on the outside she would have already fired off some questions, on the Rez things moved at their own pace. Respecting that, she remained still, wondering if the person on the other end of the line would be as patient as she was being forced to be right now.

"Our new FBI resident agent, Andrew Thomas, apparently interrupted a Sing last night. Now he's missing. Thomas never returned to his office, called in, or e-mailed his supervisor. He's been completely out of touch since around seven last night—over sixteen hours."

The bad feeling she'd had suddenly got worse. Andy Thomas was in a world of trouble. If he didn't turn up quickly, alive and well, dark times lay ahead for the missing agent—and the reservation.

TWO
——— ✖ ✖ ✖ ———

Ella gathered her thoughts quickly, mentally checking off the information she'd need to formulate a plan of action. "Interrupting a Sing is a major offense. If that report is true, Agent Thomas's disappearance is going to be a real bear to investigate. A lot of folks are going to think that the gods have punished him and that's why he's missing. They'll fight any attempt we make to find him."

He nodded. "Our traditionalists will be especially hard to deal with, but that's the way it stacks up."

"I'll get started on this right away, but I'm going to need more to go on, like who was the patient at the Sing and which *hataalii* performed the ceremony? Also, where did it take place?"

Big Ed shook his head. "We don't know any of that yet, but the FBI area supervisor should have some of that information by now. He's looking through Thomas's case files as we speak."

"So there's a chance our information is wrong and Agent Thomas didn't really interrupt a Sing?"

"No, our information about that is right on target. Agent Thomas followed local law-enforcement protocols, at least. He called our dispatcher to report that he was pursuing an investigation on tribal land and was on his way to question a suspect he believed was attending a Sing. Thomas didn't give any more details other than that and told Dispatch he'd call back and let us know when he was finished."

Ella nodded thoughtfully. Senior agent Dwayne Blalock handled cases here on the Rez, out of his Shiprock office. From what she knew of local Bureau procedures, Andy Thomas, though he was currently sharing Blalock's office, usually handled cases off the reservation unless tribal officers called him for support. But that couldn't have been the case, at least in this instance. "Didn't Dispatch give him a heads-up about Sings?"

"Dispatch warned him to keep his distance and not to interfere, but Thomas said that he was going to wait until it was over, then question the suspect. Dispatch told him that Sings could take up to a week, but Thomas said that, according to his information, this particular ceremony wouldn't take long, so he intended to hang around until it concluded."

"In his ignorance, he might have thought it was a fair compromise. But just to be seen in the vicinity, if he wasn't invited, could be construed as interrupting—not to mention bringing misfortune to those present," Ella said, her insides tightening. Young agents like Andy Thomas came out of Quantico with equal portions of confidence, arrogance, and ignorance. Thomas had only been assigned to the area a short time and probably still didn't know much about how things worked on the Rez. If veteran agent Dwayne Blalock hadn't been on vacation, Thomas would have never gone to question anyone on the Navajo Nation alone.

Unfortunately, she had a strong feeling that Thomas had assumed that a Sing was akin to a church service or doctor's appointment. He'd just wait outside until the suspect emerged and then confront him. But different rules applied here.

Big Ed stopped rocking in his chair and sat up straight. "Thomas called Dispatch mostly to make sure his butt was covered. But because he never called back and no one's heard from him since, I think we can safely assume he's in some kind of trouble. Blalock's out of touch so I contacted Agent Simmons, the FBI's area supervisor, at seven this morning."

Ella glanced at the phone's blinking red light. Whoever was on hold was probably seething by now.

"I've got Agent Simmons on the line," he said, glancing down at his telephone. "You probably know Thomas and Blalock were sharing an office because of budget cutbacks, so Simmons is over there now, trying to find any open case files that'll give us an idea of what Thomas was investigating."

Big Ed paused, staring at the phone, then continued. "Off the record, Simmons is one major pain in the butt and there's a history of bad blood between him and Blalock."

Ella nodded. "I remember Blalock talking about him a few times. Simmons likes to micromanage every case, and it drives Blalock nuts. But what's Simmons's next move? If the FBI plans to flood the Rez with agents, that's going to backfire big-time— particularly under the circumstances."

"Let's hear Simmons out." Big Ed pressed the button. "Agent Simmons, I've got Special Investigator Clah in my office now, so I'm putting you on speaker. Why don't you fill us in on how you want to proceed."

"My priority right now is locating Agent Thomas, but the Bureau has run into major brick walls on the reservation before. Sending in teams of federal agents who are unfamiliar with the area isn't going to help us find our man quickly. We need the help of the tribal police, and we need it *now*. Thomas could be almost anywhere, injured, stranded, lost, or maybe dead. We can't pick up the locator signal from his cell phone, and his unit didn't have a GPS installed. That means we've got to find him the hard way. We've got to move fast on this while people's memories are still fresh, and to prevent any cover-up from taking place, if that's an accurate assessment of this situation. After thirty-six hours, you know as well as I do that it'll be nearly impossible to pick up his trail."

"Does Agent Thomas live in Farmington?" Big Ed asked.

"On the western outskirts. He has an apartment." Simmons gave them the address quickly.

"That's in county jurisdiction. Sheriff Taylor will have to be notified," Big Ed said.

"Already taken care of," Simmons answered coldly. "What I need is for your department to search the reservation. My feeling is that he's still there."

"We'll get on it," Big Ed said.

"Contact me directly if you get any leads at all. You've got my cell number and you can reach me on it day or night." He paused, then added, "Officer Clah, I need you to come over to Agent Blalock's office ASAP so I can fill you in on the particulars. I've got to leave town shortly, so the sooner the better."

Before she could answer, Simmons hung up.

Ella looked at Big Ed. "Should I call him back and remind him that I'm not with the Bureau anymore and I take my orders from you and the tribe?"

Big Ed grinned slowly. "You'd do that, wouldn't you?"

"In a heartbeat."

"You know, I can't even imagine you in the Bureau, Shorty. I have a feeling you'd be busting the chops of those good ole boys left and right," he said, chuckling, then took a deep breath and grew somber. "But right now we have to stay on target. Simmons may be reluctant to send in an army of special agents, but I think he will if we don't get results fast enough for him." Big Ed leaned back in his chair.

"It shouldn't be that hard for us to track down Agent Thomas once we find out what he was working on and get his last known location. A Navajo suspect can hide in plain sight on the Rez, but a redheaded Anglo like Thomas is really going to stick out."

"Good. Work fast, Ella. We aren't going to have any peace until this is settled. I had to report the incident to the council and I've been getting nonstop phone calls since then. Even the tribal president's office left a message. Everyone wants Thomas found before half the federal agents in the country start racing around the Four Corners in their gas-guzzling SUVs."

"What about my other cases?" Ella asked. "One is critical right now. Unless I track down the witnesses to the Twin Lakes hit-and-run ASAP, the woman will have all her tracks covered. We'll never get enough for an arrest."

"Her ex still in intensive care?"

Ella nodded. "Not that he didn't deserve it. He beat her with a baseball bat not long ago, I heard."

"At least she'll have her day in court. I'll farm that one out to one of the officers at Window Rock." Big Ed shook his head slowly. "And the rest I'll hand out to our patrol officers—for the time being. Just put the folders on the duty officer's desk. Until Thomas is located, the FBI case comes first. Make it a top priority for your Special Investigations team."

Ella had just stepped out of Big Ed's office when she saw Justine down the hall by the candy machine. She'd never quite figured out how Justine managed to stay so thin. Her cuz was practically addicted to peanut butter and chocolate. Ella joined Justine and quickly brought her up to speed while she retrieved the active files from her office and turned them over to the duty officer.

Three minutes later they were at the main entrance to the station. "Do you want me to go with you to meet Simmons?" Justine asked at the door.

"No. I'd rather you drive to Thomas's apartment and check it out. The address is in a computer file Blalock mails to me periodically to keep me updated. It's got his and Thomas's addresses and phone numbers, blood types, next of kin, and so on," Ella said. "When you get to Thomas's place, try to get around not having a court order by persuading the landlord to let you in. If that doesn't work, I'll see if Simmons can cut corners and get a warrant for us quickly," Ella said as they walked out to the parking lot.

"Why search his apartment?" Justine said, almost as if she'd read Ella's mind. "Are you thinking that Thomas's disappearance might be personal and that it has nothing to do with the Sing? But if that's the case, why did he call Dispatch in the first place?"

"I admit it's not likely, but we've got to check out all the possibilities. I also want to know *everything* about Agent Thomas—his routines, who his friends are, what he does when he's not working, also if he's put away any local bad boys recently that might have sent someone to even the score."

"Got it. I'll get on it right now." Justine waved and turned, jogging toward her own unit, parked across the lot.

Ella drove north onto the mesa where the FBI's bland, brown brick-and-glass office was located among several tribal agency buildings. Although it was turning out to be the worst possible time for the senior local agent to have gone on vacation, she understood why it had been important for him to get away, turn off his cell phone, and find a quiet place to clear his head.

Agent Blalock—-FB-Eyes as he was known locally because he had one brown eye and one blue—had been working long hours with Thomas. After a disagreement with Simmons over some of Agent Thomas's reports, Simmons had come down hard on Blalock. Angry and frustrated with bureaucratic protocols, Blalock had announced that he was taking time off. Simmons had actually encouraged him by urging the workaholic Blalock to use his leave before he lost it.

On the face of it, she sure wished things had gone down differently. It would have been an advantage to have an agent like Blalock, who was well acquainted with the reservation and Navajo customs, acting as liaison between the tribal police and the Bureau. Not that Blalock would have jumped at the chance. The last thing he needed was one more job.

Since Blalock's last partner, Lucas Payestewa, had been transferred back to northern Arizona, Blalock's workload had been brutal. Paycheck, the nickname some of the Navajo officers had given the young Hopi agent, had turned out to be a real asset to local law enforcement, but his continual call for more resources in the Four Corners states had annoyed his supervisors, and he'd been transferred in May.

All things considered, Lucas would have been a great ally to have in a case like this. Trying to find an FBI agent who'd interrupted a religious and healing ceremony would take skill and patience, and Paycheck would have understood that well from his own background. And now, without either Blalock or Payestewa around, she was afraid that the Bureau might try to rush things, not realizing until it was too late was that they'd have to adapt to the rules here to make progress. Thinking outside the box and working around cultural differences was what the Bureau did least well, in her opinion.

For the tribal police it was a no-win situation, no matter how she looked at it. Any efforts they made to find the agent would be perceived as siding with the Anglos—and working against the Dineh's cultural traditions. Anyone interrupting a Sing was supposed to be punished, and virtually every Navajo would back that notion.

But if Agent Thomas turned up dead, then the Rez could become an armed camp. The Bureau wouldn't let one of their own go down at the hands of a Navajo, or Navajos, without insisting someone pay the price. Law-enforcement people lived with a lot of anger, and that came to the forefront with a vengeance when an agent or a cop was killed.

Ella arrived at the Bureau's office in less than ten minutes. The door was halfway open, so she stepped inside. A slightly balding Anglo man in a suit was sitting behind Blalock's large metal desk going through a stack of files. Except for the tall stacks of paperwork on both desks and an open file cabinet, the place looked completely normal to her, having been there often over the past two or three years.

The man looked up as she came in. A scowl was on his face. "About time. Tribal police, right? Ella Clah?"

Ella looked at the badge hooked to her belt, then back at him. "Either that or I've stolen her badge."

His expression didn't change. "Sit. We've got a lot of ground to cover quickly. I've got to leave soon to catch a plane to D.C."

Papers were stacked high on Thomas's desk chair, so there was no place to sit without moving a foot-high stack of folders. Ella stood instead, eyeing the man.

Simmons looked vaguely familiar to her, but she couldn't place him. He was a fairly nondescript man with ruddy cheeks, graying brown hair, wire-frame glasses, and relatively fit for a man around fifty years old. All in all, he looked like a midlevel bureaucrat who worked out at the gym after hours but rarely ventured outdoors except to walk to his car.

"I was hoping to find something I could use, but all these reports are old and mostly generic crap. Blalock was supposed to supervise the kid and make sure everything was done right—for a change. What was I thinking? Blalock's reports blow, and so do the kid's."

Simmons shook his head and continued. "New resident agents like Thomas are the worst. Once they finally earn their badges they think it'll all be downhill from there. A little overconfidence goes a long ways, and too many college punks coming out of Quantico just can't cut it on the streets. The Bureau invests all that time and money trying to bring them up to snuff, then has to weed them out. You know what I mean. Those agents who can't cut it drop out after a year or two, then take some BS job in local law enforcement." He stared hard at her, leaving no doubt that he was including her in his assessment.

Ella met his gaze coldly. It was a snarky comment meant to put her down, to imply that she wasn't quite as good as he was because he'd stayed with the Bureau and she hadn't. Ella bit back her anger knowing Simmons was looking for a reaction. She'd lose her temper, he'd keep his cool and, in the process, make her feel that she'd just proven his point. But she wasn't playing his game.

"You're the one who has lost an agent, so maybe you should stop wasting time and tell me what you've got. I need a starting point," she said.

He looked at her in silence, then to hide the fact that it had taken him a moment to reconnect his brain cells, he cleared his throat. "All I can find out from this debris is that he was in the middle of a suspected fraud case that led him to an area southeast of Shiprock near someplace called Sanostee."

"Not a lot of people live out that way. And fraud's not generally federal turf unless a government agency is involved. What's the rest of the story?" Ella pressed.

"That's the sum total of what I found in his log book." Simmons pointed to a black leather portfolio on an office chair beside a small table also covered with papers. "If he ever did compile a file on the case he was investigating, he has it with him. But maybe you can find something useful in this mess. You're welcome to try," he said, waving his arm over the dozens of files stacked on Thomas's desk and beside his chair on the floor. "But keep this to yourself 'cause, officially, I can't have non-Bureau personnel go browsing through our files."

Ella knew that Blalock was far from neat, but he did file things. Maybe Thomas was worse, but nothing could compare to the damage Simmons had already done to the office. "You must have pulled out every file."

"I was looking for anything that involved fraud—current or archived. But since I haven't even got a name, I didn't know where to start. To get into Blalock's computer I would have needed his password, which I don't have. Since this office isn't guaranteed secure, his software erases the files after two failed attempts to hack in."

He waved a hand toward the other desk. "Thomas's computer crashed three days ago and his files were deleted," he continued. "I tried to retrieve the data anyway, but it's lost except for bits and pieces. I'll take the CPU back with me to Albuquerque and let our tech support try to reconstruct some of the missing files."

Simmons glanced at his watch. "After that, I'll be on my way to D.C. to make a presentation. It's a Bureau seminar I can't get out of now, but I should be back tomorrow evening. Other agents are already in the field as we speak. I've got teams searching off the reservation in San Juan and adjacent counties, and outside New Mexico as well, especially northeastern Arizona.

"If they turn up anything, they'll forward it to me through the Albuquerque field office and I'll pass it on to you. I expect you to do the same for me." He scribbled a number on the back, then handed her his card containing the Albuquerque numbers.

"Of course." Her tone brought the office temperature down

by at least twenty degrees. "By the way, is there the remotest possibility that Agent Thomas's failure to remain in contact is due to personal reasons unrelated to his work?"

"Hell, Clah, I suppose if you wanted to consider *all* the possibilities, he could have been abducted by aliens. Or maybe he just got lost or ran off the road into a ditch. Either way, he's missing and has to be located."

"I'll find him if he's on the Navajo Nation," Ella said.

"One last thing, Clah. You report only to *me*. Get it?"

"No, actually until the FBI starts issuing my paychecks, I report to Chief Atcitty. He, in turn, will keep you in the loop."

Simmons cursed. "You know what I mean. You're not to call the Bureau directly—you speak to me first and I'll handle any requests you make, and direct them down the proper channels. This includes any search warrants, which shouldn't take long because I've already contacted the U.S. magistrate. My cell number is on the back of the card."

She nodded, suddenly realizing what was going on. Politics were at hand. The Bureau didn't want word to get out, except to the agents already on the case, that Navajo officers were helping them track down one of their own.

"We'd also appreciate extreme discretion when you talk to anyone outside the reservation about this case," Simmons said, and looked at his watch again. "I've got to leave right *now* or I'll never make it. I'll expect a preliminary report in four hours or less," he said, standing up.

Simmons grabbed Thomas's CPU, which had already been disconnected, looked around at the piles of folders, then groaned. "Good luck sorting through everything here, Clah. Close the door for me, will you? It locks automatically."

Before she could comment, Simmons was out the door. Ella exhaled softly then turned around, taking in every detail. In his zeal to do a quick search, Simmons had just made things worse by pulling folders out randomly. Nothing followed a logical sequence now.

Ella walked over to Blalock's desk and decided to have a

quick look at his computer. Although she hadn't told Simmons, she knew Blalock's current password. Years ago he'd started giving her the new one each time he'd changed it. She understood it was only to be used in case of an emergency—and this certainly qualified as one. If Agent Thomas had filed duplicate reports with Dwayne Blalock, she'd find them.

Ella turned on the computer, waited for the system to boot up, then typed in "NBR1RDNK," Blalock's latest password—short for number one redneck. Once on, she searched the data files, starting with the most recent date. She was familiar with the software, and recognized most of the cases Blalock was working because they were connected with the tribe, but none of them were in any way related to fraud. Logging back out, Ella started to check the file folders, but soon realized that it would take hours.

Picking up her cell phone, Ella dialed Officer Tache, the third officer permanently assigned to the Special Investigations unit. Taking him off his other duties, she gave Ralph the job of sorting through the files while she concentrated on gathering everything she could about the Sing. Simmons didn't have to know.

Suddenly she heard the sound of footsteps over by the door and remembered she hadn't bothered to shut it. Ella glanced up and saw a face she recognized.

THREE

✖ ✖ ✖

Hey, Teeny. How've you been?" she greeted him warmly. She'd known Bruce Little almost all of her life. Theirs was a peculiar friendship and, to date, she was still the only human being since third grade who could call him Teeny and not end up requiring facial reconstruction, or worse.

Teeny had always had a soft spot for her. Ella knew it, Teeny knew it, but nothing had ever been said or done about it, and probably never would. Teeny had joined the department before she had, but his skills with computers had persuaded Big Ed to take him out of the field and reassign him to a desk.

Teeny had become their information technology expert and had set up and maintained the computer network in the department and kept the system going even after it had become obsolete. A year after he'd installed and debugged their most recent system, Teeny had been laid off due to budget cuts. Big Ed had protested, knowing how valuable Teeny was, but he'd been overruled by the tribal leadership.

Teeny had quickly set up his own business, serving as a computer and Internet consultant in the Four Corners area and now the tribal police had to hire him frequently to maintain or repair their network and computers. Using his police training and imposing appearance, Teeny also did more traditional police-type jobs, like providing security for big events in the area.

"How's business?" she asked.

"Not bad. Got two shops now. One across the hall and another in downtown Farmington. People still have problems with their networks, but they don't usually want to hire someone full-time as a computer geek. The other half of my work, handling security, is also booming. It's got me thinking of applying for a private investigator's license. I could expand and take on a variety of jobs. There's lots of times when people need a big guy on their side, you know, even if it's just collecting from deadbeats."

And big he was. Ella was pushing five ten, but Bruce Little towered over her like one of the rock formations in Monument Valley. He hadn't sculpted himself a body builder's torso either. Teeny had meat on him, like two oil drums with a basketball on top. Yet anyone who thought he was fat or lazy quickly discovered the man was not only as strong as a bear but surprisingly quick.

During his days in the police department, Teeny had kept his hair shorter than regulation, but now it was just a shade longer than peach fuzz. Combined with his small, dark eyes and often spaced-out expressions, Teeny gave the impression that he had the IQ of a tree stump, which just went to prove that appearances could be deceiving.

Teeny was a self-described big, ugly dude, but Ella had always liked him. He was intelligent and inventive. More often than not he used his head and common sense to avoid confrontations even though he could have bullied others into giving him what he wanted by sheer size alone.

"What's with the 'I'm important' *bilagáana* in the suit?" he asked, using the Navajo word for "white man." "Simmons—I think. He Agent Thomas's boss?"

"Yeah."

"I hope Andy Thomas hasn't stepped in something serious. The kid loves his job, but he's still not with the program." Teeny walked into the office, looking at the stacks of files curiously.

"What do you know about Agent Thomas?" Ella asked.

"Andy's a hard worker. He never gives up. If he had, he

wouldn't be in the FBI," he said, then pointed to a photo on Thomas's desk.

Ella picked it up. On the fading print was a young Andy Thomas standing by an old VW van that could have optimistically been described as falling apart. A middle-aged woman was next to the red-haired, freckle-faced teen. "Not from a wealthy family, I take it?"

"I commented on the VW one day and he told me that was his home the first two years of college. Andy got a scholarship that paid for books and tuition, but the money didn't go far, so living in that vehicle was the only way he could afford to stay in school. During that time he lived on bread and cans of pork and beans, and, to this day, he says he can't eat beans without gagging," Teeny answered. "That's his mother with him. She worked as a housekeeper and sent him money when she could. Now that she's older and sick, he supports her."

Ella thought of her own mother, Rose, and how close they were. In Andy's shoes, she would have done the same thing.

"I don't know about you but my tribal scholarship paid for nearly all of my school-related expenses. I'm not sure I would have stuck with it if I'd had to live in a van," Teeny said.

"I only applied for a partial scholarship the first year, thinking that I could make it on part-time jobs. That was a mistake. I didn't live in a car, but I had to move in with a friend for half a semester."

Teeny chose Blalock's extra-large brown leather chair and made himself comfortable. "Andy's heart is in the right place, but he's really clueless about the way things work around here. The first week he was on the Rez he went out to interview people wearing a suit, like the guy who was just here. Old Navajos would see him coming and never answer their doors. Andy would end up with nothing to talk to except a horse and some sheep—that's if the dogs didn't run him off first."

"Did you say anything to him about that?"

"Me? No way. It's none of my business. I get crashed networks up and running, do troubleshooting, and tweak custom-designed software for virtually every law-enforcement agency in the Four

Corners. And when I'm not doing that, I protect paranoid enter-
tainers from screaming fans at concerts. That keeps me busy. I
don't have time to open an advice column for the feds. But FB-
Eyes must have had a talk with Andy about the clothes because
Andy finally lost the suit and discovered bolo ties and western-
cut boots," he said, then added, "All that said, I have a feeling the
guy's in trouble right now."

"What makes you say that?"

"Yesterday afternoon Andy asked me about Navajo
ceremonies—then took off. But he didn't show up this morning,
something he always does like clockwork, and now both his boss
and you have come by to check out his office. In my experience,
the only time the FBI gets the tribal police involved in anything is
when they have no other choice and they *really* need something.
The fact that you're here now proves it. They must be desperate if
they left you here alone to search his office."

It was all resoundingly logical. "Wait a sec. Back up a bit. What
kind of ceremonies did Agent Thomas want to know about?"

"He didn't say—maybe he didn't know exactly. But he
wanted to know who did ceremonies around here, where they
were held, and if there were any scheduled soon. He told me that
he'd tried asking several Navajos around town but they wouldn't
tell him squat."

She rolled her eyes. "Really. So what did you tell him?"

"That I didn't know of any ceremonials, public or private
right now, but that didn't mean anything because I wasn't in the
loop when it came to that kind of thing. I've been kind of an out-
sider since I moved off the Rez, and, hey, I'm Catholic. I did warn
him that some Sings were *very* private affairs and that he could get
himself in a truckload of trouble. But I could tell that he was chasing down a lead and wasn't about to let go." He paused. "Then today Mr. Suit—Simmons—came into my office asking if I'd seen
the kid. Stuck his badge in my face, too."

"What did you do?"

"Nothing. I just shook my head and stood up. He kind of
backed off, as I recall. Then I saw him out."

Ella bit her lip to keep from laughing. Simmons was around six feet tall, but practically a skeleton in comparison to Teeny.

"You haven't said why you're involved in an FBI case. Jumping ship again?" he asked, alluding to her days in the Bureau before joining the tribal force.

"No, but your theory about what's going on is right on target," she said, seeing no reason not to tell him. Teeny was obviously acquainted with the missing man and might be able to provide a lead. "Agent Thomas went missing yesterday, or last night, I guess. If you hear anything I can use, pass it along. I need to find him ASAP. And keep this confidential, okay?"

His eyes narrowed as he studied her expression for several long moments. "This isn't just business as usual for you, is it? You've got a stake of some kind in this."

Teeny had an absolute gift for picking up nonverbal cues.

"You're right," she admitted slowly. "Blalock asked me to keep an eye on Thomas before he left on vacation. But I got wrapped up in other stuff and didn't take the time to check in on the rookie. Thomas called about a week ago, asking if we could get together over coffee, but I put him off because I was concentrating on a case. Said I'd call him back and never did."

"So you're thinking that this is partly your fault?"

"I could have made sure he understood that he can't run roughshod over the Rez just because he carries that gold badge. But I never got around to it."

"Did either Blalock or Thomas ask you for cultural lessons?"

"No, but I should have seen this coming. Blalock reins him in. Without Blalock around . . ."

"It wasn't your responsibility, Ella, you're not teaching lesson twelve in the special-agent real-world curriculum. Like most inexperienced, aggressive people I've met in law enforcement, Thomas wanted to do things his way," Teeny said. "Apparently, once he was really on his own, that's exactly what he did, and all you can do now is try to sort out the mess."

His cell phone rang, Teeny muttered some quick words, then

glanced over at her. "I've got to get going, Ella. The server at the county courthouse has locked up again."

"Before you go. Any idea how I can get hold of Blalock?" she asked as Bruce made his way to the door.

He shook his head. "Dwayne—don't you love that name— didn't want to be found—at least that's what he told me. He swore he wasn't going to turn on his cell phone again until his vacation was officially over. But he did mention that after he had a chance to do some fishing and camping, he planned to visit his sister in Denver."

After Teeny left, Ella shut down Blalock's computer, then checked through the address book on his desk. He'd never been much on computerizing what could be easily written down. Mercifully, a quick look through the names revealed a Phyllis Blalock. She hoped it would turn out to be his unmarried sister instead of an ex-wife who also lived in Denver and had kept his name. Although she'd known Blalock for a decade, and had grudgingly grown to respect him and his abilities, Ella knew very little about his personal life. In fact, although his first name was Dwayne, she felt much more comfortable calling him Blalock. It was that kind of relationship.

A quick phone call verified that Phyllis was indeed Blalock's sister. Ella introduced herself, then left a message asking that Blalock get in touch with her as soon as possible. That done, she grabbed a set of office keys from Blalock's desk just in case, and headed out to her car.

Her brother, Clifford, a well-known *hataalii*, a medicine man, might know about the ceremony—who'd conducted it, who the patient was, and all the other details Ella needed to get. It was also entirely possible he'd done the Sing. If so, she'd try to persuade him to share some information she could use to track down Thomas.

As she reached her unit, her cell phone rang.

"This is Agent Simmons. I just wanted to let you know again that I *will* be back on the Navajo Nation as soon as I possibly can.

I'm not just dumping this in your lap," he said, then added, "Were you able to find anything useful in Agent Blalock's office?"

"Not yet, but I've been on the case less than an hour, Agent Simmons. You, on the other hand, have had around five hours since the dispatcher called you to report that Agent Thomas was missing. Not asking for the tribal police's help immediately has only made matters worse."

"Don't tell me how to do my job," he snapped. "I've been an agent for twenty years, and I don't need advice from a tribal police officer who couldn't cut it in the Bureau."

As anger flooded through her, she gripped her cell phone so tightly her hand began to shake. "I do *not* have to justify my career choices to you," she said, her jaw clenched.

"You misunderstand me, Clah. I'm not saying that it was your fault. Affirmative action just hasn't done anyone any favors."

"I got through Quantico on my own ability, Agent Simmons, not through affirmative action." Even the implication that she'd made her way into the Bureau through a back door rankled her. She'd worked very hard for everything she'd ever attained.

"You really were up and coming . . . once," he said, then continued before she could respond. "But we're getting off track here. I just wanted you to know that I'll be back on the reservation as soon as I can to oversee this case."

"Understood," she clipped, then hung up and looked at her watch. It was nearly 1:00 P.M. She was on the highway driving south in the general direction of her brother's medicine hogan when her cell phone rang again.

Justine's alto voice came through clearly. "One of our uniforms found Agent Thomas's sedan. It's at the bottom of a big arroyo west of the Sanostee Chapter House. If Officer Curtis hadn't gotten a tip from one of his relatives, we probably wouldn't have found it for days. The man was riding his horse up in the foothills and happened to come across it."

"Was the car anywhere near a medicine hogan?"

"About half a mile uphill and west from one, according to Officer Curtis," Justine said.

All this time she'd clung to the faint hope that their intel was wrong and Agent Thomas hadn't gone anywhere near a Sing. But reality now shattered that fragile illusion. "Give me the exact location and meet me there. Call Tache, too. I want him to process the scene."

Directions on the Rez didn't always entail the use of street names and house numbers. In this particular case, she had to proceed south down the highway leading to Gallup for around twenty-five miles on good road, turn west for another ten toward the Chuska Mountains, then continue another few miles on a primitive dirt track that would be hell this time of year even with the scant rains. The entire area was lined with overgrown trails that had at one time served as roads to the mines that had been in operation during the '50s and '60s.

The drive took her nearly an hour. It was just past two o'clock when she parked beside Justine's dusty white department vehicle at the top of a small piñon- and juniper-lined canyon in the rocky foothills. The terrain was rough, and she'd nearly gotten stuck during the last half mile because she'd kept to the vehicle tracks of those who'd arrived ahead of her.

Justine was already on the scene, standing beside the dark blue FBI unit, and waved as Ella exited her SUV. Officer Tache, in the department's crime-scene van, had nearly caught up to Ella just before they'd left the surfaced road, and Ella could now hear the low gears and bouncing tires as the officer approached from a rocky outcrop to her right.

The familiar scent of pine resin, fresh sagebrush, and late summer flowers reminded Ella that her father's mother, her *nálí*, had lived not too far from here. This had been a place of happy memories for her at one time, but now the area held only echoes of tragedy and danger.

Ella brought out her evidence kit, donning a set of latex gloves so she wouldn't leave her own prints behind. When a body was part of a crime scene, two pairs were usually worn by the Navajo officers in order to prevent touching anything that had touched the dead—a taboo even most modernist Navajos respected.

Not waiting for Tache, Ella climbed down the rock strewn slope, picking her way around the footprints and vehicle tracks that would need to be recorded and processed. As they approached Agent Thomas's vehicle, Ella saw that it had been damaged.

"Vandalism, or the result of an attack?" Ella asked, then saw the answer for herself as she came up to it. Both headlights had been smashed, along with the windshield, and someone had scratched "F-BItes" into the surface of the hood using a rock, apparently. Another rock was still embedded in the windshield.

"No sign of the agent. I did a spiral search for about a hundred yards while I was waiting for you, and called out several times," Justine said. "But the truth is he could be anywhere. There are a lot of mines around here."

Ella nodded, checking the ground carefully from several viewpoints, like a golfer lining up a putt. "There were two groups of people here," Ella said, waving her arm in the immediate area around the vehicle. "At least five individuals. Two people arrived on foot but, later, there was also an SUV or a pickup here. There was a struggle, too," she said pointing to the tracks on the ground. "See the undisturbed boot marks by the driver's door where Thomas first got out? He was okay until he started to come back to his vehicle, then he was jumped."

"Someone must have caught Thomas looking in on the ceremony and sent two helpers to deal with him."

"Those larger footprints—two sets—are over the smaller ones, which means they were here last. It's anyone's guess who vandalized the sedan. In some places there are so many tracks it's difficult to make heads or tails out of them. Take plenty of photos, Ralph," Ella said to Tache, who'd just arrived carrying a big box that held his cameras and other gear.

Officer Tache, a slender, glum-looking man who rarely smiled, nodded. "Right, boss. Anyone else coming I should know about? Want me to put up the tape?"

"Don't bother. We're on a rush job right now. We need to find something quickly that'll lead to locating the Anglo FBI agent."

Tache nodded and brought out his camera, getting to work immediately while Justine continued to examine the agent's vehicle.

Studying the area of the struggle about six feet from the sedan, Ella found a few drops of blood on the sand. She waved first to Tache, who took a few photos, then had Justine come over and bag a sample.

"Someone got injured but we would have seen more blood if it had been a severe wound," Ella said, as Justine recorded the date, time, and other identifying information on the bag's label. "See if it matches Agent Thomas's as soon as you can."

Ella's muscles tensed, dark images filling her brain. With effort, she pushed them back, knowing that neither anger nor guilt feelings would help her now. She was here to do a job. Self-discipline was the key now and fortunately that came easily to her, particularly in circumstances like these.

"I caught a glimpse of the hogan on the way in," Ella said. "I'm going down there now to take a look around."

"Watch your step," Tache reminded. "The ground west of here is pockmarked with uranium mine shafts. You must have seen some of the old markers along the road on the way in. Most of the openings have been overgrown with brush, so make sure you don't fall into one."

Seeing Justine's attempt to hush Tache up, Ella smiled. "I won't make the same mistake twice, Ralph. But thanks for the warning," she said, remembering her last experience. She'd been lucky to come out of it alive, but the nightmares would haunt her for the rest of her life.

Justine picked up her own camera and walked along the narrow canyon with Ella, occasionally spotting tracks leading to and from the hogan as they scrambled over solid outcroppings, beds of coarse sand, and hard, rocky ground.

"One group came up this way, then went back down," Ella said, then let out a harsh whistle to catch Tache's attention. He looked over and she pointed to the ground, then saw him nod.

"I've never been able to whistle that way," Justine said. "I wanted to learn and my brother tried to teach me, but I never got the hang of it. And forget about my sisters. All they can do is scream."

"Once Clifford started whistling, I had to figure it out so I could do it too. It's this sibling thing we have between us," Ella said, and grinned.

As they approached the hogan, Ella heard a rumble of thunder and glanced up at the clouds creeping down the mountainsides. "We better move fast, photograph everything, and secure all the evidence we can."

"Maybe it'll just threaten to rain—the usual. But the wind certainly won't help."

"No, today it'll pour—mostly 'cause we need it to stay dry," Ella answered with a wry smile as they approached the medicine hogan. Ceremonial hogans were usually larger than those intended as residences, and more traditionally constructed. This eight-sided structure constructed of interlocking pine logs was topped with layered branches and a sealing layer of clay on the roof. No blanket was hung in the simple doorway here.

Ella crouched near the hogan's entrance, studying the tracks left on the sandy ground outside. "The ceremony was attended by a fairly large group—maybe a dozen or so people, judging from all the different sizes and types of tracks. I can see moccasins, boots, and even a few imprints from athletic shoes."

Ella stepped inside the rounded interior, her gaze taking everything in as Justine snapped photos. The fire pit had been used recently and the dirt floor had been cleared of any debris or plants and smoothed out. "This place has certainly been used as a medicine hogan, but I have no idea which medicine man, or men, work here. Maybe my brother will know."

Ella studied the ashes scattered about, then picked up a bit of blackened animal fat. "Blackening must have been part of the Sing that was done here, but all I know about this is that the black comes from charcoal. My brother will be able to tell what kinds of ceremonies incorporate that ritual and, with his help, we may be able to track down the *hataalii* who conducted it."

Sings were based on knowledge and no one medicine man knew all them. Some could last for days and were extremely complicated, so *hataaliis* specialized, sometimes memorizing only one ceremony.

When her cell phone rang, Ella stepped outside and answered it. Big Ed's booming voice came through clearly.

"Our front desk just received a call from someone claiming to be Agent Thomas," he said. "The caller, a man, said that he was injured, unable to move, and trapped in a dark place. The call was made from a cell phone, but the transmission was weak, and faded before we could get any more details. Unfortunately, every attempt to call him back has failed. I wanted you to know right away and I'll be calling Agent Simmons next to tell him about it. If he's on the flight and I can't get him, I'll leave voice mail. Is there anything you'd like me to pass on to him, Shorty?"

"Yes. See if he can get the Bureau to try and pick up the GPS signal from Thomas's cell phone. Maybe his battery still has enough juice to home in on. If you can't reach Simmons, call the Albuquerque office. That's all I can offer at this stage," she said, and told him what they'd found. "But once I have something more definite, we'll pass it along."

"It's your call."

Sensing Justine's curiosity, Ella folded up her cell phone and briefed her partner quickly. "We've got to pick up the pace. If the caller was really Andy Thomas, then he's injured and trapped, so there's no telling how long he'll be able to hold on."

FOUR

✖ ✖ ✖

Working quickly, Ella helped Justine and Tache collect the evidence around the missing agent's sedan. Search dogs had been called, but they and their handlers were still en route, and the air now felt thick with moisture. Rain wasn't far.

"There are more footprints leading to the west where the mine shafts begin. Do you think Agent Thomas fell into a hole trying to escape?" Justine asked. "That might block out any signals he's sending, or cause interference, at least."

Tache made a low, guttural sound. "If he's underground, he's screwed. I heard there are more than a hundred uranium and coal mines along these mountains and, these days, their exact locations are anyone's guess. That knowledge, along with the maps, was lost when the mining companies went out of business."

"Don't be so quick to give up on Agent Thomas. You both know I fell into one of those and I'm still here," Ella said.

"Yeah, but that was different. We all had a pretty good idea where you were. It was just a matter of getting you back out," Tache said.

Ella exhaled softly. Ralph made it sound so simple, but to her, it had been like an extended visit to the eighth circle of hell. Every second she'd fought to claw her way out of the mine shaft had felt like an eternity.

Those memories were now as much a part of her as the beat of her own heart. She could still recall the terror she'd felt. Knowing that if Agent Thomas was trapped in a mine shaft he'd be going through the same ordeal renewed her energy. She knew what it was like to cling to hope when the odds were stacked against you and how fear became like an undertow that dragged you down into a fathomless well of despair.

Feeling a sudden gust of wind, Ella focused on her surroundings once more. Without warning, the dark gray clouds that had covered the sky opened up and a thunderous rain began pounding the ground. "Call off the search dogs," Ella told Justine as she zipped up her jacket, then glanced at Tache. "Take one last, fast look around. If there's any evidence left at all, we have to find it *now*."

They searched again quickly but within a few minutes it became obvious that to continue would be fruitless. "Saddle up. We're not going to be able to find anything else for a while. Go back to the station with what we have," Ella called out over the noise of the downpour, then joined them as they ran through the mud to their vehicles.

Back in her unit, watching as Tache, then Justine, used their four-wheel drives to work their vehicles out of the water-soaked ground, Ella called Big Ed on the phone and gave him an update. Her boss was disappointed when he learned of the rain, but could see the storm from the station all the way back in Shiprock.

"Shorty, I had to leave a message for Simmons, but I got the Bureau to try again with their GPS system. They couldn't get a peep from Thomas's phone. If that call from Agent Thomas was the real thing—and we have no reason to doubt that at this point—then that Anglo boy is in a world of trouble."

"I can find him," Ella said firmly. "But I'm going to need search teams out here scouring the ground and peeking down mine shafts while I follow up on other leads. The rain looks like it'll be ending before long, but make sure they're equipped with four-wheel drive."

"Right. I'll get some people into the area even if I have to import them from the county," Big Ed said. "I still haven't gotten through to Simmons. My phone's been ringing off the hook here. Try to call the man yourself and give him a rundown," he said. "You have the number?"

Ella swallowed the bad taste in her mouth. "Yes, sir. I'll get on it now."

Not wanting the call to hang over her, Ella decided to get it over with. She'd hoped to be able to leave voice mail, then hang up and drive back to the highway with both hands on the steering wheel, but it wasn't to be. Unlike Big Ed, she got Simmons on the first ring.

Ella put the vehicle in gear and drove slowly, inching her way along the slippery path, phone in her left hand. Steering with her right, she filled him in on the discovery of Thomas's car and the phone call, and the attempt to find his cell phone using the GPS signal.

"My guess is that it was probably a crank who found, or stole, Thomas's phone and is now playing games with the police," Simmons said. "But, on second thought, nix that. It's too much of a coincidence—a guy making a call like that without knowing Thomas is missing." He paused, then added, "Thing is, if it isn't Thomas, then the caller may be one of those who saw him last night, so you've got to follow it through."

"Can you get me what's needed to make a trace if we get another call?" Ella asked. "And keep someone monitoring in case Thomas's GPS starts working?"

"I'll make sure we have someone listening in for his GPS signature, but I'm not sure if I can get a tech for you to trace a call from a civilian's cell phone, or Thomas's if his GPS sender is down. Operations like that require a full-time tech and state-of-the-art equipment. Very expensive." Simmons said.

"How much is Andy Thomas worth?" Ella had already had enough of Simmons to last a lifetime.

"Yeah. Well, okay. I'll make a call. We may be able to get what we need through the Albuquerque office. They have access to some hardware, with all the research labs around New Mexico."

"The sooner the better, Agent Simmons." Ella considered telling him about her plans to talk to her brother and follow up on the Sing, but decided against it. She'd call him when she had answers, not possibilities. "I better get back to it, then," she said, intending to hang up. But he spoke again.

"Right now I'm waiting to take off to Denver, and from there I'm on to D.C., but I'm available to you twenty-four/seven. Make sure you keep me updated, particularly if you get another one of those phone calls allegedly from Thomas. Just remember, don't assume anything. Something like that bears closer scrutiny."

Ella put her cell phone down and concentrated on manhandling the SUV through a small arroyo which had water flowing in the bottom. But Simmons's last phrase stuck in her mind. Most people would have said something simple like "is worth following up" or maybe just a simple, "keep digging." But "bears closer scrutiny"? Who the heck sounded like a Sherlock Holmes dictionary when they talked?

The phrase continued to bug her and, within seconds, she suddenly remembered why. Back in her Bureau days, like many green FBI agents, she'd worked hard to try to get assigned to the Los Angeles Bureau where the action was. Careers had been made at posts like that, or in Washington D.C., or New York City. But she'd faced tough competition for the one available opening that happened to pop up just at the right time.

Gregory Simmons, already a seasoned agent, had been one of those also angling for the job. They'd both interviewed with the special agent in charge informally at first and, as she'd waited for her turn to speak, Simmons had told the SAC that a post in the L.A. Bureau should belong only to the best, and any candidate who "wasn't worthy of close scrutiny" wasn't worth having. He'd then listed his years of experience and impressive qualifications, capping that off by saying that he'd taken no shortcuts. He'd met the highest standards at the Bureau through his own merits and hard work alone, not via the back door.

Everyone in the room had known he was referring to the minority recruitment program. At that moment, more than anything, she'd wanted to grace him with an elbow smash to the hinge of his jaw.

She'd gone through the official interview that had followed, wondering if the SAC was part of the "old school"—in which case he probably disapproved of women agents and she was out of the running—or if she really had a shot at the spot. To her own surprise she was offered the assignment and, after that, she never saw Simmons again. Although she'd forgotten all about him, she was dead certain he hadn't forgotten her.

Thirty minutes later, Ella arrived at her brother's place, which was farther north and a few miles from her mother's home. Clifford's medicine hogan was about one hundred feet from his house, and she could tell that he and Loretta were both at home. His pickup and her old beat-up white sedan were parked on either side of the front entrance to their home. Since the Sing the agent had interrupted hadn't been done here, she was fairly certain that her brother hadn't been the *hataalii* who'd conducted it. But he might know who had.

Ella pulled off the dirt track and parked, then got out of her unit and looked around. There was a small cloud of dust rising from the direction she'd just come. It was either another vehicle or, more likely, a dust devil crossing the road. If they got lucky they'd have rain tonight in this area too, and that would settle some of that dust. She could see another promising thunderboomer still building over the dry deserts to the southeast.

The rocky ground here, well above the river valley to the north and east, wasn't much good for farming. There was dirt and sand, but no real soil. Only stunted grass, sage and rabbitbrush, and a few scrawny junipers grew here, but she loved the area. This was the land that the tribe had originally given their family. On the reservation no one except the tribe *owned* land, but allottees could hold on to what they'd been given for as long as they remained on the Rez and in possession of the land.

Leaning against the door of her unit, Ella waited for her brother to extend an invitation for her to approach. It was a courtesy many Navajos, mostly traditionalists, still granted their neighbors.

Minutes passed and Loretta, Clifford's wife, came out to the front porch. Loretta was a beautiful Navajo woman with long, black hair and almost Asian features. Nearly ten years younger than her husband, she was nevertheless a staunch traditionalist and usually dressed in long skirts and simple blouses, like the ones she was wearing today.

Loretta waved at Ella and called out. "My husband's not in the medicine hogan, sister-in-law. He went to gather herbs in the moist spots along the cliffside. There's a place where water stands long after the summer rains. It's one of his favorite sites."

"I know where that is," Ella called back, and with a wave, walked across the road in the general direction of the hogan, knowing it would be easier to hike up the path that ended there than drive—and it would take less time, which was even more important at the moment.

Despite Clifford's skill as an outdoorsman, he left tracks just like anyone else unless he was deliberately trying to hide his passage. Today, his path of travel was distinctive and she knew it would be no problem catching up to him.

The long, low mesa where she was headed could be seen for miles. Nearly vertical in places, the flat-looking summit held piñon and juniper trees in greater abundance than down below. At the base of the cliffs were boulders that had broken away from the mesa, depositing a jumble of large and small sandstone rocks—what geology teachers called a talus slope.

In some places water rushing past at the base of the cliffs, following much-appreciated rainstorms, had worn small hollows and exposed bedrock, or deposited sediments into cool, shady spots. The drainage of water off the mesa in places had created temporary waterfalls and resulted in intermittent pools where children could cool their toes on the hottest summer days. Around these spots the soil retained more moisture, making them fertile spots for vegetation.

As she made her way along the base of the mesa, which extended for miles in a general north-south direction, Ella began to experience a vague uneasiness that soon penetrated to the forefront of her thoughts. At first, it was nothing more than the uncertain but creepy feeling that someone was watching her. Then the badger fetish at her neck began to feel hot—a sure sign that she was in danger. She'd never been able to figure out why the fetish her brother had given her always grew warm when she was in trouble, but that warning had never failed her, so she'd learned not to discount it.

Ella stopped behind cover and studied the area around her. Something wasn't right. She wasn't sure what that was, exactly, but her instincts were telling her to stay sharp. She started to move forward, then froze to the spot. Intuition told her to wait, and that instinctive knowledge could be trusted. It came from that part of her that never lowered its guard, that always weighed actions against words, never quite trusting anyone or anything. Cop radar.

Ella waited, listening. She couldn't hear or see anything out of place but she knew in her gut something or someone was out there. Not wanting to lead danger right to her brother, Ella circled around, staying behind cover. If it were an animal, like a mountain lion that had wandered down from the mountains in search of prey, she'd soon spot it, providing she remained watchful long enough. Patience was the key.

Like a skilled hunter, her passage through the underbrush was as silent as snowfall. Ella doubled back, then pivoted randomly, attuned to everything from the scent of sage in the air to the birds, lizards, and occasional cottontail that scurried out of her way. After exhausting everything in her bag of tricks and finding nothing, she headed back along the mesa trail that would take her to where Clifford was. If nothing else, she was certain she'd lost whoever or whatever had been following her.

Although her approach had been silent, her brother looked up as soon as she got within twenty-five yards, a worried frown on his face. His gaze took in the area around them in a split second.

"Behind you!" he shouted abruptly.

Ella dove to the ground just as a thunderous blast came from the bushes somewhere to her right. She rolled to the side, intending on reaching for her gun, but unfortunately her move dropped her down into a narrow arroyo she didn't remember was there until it was too late. Sputtering and blowing the sand out of her teeth after landing facedown, Ella rolled onto her back and found her pistol by feel.

Clifford jumped down into the arroyo beside her. "Are you all right?"

She nodded. "Give me a hand up. I'm going after him," she said.

Clifford pulled her up in one fluid motion, turned, and pointed. "Guy with a shotgun, I think. He ducked back into the brush, then I heard him running east." As he spoke they both heard a powerful engine start up and a vehicle roaring away.

"A diesel, judging from the rattle. I had a feeling I was being tailed, but even though I looked, I never did spot him."

"I *felt* him—and you. That's why I looked up and saw him when I did."

"What did you see, in addition to the shotgun?" she asked quickly.

"All I got was a glimpse. He was dressed like a lot of Navajos—a straw western-style hat, blue jeans, and a greenish gray shirt. The shotgun was a pump."

"I don't know how he managed to stay hidden. I circled around and double-backed, looking and listening. But I never saw him."

"Then that tells us something else. Judging from the way he trailed you, he *knows* our land," Clifford commented. "And he's as good a tracker as you are."

"Let me go take a look around, then I'll catch up to you again in a few minutes."

Ella went to the area where the shooter had been, and found the place where he'd taken cover. The impression left on the hard ground was barely discernible, and the smooth footprints showed he'd either worn flat soles or moccasins. There was nothing to find here, not even a heel mark. He hadn't ejected the shot shell, and having used buckshot, it would be almost impossible to find or trace.

Clifford stood and waited for her as she called it in on her cell phone. Minutes later, they were hurrying back, Clifford anxious to make sure Loretta was all right. His pace was difficult for Ella to maintain, but she kept up, her breathing steady.

"What brought you here today?" Clifford asked as they ran alongside each other.

She told him about the missing agent between breaths. "I have to find the *hataalii* who did the Sing. All I know is that it entailed a blackening."

She told him about the blackened animal fat she'd found in the hogan, and everything else she knew. As they got within view of his home, and they saw Loretta out back bringing in laundry from the clothesline, Clifford slowed to a walk and Ella followed suit.

Reaching into her jacket, she pulled out the evidence pouch with the bit of animal fat. Since the ritual itself wasn't part of the investigation, it wasn't official evidence. "This is what I found. Does it tell you anything?"

He nodded. "That's used for an Evil Way. It's a special mixture of mutton and deer fat that's mixed with ball charcoal. It's powerful medicine against the *chindi* and it's used in a one-day ceremony. What you have in your hand is the blackening agent that's used on the patient. Afterwards, he's not supposed to wash it off for four days, which, come to think of it, should make it easy for you to identify him. He'll have a line drawn on his face that goes down from his ear to his jaw, then back up to his other ear."

"Thanks for the heads-up. Who does that kind of ceremony?"

"*Hastiin sání* and his son," he said, using the Navajo expression for "old man" to refer to John Tso. Traditionalists still held the belief that names had power and to use them would diminish the person spoken about. "The father was the one who did the Sing for you, remember?"

"Of course. You know it's remarkable that anyone that age can remember every word of a Sing as complicated as that one. It's the equivalent of the entire script to a very, very long movie."

"The gods have shown him favor," he said.

"Would either of those *hataaliis* use that particular hogan?" she added, describing the one she'd seen and giving its location.

"The two I mentioned have their own medicine hogans. But it's possible that particular hogan belongs to the family of the patient, or a relative, and they wanted the ceremony done there. It happens that way sometimes."

"I need some leads. Can you ask around and try to get me the name of some of the people who attended the Sing?"

"I'll do my best."

"In the meantime I'll speak to the two men you mentioned. Can you give me directions to their homes?"

"Sure." Clifford gave her the information she needed, then pointed to her unit, which was across the road from where they were standing. "Looks like you're not leaving right away. You have a flat tire—no, two of them, it looks like, both on the left side."

"Crap. Must have picked up some nails on one of the back roads I've been on today." But as she got closer Ella saw that someone had punctured the sidewalls with a knife or screwdriver. "This is the last thing I need now," she hissed. Time was slipping away from her and, more importantly, from Agent Thomas.

"I'll help you change them. You'll be out of here in ten minutes, if we hurry."

"But I've only got *one* spare," she said.

"Take my pickup, then," he offered. "We still have my wife's car."

Ella shook her head. "Need my radio. How about if I just take your truck spare? It's a different tread and width, but the right diameter. That and my own spare will do the trick."

"Okay. Let's get to it," he said.

"Can you start while I go around back to ask your wife a few questions just in case she saw something?" Seeing him nod, Ella tossed Clifford her keys so he could get to her spare and jack.

Ella questioned Loretta but she hadn't seen anything. While ironing she'd heard a vehicle stop outside. By the time she walked to the window to see who it was, the car was already gone. Later she'd also heard a shot, but had assumed someone had been hunting. After that she hadn't heard a vehicle go by, so the suspect had clearly used a different escape route.

Wishing Loretta had been more observant, Ella hurried to help Clifford. The sun was low in the sky and would be setting in a couple of hours. If Agent Thomas was still conscious, he was in his own version of hell by now. His moods would swing like a pendulum between fear and hope, each having its moment, then slipping away, leaving him with only his will to live. But that too would desert him eventually, no matter how strong he was.

Ella helped her brother with the second tire, then thanking him, was soon back on the road. As she headed for the main highway, Justine called.

"I've got the results of the blood test, and the type matches Agent Thomas's," Justine said quickly. "We'll get a confirmation through DNA tests, but that's going to take longer even though I called the FBI and they're putting an emergency rush on the job. Right now I'm trying to identify tire marks, and go over the evidence we found in and around Agent Thomas's car."

"I've got two possible leads on the medicine men who might have done the Sing," she said, explaining. "Can you take Ben Tso while I question his father?"

"I could do that, but that'll mean that no one will be here processing the evidence."

"Where Ralph Tache?" Ella asked.

"He's working on the photos, then he'll be figuring out the sequence of events based on the foot and tire prints."

Ella exhaled softly. There was never enough manpower and that always became even more apparent during a crisis. "Is Sergeant Neskahi around the station? I'm going to recruit him for this case."

"You'll have to wait until this evening, Ella. Joe's testifying in court right now."

Frustration bit at her, but she pushed the feeling back into a dark corner of her mind. "I'm on my way to see John out by Four Corners. He doesn't have a phone, so I have no other option. Tache's work is less critical than yours, so have him go speak to Ben. The son lives closer to the station, north of the Nenahnezad Chapter House, but like his dad doesn't have phone service."

Off the Navajo Nation, phone service was taken for granted even in most rural areas. On the Rez, a lot of people still did without it because they didn't have a telephone line in their area, or money for the monthly bill. "With luck, he'll reach Ben's place and get answers before I turn off the highway. That may save me a long trip down another bad road," Ella said.

"But Tache's working on the photos right now and he's in the darkroom. . . ."

"Interrupt him and tell him I need him to talk to Ben," Ella snapped, then took a deep breath. "If we don't find Agent Thomas soon, the Bureau's going to send in an invasion army. Once that happens, whatever chance we had of finding Thomas will disappear in a flash."

"I'll go get Ralph," Justine said.

FIVE

✖ ✖ ✖

It was nearly 4:30 P.M. now. Ella drove northwest farther into the Rez toward Teec Nos Pos. John Tso lived in the extreme northwestern corner of New Mexico beside the San Juan River. The quickest route there lay in going just west into Arizona, then turning northwest on Highway 160. Just before the turnoff leading to the Four Corners monument was a dirt track leading southeast. Down that road was a shallow valley between rocky mesas where the river flowed out of Utah, cut across the tip of Colorado, then into New Mexico.

After his former home by Rattlesnake had burned to the ground last winter, Tso had moved here. The house stood alone just above the river in the narrow bosque. Because of the location, Ella was sure that his electricity came from a generator, but at least he had a well, being close to the water table.

Ella pressed on the accelerator, trying to eat up the thirty-five or so miles of good road before the turnoff. The high speed gave her the illusion of progress, and she found it comforting. Miles became a blur but soon she had to slow down as she passed through Beclabito, the last significant New Mexico community before entering Arizona.

The country around here was higher in elevation, with many more junipers and a few piñons, small hills and sandstone cliffs. The reds and browns in the soil contrasted with the dark greens of the low, wide trees, and even the grays of the brush were beautiful. Farther ahead, to the north, the area right around Four Corners itself was flat and dry, almost expressionless.

Despite the seriousness of the situation, Ella couldn't help but smile, recalling the many times she'd roamed around the countryside in this area as a child. She'd sneak away chasing rabbits while her father preached from a big tent and served lunch to anyone who'd come to sit and listen to his Gospel.

Ten minutes later, as she turned onto the dirt track that led back east toward the river, Tache called over the radio. "You're going to the right place," he said. "*Hastiin sání* did the Sing. I just spoke to his son."

"Thanks."

After ten minutes of a sand and rock roller-coaster road that rarely let her use anything but low gear, and conscious of the fact that she had no spare tire now, Ella reached John Tso's place without incident. His cinder-block house stood at the edge of a dry plateau just above the narrow bosque of willows and brush that lined the river. Mountains rose in every direction except the southeast.

A large medicine hogan stood about fifty feet from the main house, closer to the river. Sheltered from the westerly breezes by a low embankment was a peeled cottonwood log pen holding about a dozen sheep. If there was a dog, she couldn't see any sign of it.

Noticing smoke coming from the hogan, Ella parked in line with the blanketed entrance, then got out of her unit and leaned against the door so he could see her clearly. Custom dictated that she wait, but as the minutes ticked by, her impatience grew. Agent Thomas was in a life-or-death situation, and after racing over here, being forced to wait out of courtesy seemed inappropriate—and dangerous.

After the longest five minutes of her life, Ella decided to throw convention to the winds and began walking toward the blanketed doorway. She'd only taken a few steps when she reconsidered, stopped in midstride, then returned to the SUV.

She knew better. A disrespectful approach would get her

nowhere, and if wasting five minutes now would save a day's searching later, she'd just have to stay still a while longer.

Another two minutes passed and John failed to appear. Ella was certain that he knew she was there. She'd seen the blanket in the doorway billow out and part slightly as she'd started toward the hogan. John had probably noted her impatience and decided to teach her a lesson in manners by making her wait some more.

Ella weighed her options carefully. It was time to get creative. Reaching inside her unit, Ella pulled out her clipboard, then began walking around, searching the ground and occasionally crouching down and pretending to take notes. She'd only done that for about a minute or so when John Tso came outside.

"What are you doing?" he asked.

Ella smiled at the medicine man, whom she suspected was in his nineties. "I was studying the plants around here," she said. Noting his annoyed expression, Ella knew that seeing her approach his hogan uninvited *had* angered him. If she wanted him to cooperate, she'd have to find a way to put him in a more receptive mood. Otherwise, he might choose not to give her the name of his patient or any other information pertaining to his Sing. All things considered, getting him to tell her anything at all was bound to be tricky. He'd probably taken Agent Thomas's intrusion on the ceremony as an affront and wouldn't be eager to interfere with whatever punishment the gods had meted out.

"You're lucky to have so many plants around here that are good for grazing, like blue gama and winter-fat," Ella said.

"You remember such things?" John asked, surprised.

Ella nodded. "When I was a little girl, my mother taught me which were the best plants for grazing sheep and goats. She even encouraged me to put the pieces of each in my mouth. I discovered one in particular that tasted really salty. When I told Mom, she smiled and told me that it was because the sheep peed on them. I spit that plant out so fast, I nearly gagged. Then I saw my mother laughing and realized she'd only been joking."

John laughed. "I know your mother, and that's her, all right!"

He cocked his head toward the hogan. "Come in. We'll talk inside. Even a small breeze chills these old bones of mine."

Ella followed *hastiin sání* inside, taking the woman's place on the north side, and accepted the warm cup of herbal tea he offered her. Though she was anxious not to waste time with pleasantries, on the Rez these rituals were far from inconsequential.

"Uncle," she said, using the name out of respect, not kinship, "I'm searching for an FBI agent who I believe may have intruded on one of your Sings. A red-haired Anglo man."

"Yes, I know who you mean. He showed up uninvited at a ceremony I was conducting in a medicine hogan that belongs to my patient's family. Someone spotted him watching from behind a tree and two of the men went up to chase him off."

"What happened to the agent?"

"I didn't see. My patient and I remained in the hogan. But that *bilagáana* made a very big mistake. My Sings have a lot of power so everyone there with the right attitude can benefit. But if the prayers aren't said exactly right, or if something disturbs the harmony, then bad things happen and the gods aren't always quick to forgive. You know this, your brother is a Singer like me."

"Who was your patient?"

He shook his head, dismissing her question. "I don't have to answer that."

Ella said nothing for a while, staring instead at her lap, deep in thought. At long last she looked up. "Uncle, unless I find this agent, the federal government is going to send in dozens of their law-enforcement people. If they come in, there'll be no peace or harmony for anyone, and it could go on for weeks. This has happened before."

John nodded, then considered it carefully, sipping his tea. "I know nothing about the *bilagáana,* but my patient's name is Melvin Rainwater," he said in a hushed tone, respecting the use of a proper name. "His family has used that particular hogan before, I was told, but I don't think it really belongs to them," he added, shrugging. He looked down and noticed a spider crawling across the dirt floor. Finally he looked up again. "I suppose I'm partly to blame for this trouble. I should have stopped the Sing after the men spotted the intruder. Everyone was really angry about that and I knew it was dangerous to continue. But my patient insisted. It would be improper for me to interpret the effectiveness of the Sing, but my patient will know soon enough."

Ella knew that Sings were sometimes repeated, or other ceremonies performed if the problem persisted. "What else can you tell me about your patient? I'd like to find him so I can talk to him."

"His clan is Red Running into Water—Táchii'nii, and he was born for the Cove of the Mountain clan—Dziltl' ahnii. The man is in his twenties, with short hair and a wide nose that looks like he got it broken a few times. His Navajo is better than most young people speak today, and his English is very good."

Ella wrote it all down in her memo pad, then looked up. "Is there anything else you remember?"

He shook his head. "He wouldn't tell me much about himself, only that he really wanted the Sing done. After the ceremony was over, he apologized for the Anglo government man. He said he'd known that the man wanted to talk to him, but never expected him to show up at the Sing."

"Did your patient tell you *why* the agent was looking for him?"

"He didn't say and I didn't ask," John answered.

"Who else attended the Sing?"

He shrugged. "I assumed they were all members of his family and friends, but I didn't know any of them. They wouldn't have introduced themselves to me using their Anglo names, so I can't really answer your question. But there's just no excusing what that Anglo agent did. We need to be free to carry on the traditions of our people without interference from an ignorant *bilagáana* who thinks a gold badge is all the authorization he needs."

"Thank you, Uncle, for taking time to talk to me."

A few minutes later, Ella was on the way back to the station. She hadn't had more than a bite to eat since early that morning, and she was starving. She didn't remember if there was a fast-food place in Beclabito, but Ella consoled herself with the thought that she'd be back in Shiprock within the hour and she'd be able to grab something then. From the looks of it, she'd be working nonstop through the night unless they got an unexpected break.

That, of course, brought up another problem. Ella reached for her cell phone with one hand and called home. A moment later Rose answered. Over her mother's hello she could hear Dawn chattering in the background.

"I already know why you're calling," Rose said softly. "You won't be home until late, right? Your brother said you were looking for someone. I promised not to mention it to anyone, so don't worry about any gossip, daughter."

"I won't have anything resembling regular hours until this man's found. His life is on the line."

"I understand, and so will your daughter. Would you like to speak to her?"

"Yes, please." Ella heard footsteps on the kitchen floor as Dawn ran to the phone. A moment later her daughter's excited voice greeted her.

"Mommy! Guess what? I got to ride *bareback* today. Boots led Wind around the corral and I was able to stay on even when we trotted! Then she let me go around on my own three times."

"Good for you!" Ella said, wishing she could have been the one to give Dawn her first bareback lesson. Before Dawn could chatter on, Ella got serious. "Pumpkin, I have to work late tonight and maybe tomorrow too. Someone's lost and I've got to help find him."

"Okay." Dawn said, then added, "Can I ride Wind one more time before dinner?"

Ella sighed. Sometimes she had the distinct feeling that if Dawn had to choose between her and Wind, the pony would win. "Ask Boots," Ella said, referring to Dawn's baby-sitter, "and your *shimasáni*," she added, using the Navajo word for "grandmother." "Whatever they say is fine with me." Ella heard Dawn drop the phone and run off to talk to Boots.

A second later Rose picked up the receiver. "She really *does* miss you," Rose said gently, guessing what had gone through

Ella's mind. "It's just that she knows you'll be home sooner or later, and, in the meantime, she has Boots and me. Remember that time doesn't mean as much to her as it does to older folks like us."

"Mom, if something comes up while I'm working on this case and you find that neither Boots nor you can stay with my daughter, call her father and ask him to help."

"We'll manage. Don't worry about us."

"Thanks, Mom."

The sun was resting atop the Carrizo Mountains when a pale brown or gold SUV passed her at high speed, racing east. A blinding glare reflected off the rear window, and even though she'd been wearing sunglasses, Ella had to take her foot off the gas and concentrate to keep her unit in the lane. With bright dots still dancing in her eyes—much like the aftereffects of a flashbulb—she looked ahead, hoping to catch a better description of the SUV, and maybe the license plate.

The vehicle—from the size and shape a Ford Excursion—was still accelerating, and Ella saw it whip around and pass a pickup loaded with firewood less than an eighth of a mile ahead. The glare must have blinded the pickup's driver as well because he hit the brakes hard and swerved, wobbling in the lane and spilling a dozen or more split logs onto the highway. The chunks of wood struck the pavement at forty-five miles an hour, bouncing and flipping end-over-end like bark-covered footballs.

Ella tapped the brakes heavily, trying to slow enough to maneuver around the logs, which bounced randomly all across the highway. She had to pull hard to the right to avoid a particularly large chunk tumbling right toward the center of her onrushing vehicle.

Due to the extra-wide tire on the back left, the rear end fluttered and lifted up off the pavement on the right side as the unit reacted to her abrupt maneuvers. She compensated quickly, but a chunk of wood struck a front tire and the vehicle shuddered. With all four tires making contact again, and no oncoming vehicles, Ella pumped the brakes, easing off onto the shoulder, needing only a last-minute adjustment to avoid a rolling log.

Her heart beating a hundred times a minute, Ella glanced up, and through a big cloud of slowly clearing dust, saw that the pickup with the firewood had run off the road. It had also taken out a section of wire fence along the way, finally coming to a stop fifty yards into the brush. From her angle, she couldn't see the front end, but the vehicle was upright and looked intact.

Ella called it in with her radio, then ran to check on the driver. As she approached the oversized white four-door truck, her blood turned to ice. The pickup belonged to Herman Cloud, her mother's friend, and hers too.

"Herman!" she yelled, then breathed a sigh of relief when she saw him step out of the truck slowly and turn back to look at all the scattered firewood. He wasn't injured as far as she could see, but he looked angry as hell.

"The people in that big Ford are crazy!" he called out to her. "Did you see what happened? That stupid game of theirs caused all this! They should be arrested!"

"Game . . . you don't mean glare?"

"There was someone in the back of the SUV wearing a red cap playing with a big mirror. He was actually aiming it. I only saw him for an instant before he got me right in the eyes, but he was trying to make me wreck!" He rubbed a reddish welt on his forehead.

"Are you all right?" she asked gently.

"Yeah. I just got bounced around a bit. But *my truck!*" he grumbled, looking back at. "I better check the oil pan. I scraped something real hard."

"Did you get a look at the plates on that Ford?"

Herman shook his head. "Wish I had," he muttered, crouching down gingerly to look beneath the truck.

Ella insisted on calling the EMTs for him despite his assurances that he was okay, then jogged back to her unit to put out an APB on the vehicle. Not that she was hopeful it'd get results—all she had was color and a probable make and model. She'd never seen the plates. But it was the recklessness of the incident that bothered her most. The dark side of human nature seldom made sense to her. Malicious behavior all too often existed in defiance of logic.

Unfortunately, this was just another thing slowing her down at a time when she could least afford it. First the shooting near her brother's home, the vandalized tires, and now this. She strongly suspected that someone was deliberately trying to divert her away from the search for Agent Thomas.

Still weighing the implications, Ella glanced up and saw Herman come out from beneath the truck, try to stand up and stagger. Ella rushed over to steady him.

"I'm all right," he grumbled.

Despite his protests Ella held on to him and felt him sway. She wouldn't leave Herman until help arrived and she was sure he was safe and in good hands. Whoever had been determined to slow her search had won this round.

SIX

—————— ✖ ✖ ✖ ——————

While clearing firewood from the highway, Ella had called Rose, knowing her mother would have never forgiven her if she hadn't told her about Herman's accident immediately. Rose now stood a few feet away from her, watching Herman checking his truck one more time as paramedics collected their gear, ready to leave.

"Mom, I wish I could stay with you," Ella said as the medical team climbed into the ambulance, "but I've got to get going again."

"The missing agent," Rose said in a soft voice and nodded. "The temperature is supposed to really drop in the foothills tonight, too," she added.

Ella nodded. "It's already getting chilly," she said, zipping up her jacket. What worried her even more was the possibility that it had rained wherever he was. If he was cold, wet, and injured, he wouldn't stand much of a chance when hypothermia set in.

Ella checked with Herman and confirmed that his vehicle was operational, then nodded her approval as Rose volunteered to follow Herman home in case his pickup had a delayed-reaction malfunction.

Ella said good-bye, then called Justine as she drove toward Shiprock and the station. "I need everything you can get me on Melvin Rainwater, and I want it yesterday."

Ella heard Justine type in the name after verifying the spelling. "Nothing—no arrests, not even a parking ticket. But DMV has a Melvin Rainwater with a NM chauffeur's license and a listed Farmington address. There's also a telephone number."

"Give me that information, then keep digging with all the databases you can, credit reports . . . everything you can find. We need to know where he works, where he banks, what he drives, whatever."

Ella wrote down the address and telephone number, then hung up. Thinking about it only for a second, she decided to call Rainwater's home. She'd pretend to be a telemarketer. That would give her confirmation of his location without revealing who she was. All calls from her cell phone were blocked. After that, she'd head for Farmington.

She dialed, then got a recording stating that the number had been disconnected. Either Melvin hadn't paid his bills or he'd switched to a cell phone or maybe moved out.

Ella called Justine back and asked her to find any other possible phone numbers or addresses listed for Melvin Rainwater. "Do your best, and remember—in this case, faster *is* better," she added, then hung up again.

Ella put the phone away and considered her options. To find Agent Thomas quickly she'd need to pull in every resource available. Ella called the county sheriff, Paul Taylor, and, within a minute, arranged for a deputy to go check Rainwater's listed address. Melvin, if home, would be detained until she could get there.

Ella was just passing through Shiprock, heading east, when she got a return call from Taylor. The sheriff had a laid-back good ole boy manner and a slight southeastern New Mexico accent, but he was sharp and very capable. "Ella, the deputy stopped by the Rainwater address and the apartment was occupied by a retired black man. According to a neighbor, Rainwater moved out three months ago. I've got his vehicle's plate number—providing that's more accurate than his address of course—and he owns a blue-green Chevy Blazer. You want me to put out a bulletin to stop and detain the man?"

"That would be great, Paul. Could you give me a call right away if he turns up? You have my cell number, right?"

"Of course. Glad to be able to help the tribe again. Why are you looking for Rainwater?" Taylor asked.

"Just for questioning at the moment. He may have information about a missing-persons case I'm working on."

"Oh, *that* missing person. Okay, I'll put out a bulletin now. I have Rainwater's physical description from his DMV record. Anything to add to that?"

"I don't remember having seen Rainwater before, but he *might* have some black markings on his face from a recent healing ceremony, though I can't guarantee that. I'll have one of my officers send more details if they become available. Thanks, Paul."

"Right, Ella. Happy hunting, and take care."

Ella couldn't afford to wait until somebody stumbled across the man, she needed help finding him *now*. But she didn't have the authority to enlist anyone off the Rez full-time, not without going through channels, and that would take hours, maybe even days.

Pulling off the road into the Totah Café parking lot, she took a moment to search her mind for available resources she could tap into. Then she remembered Teeny. He did contract work for the department from time to time, was a trained former Navajo cop, *and* lived in the Farmington area. Maybe she could talk Big Ed into agreeing to put him on the job. She'd been given the authority to use all tribal resources, and the tribe did employ Teeny on occasion . . . even if it was usually for technical work, not tracking down witnesses.

Adhering to the old adage that it was better to ask forgiveness than permission, Ella decided to put Teeny to work right away then call Big Ed afterward and convince him to sign off on her decision. She was certain the chief would go for it, and, after all, timing was critical.

Ella got Bruce Little's number from information, then dialed. After exchanging a few pleasantries, she got right to the point. "I want to put you back on the tribal payroll, Teeny, at least long enough for you to help my SI team on a case. I'd need you right now. Can you help?"

"Hey, did you really have to ask?" he said, then added, "But since this calls for me to drop everything else, I insist on a bonus. You owe me dinner—and I eat a lot."

Ella laughed. "You've got it. But don't you want to know what the job is first?"

"If it's for you, it doesn't matter. But okay, what's the job? Finding Andy Thomas?"

"It's related to that. What I need you to do is track down a Navajo man named Melvin Rainwater." She gave Teeny Rainwater's former address, a physical description, and the vehicle information he had listed with the Department of Motor Vehicles.

"I know Rainwater from somewhere, and I'll probably remember why once I hang up. Either way, I'm on him right now, Ella. You want me to collar him for you?"

"Not unless he makes a run for it. Just give me a call and stay on him." She gave him her cell number, then added, "I need to interview him ASAP. Deal?"

"Deal. I'll get back to you."

It didn't take long for Big Ed to officially approve her decision to hire Bruce Little. After all, the tribe sometimes paid private investigators to assist their attorneys, so this wasn't totally unprecedented. But Big Ed had asked that Ella keep him updated on Teeny's progress every step of the way. A fair deal, all in all.

Already parked in front of the Totah Café and smelling the aroma of freshly roasted chile, Ella decided to go inside. Her stomach was so empty it hurt. She'd get something to eat, talk to the staff, and hopefully pick up some useful information.

Ella passed through the glass foyer, stepped into the air-conditioned interior, then walked up to the counter and placed an order. It was busy, dinnertime for most, but she was still able to make conversation with the waitress and the cashier between customers. She asked them about Melvin Rainwater—there were few traditionalists here judging from what they were wearing, so using his name was appropriate—but although the waitress had heard of Melvin, she had no idea where he might be living now. The woman thought it was Farmington from the way he'd talked at the cash register about the Scorpions, a local high school team.

Ella had just paid for her order when her cell phone rang.

"It's me," Teeny said, knowing his voice was distinctive. Someone had once compared it to a person who'd swallowed a large chunk of pumice stone. "I'm at my Shiprock office now. Where are you?"

"I'm at the Totah," Ella answered, wondering if he'd already found Melvin. It was entirely possible that Teeny had known exactly where to find him all along and had just wanted to justify his employment by making it look like he'd worked for it. Even ex-police officers rarely placed all their cards on the table.

"I've got news you need to hear. Be there in ten," Teeny said.

He hung up before she could say anything else, but Ella knew Teeny well enough to know that whatever he had to offer would be worth the wait.

Teeny actually arrived a minute early. Spotting Ella, Teeny nodded, then walked over to join her, pulling up a chair from an empty table near her booth. "Sorry for the need to make this face-to-face, Ella, but I just didn't want to discuss this over the telephone. I know you needed fast answers, so I went to plan B instead of wasting time with legwork."

Ella didn't know if she really wanted to hear about plan B, but Teeny was right about the need for quick results. "Go on."

"I remembered that Melvin was dating a cousin of mine a few years ago. He was working for Yazzie Construction and living with one of his brothers. I couldn't reach my cousin, so I hacked—"

She held up a hand. "Whoa, *too* much information. Just give me what you've got."

"I *acquired* the address Melvin gave Yazzie Construction. But there wasn't much else in his personnel file. He only worked there a few months, then quit to work for the *Dineh Times*," Teeny said, slipping a piece of paper across the table.

Teeny's gesture was so guarded Ella was reminded of a similar action many years ago while she was still in the FBI, working undercover. The circumstances at that time made today's gesture seem innocent by comparison.

"The location's on the reservation, so it's completely within your jurisdiction," Teeny said. "Just keep in mind that I don't know if either brother is still living there." He studied her expression, then added, "If you're planning to check it out, take me as a ride along. I know backup is a pain because it can take forever, but you shouldn't solo this one."

Ella thought it over. With Justine and Ralph Tache already busy and Neskahi tied up in court, it wouldn't hurt, and it was possible Teeny's presence would give her the leverage she needed to get some fast answers from Rainwater if the lead panned out.

"Let's go," she said, looking around for the waitress. Three minutes later, her chile cheeseburger and fries in a foam container, Ella walked with Teeny to her unit.

"Hey, Ella, I'll drive while you eat, okay?"

"Thanks." She handed him the keys, and they were soon under way.

"I always wanted to work with your SI team. Just my luck I became the department's tech head. But it all worked out in the long run. I like running my own business," he said, picking at the fries she'd offered. "What about you? You've been a tribal cop long enough. Why don't you consider becoming a PI? There's more money in it."

"Nah, we all have to do what we do best. You're good with software and communications gear, so you ended up in the right place. Me, I'm a field officer, first, last, and foremost."

"I hear you," he said.

"But doing PI work might be right up *your* alley if you really want to get out of the office more often."

He smiled, but the gesture didn't make him look much friendlier than a bear showing its teeth. On Teeny, smiles never looked quite natural.

"I'm glad to help you and the tribe this time—not as a tech head, but on an in-your-face investigation. It'll give you a taste of what I can do, you know? Then, in the future, maybe you'll call on me again."

"You've got it."

"Now fill me in a little more. Why do you need Rainwater? Something to do with Agent Thomas, obviously. But what's Melvin into?" Teeny asked.

It was a fair question under the circumstances. Ella knew that he was simply trying to determine what kind of reception to expect once they caught up to Melvin and possibly his brother.

"I honestly don't know. Thomas didn't leave any details concerning the case he was working on, and with Blalock gone . . ." She shrugged. "That's why I'll be pressing Rainwater hard for information on Thomas. He's the best—no, the only—lead I've got so far."

Soon they arrived at a small wood-frame house east of Shiprock in an older tribal housing development. The driveway and carport were empty, and no one seemed to be around. In addition, there was no sign of trash cans or garbage bags to indicate anyone currently lived there.

"Cover the back for me, Teeny, just in case one of the Rainwater brothers is home and decides to make a quick exit."

"Done."

As Teeny walked around back, Ella went up to the front door, knocked, and identified herself. The rapping reverberated with a hollow echo, but other than that, no sound at all came from the interior. Waiting only a few seconds, Ella stepped around the corner of the house and, seeing a curtainless window, peered inside. The interior was vacant. There was no furniture or any other sign that anyone was living there.

"This was a bust," Teeny said, coming around the corner of the house. "From what I could tell, no one's been here for weeks, possibly months. There are cobwebs around the back door, and no fresh tracks anywhere unless you're tracking dogs and crows."

He paused for a long moment, rubbing the back of his neck with one hand. "Guess Melvin and his brother both moved on. Drop me back off at the Totah and I'll make a few phone calls."

"Okay. I'll follow up another lead based on the information you gave me."

"Jaime at the *Times*?" he asked.

She nodded and smiled, remembering that Teeny and Jaime were good friends. "I'm going to go talk to her next."

He gave her a lopsided grin that might have been truly frightening under different circumstances. "Jaime's a cool lady. She brings me some business from time to time. I've done some nontechnical work for the paper twice in the last six months."

"Doing what?"

"Well, it wasn't reporting," he said. "That's all I can tell you." He paused, then met her gaze and held it. "The address may not have panned out, Ella, but I'll earn my paycheck. Count on it. My sources are . . . different from yours."

"Which is why I called you," Ella answered with a nod.

Ella dropped him off at the Totah Café, and on the drive to the newspaper office called Big Ed and told him about Teeny accompanying her to the empty house. Her chief grumbled, but thanked her for keeping him up to date.

A short time later Ella arrived at the nondescript newspaper office, a cinder-block building that had formerly housed a potato-chip plant. The interior of the warehouse-style structure still smelled a bit like vegetable oil and fried chips despite a repainting and remodeling, or maybe it was just nostalgia playing games with her. Ella had taken a tour of the factory back in elementary school—an ice age or two ago.

As she walked down the hall past the vending machine, Ella discovered Jaime standing outside her office talking to a young Navajo woman in slacks and a loose-fitting jacket. The canvas camera bag slung from her shoulder suggested Jaime's companion was a reporter or photographer, but Ella didn't recognize her.

Jaime looked almost the same as she had in high school, except for a few extra pounds. Today her hair was up in a ponytail and she looked tired. Seeing Ella, her expression brightened instantly. "Hey, you're just the person I wanted to talk to! We've heard that there's a missing FBI agent and that the tribal police have joined the search. Care to comment on the progress of your investigation?"

The young photographer reached into her canvas bag, placing a hand on her camera. Jaime caught her eye and shook her head almost imperceptibly.

"I'm helping track down a missing Anglo, Jaime, but I was told he was a tourist interested in tribal ceremonies," Ella said, giving Jaime a quick cover story. Simmons had requested discretion and, under the circumstances, she agreed with him. There was another way to play this and still get what she needed. "I'm following a lead right now, which is why I'm here. I can't go into the particulars yet, but I'm looking for an employee of the paper, a delivery man, Melvin Rainwater."

"Never heard of him, but then our paths wouldn't necessarily cross. Come back to my office and I'll have my assistant look him up." Jaime nodded to the photographer, who left without comment.

Jaime, the editor in chief of the tribal newspaper, led the way inside to the large, sparsely furnished office, one of two actually walled in completely to the ceiling. The decor was spartan and clutter abounded. There was one desk containing a new-looking computer, two worn chairs stacked with files, and several large metal cabinets, but judging by the amount of paperwork scattered about, filing was only done here as a last resort.

Jaime pressed the intercom buzzer and spoke hurriedly to someone, then focused back on Ella. "Delbert will get the information you want in a few minutes."

"Great."

"While we're waiting, why don't you tell me more about this tourist—what he's like and so on."

"All I really know is that he's a six-foot-tall redhead with blue eyes. He should really stick out among us."

"Yeah, give him a cowboy outfit and you've got Howdy Doody. What's his name?"

"We've agreed to keep it confidential until his family can be notified. Can you make sure the important details get in your paper?"

"Sure, but I could use a photo."

"We're still trying to get one ourselves. But tall and redheaded should be enough of a description, don't you think?"

"I'll make sure we get a notice somewhere in the first two pages and include a phone number to call. Maybe it'll ring a bell with someone who saw him wandering around." Jaime poured herself a cup of coffee. "Want one?"

"Thanks," Ella said accepting the steaming cup Jaime offered. She wasn't going anywhere until Jaime's assistant got back to them anyway.

Jaime took a sip of her own brew, then spoke. "If you decide you and the department need an extra hand with this missing-persons case, you might consider Bruce Little. I know he's done computer network jobs for the tribe since he left your department, but I can tell you from personal experience that he excels at finding people—even the ones who don't want to be found. I can't go into what he's done for the paper, but you might give him a call. He's expensive, but worth every penny. Come to think of it, all *you'd* have to do is give him a big smile and he'd probably work for you for free," Jaime said, and made a face at her.

Ella laughed. "Teeny's always been nice to me, that's true."

Jaime smiled. "He's very good at the things he does, Ella. And intimidating when he wants to be. Hey, even when he doesn't want to be," she added.

"He's a good man. People are just too quick to judge him on appearances," Ella said.

"Nah, don't bother telling me he's all gentleness and sweetness in a rough package. I *know* better. Remember what he did to coach's desk?"

Ella chuckled, vividly recalling the incident. Her senior year in high school one of the coaches had been on her case, constantly accusing her of not pushing herself hard enough on the basketball court. Things hit an all-time low when, after barely squeaking to a win against their number-one rivals, he'd ragged her miserably in front of the entire boys' and girls' teams. Teeny, working as a trainer for the boys' team, had been one of those present.

The following Monday after school, when they'd all gone into the gym to practice, coach had discovered that his enormous oak desk was missing. He'd eventually found it outside, sticking out of a trash bin. The desk had been the coach's pride and joy and took six of the school's football players to carry back up to his second-story office in the athletic building.

Although kids normally talked and gossiped, there'd been no rumors at all to point to the person responsible. Coach had never been able to pin it on Teeny though everyone had known that he was the only one who could have pulled it off.

Before Ella could comment, Jaime's assistant came in and handed her a note. Jaime looked at it, then back up at Ella. "I've got an address, but I want an exclusive when you finally release the story. You're holding out on me, Ella, and you probably have your reasons, but I'm going to need some payback later."

"I agree to an exclusive, though don't get your hopes up on anything worth front-page headlines." Ella reached for the address before Jaime could add any more conditions. "Thanks."

As Ella drove away from the newspaper building, she noticed immediately how dark it was already. The moonless night chilled her spirit. Without streetlights, the dark was a yawning void that only gave way grudgingly to the narrow beams from her vehicle before it closed in behind the unit, quickly swallowing the faint red glow of her taillights.

Ella pushed her unit for speed once she was back on the main highway, but when the vehicle began to vibrate, she remembered the problem with the tires. She'd have to go back to the station and get a matching tire or risk an accident or loss of control. She could also use a spare, and so could Clifford.

Once there, she'd find Justine, and, with luck, her partner would be finished with her lab work and they could ride together. Going to interview Rainwater wasn't something she wanted to do without some kind of backup, not so much because of the potential danger but because it would be harder to prevent his escape if he tried to make a run for it.

Ella made a call to the man on duty in Maintenance, told him what the problem was, and arranged to leave her unit and the two flat tires at the garage. By the time their conversation ended, she was there. After signing the garage paperwork, Ella walked the short distance from the garage to Justine's lab inside the station and found her partner working on a report.

"I'm going to need your help," Ella said, filling her in on the latest. "I've got a new address for Melvin and I want to follow that up tonight. But we'll have to use your vehicle."

"Let's go. Anything to get out of the lab for a while. I've done all I can here now." Justine brought out a photo of Rainwater. "I got this from the Motor Vehicle Department's records, but the address listed is the same one you already checked out in Farmington."

A few minutes later, they were rolling again, but Ella's tension continued to grow and she stared straight ahead out the windshield, staring at nothing.

"It's getting to you," Justine said quietly, gesturing to Ella's hand, which was on her lap clenched into a fist.

"Yeah, it is," she admitted grudgingly. "Thomas's chances of making it out of this alive decrease with every passing hour. I can feel time slipping through my fingers like sand, and yet I can't seem to make any real progress!"

"Let's try to shake Rainwater up. But just to play devil's advocate for a moment, Ella, what's next if Rainwater doesn't have the answers we need?"

"He'll at least know the names of everyone who attended the Sing. We'll interview all of them if we have to. The trail begins at that ceremony."

SEVEN
✖ ✖ ✖

The address they now had for Melvin Rainwater was just south of the river near the small farming community of Waterflow. There were a few scattered houses in this area, even though most of the good farming land was across the river, outside the Rez. Still, with the big power plant just a few miles away, Rainwater, at least, had modern conveniences—electricity, a well, and a paved road. Stores farther east in Kirtland and Farmington offered cheaper prices than those in Shiprock, too.

Ella and Justine approached the house, a small wood-framed, flat-roofed stucco building with no garage or landscaping. A twenty-foot tall globe willow stood in front, offering some daytime shade for the front porch, a simple concrete slab. No car was visible anywhere, and there were no lights inside the house. The house and tree, standing alone on a flat, dry mesa, made the entire setting stark and lonely in the narrow beams of the headlights.

"It's too early for him to be in bed. Looks like no one's home," Justine asked softly.

Ella didn't answer. Instead, she knocked hard on the door and identified herself. Silence was her only response. Ella borrowed Justine's flashlight and walked around to the side of the house. Spotting a parted curtain, she aimed the light beam inside. An inexpensive desk against the wall beneath the window held a cardboard shoe box containing letters and papers. A coffee can beside the box contained dozens of pens of differing sizes and colors. They had logos and names from dozens of businesses and institutions. There was even one from the newspaper and the tribal council. "He collects—or steals—pens," Ella said.

At the back of the house, they found a galvanized metal trash can overflowing with garbage. Resting below the metal lid were four empty pizza cartons.

"All from the same restaurant—Perfect Pizza—in Kirtland," Ella commented. "I saw one of their pens on Rainwater's desk."

"They've got the best pepperoni pizza around but they only deliver outside the reservation. That means he had to have gone to pick them up."

"So either Melvin has had company very recently or he's a very dedicated customer with a healthy appetite." Ella put on a pair of disposable latex gloves, then pulled out an envelope from the trash. It was for Melvin C. Rainwater from a bank in Connecticut asking Mr. Rainwater to apply for a credit card.

"At least we know he's been living here recently." Ella lifted up the bottom pizza box slightly, aiming the light again so she could look farther down into the garbage. "Ugh. Several more pizza boxes from Perfect."

"He must have stock in that company," Justine said. "Or maybe he gets the leftovers or rejects."

"Reject pizzas? Oh, like 'I didn't order anchovies, but this has got anchovies' type of rejects?" Ella stepped back and took off her gloves, dropping them down into the trash where they wouldn't be seen unless someone else decided to dig through Rainwater's garbage.

Ella handed Justine back her flashlight. "I have a feeling that Melvin either works there or has a friend who does. Let's go check out the pizza place and see what we can find out." Ella gestured toward the vehicle. "But we'll want to have an officer watch this place in case Rainwater returns."

Once in the unit, Ella used her cell phone and made arrangements for the officer who normally patrolled that area to pass by the house and make spot checks. They didn't have enough officers on the evening shift to put anyone there full-time but her theory was that if Rainwater did return, he'd probably remain home the rest of the night. When the officer made his swing by, he could notify her or Justine if he saw Rainwater and they'd take it from there.

As they hurried toward Kirtland, farther to the east, Ella worked out the details of her plan. "I'm not going to call the sheriff and make this official, Justine. It's late, so we'll just go in and ask for Melvin. If we keep things casual, we'll be all right."

"Okay. Shouldn't we check and see how late Perfect Pizza stays open?"

"You drive," Ella said. "I'll make the call."

It was nearly 10:45 by the time they reached the pizza parlor, a small eatery beside the main highway. The establishment closed at eleven, so the staff was getting ready to lock up. They'd barely stepped through the door when a tall, balding man in his late forties, wearing jeans and a long-sleeved T-shirt intercepted them.

"I'm sorry, ladies, but unless you're picking up, it's too late to serve you anything but a soft drink. The ovens are shut down and we're getting ready to close."

Ella noted that he wore a blue-and-white name tag that read Mike Smith. Above his name was the word Manager.

Ella flashed her badge, but didn't bother to point out that they weren't within their jurisdiction. "I'm looking for a Navajo man by the name of Melvin Rainwater. Do you happen to know him?"

"Sure. He's one of our part-time delivery men. Is he in some kind of trouble? Speeding, reckless driving?"

"No, we just needed to talk to him."

"Sorry, but he isn't here right now. Melvin asked for a few days off. He was taking part in some kind of religious ceremony over on the reservation. I've got his home address and telephone number, if that'll help you."

Ella nodded as she wrote down the number. Unfortunately,

the address she was given corresponded to the house they'd just visited.

"He still drive the blue Chevy Blazer?" she asked.

"Yeah," he replied. He lowered his voice. "If you have any problem finding Melvin, you might try his other employer. During the day, he drives a van for a Farmington mortuary. Actually he picks up the—you know—deceased."

Ella's jaw must have dropped. Offhand she couldn't think of a less likely job for a Navajo.

"Are you sure? We're talking about Melvin Rainwater, a Navajo, right?" Justine asked, voicing what Ella was thinking.

"Yeah, that's the right Melvin," he answered in a soft voice. "I won't let him even mention his other job around here. We have a lot of customers from Shiprock, and it might creep them out."

Ella and Justine got the name of the mortuary, then drove on to Farmington. While on the way, Ella called Teeny, but reached his answering service. He was either out of cell phone reach or had it turned off. She left a message giving him Rainwater's new address, mentioned that he wasn't home, then asked Teeny to call her in the morning.

Fifteen minutes later Justine drove the unit into the mortuary driveway, which circled a central fountain and bed of flowers. The outside lighting was subdued, but the building appeared dark inside and was locked up for the night. The only vehicles present were two hearses, one white and one black, under a carport. A garage was adjacent to the vehicles, but was also darkened inside. An empty parking lot was across the street.

Ella got the business number from off the sign on the glass door and called, but there was no answer, just a tasteful recording by a woman who managed to use the terms "bereavement," "dignity," and "low cost" all in one sentence. Ella hung up without leaving a message.

"What now?" Justine asked.

"Do you know who's directing the search around the area of the Sing right now?" Ella asked.

"Big Ed is—he wouldn't delegate it."

Ella called him directly on the cell phone and Big Ed answered before it could ring a second time. She gave him a progress report, then added, "So far, Rainwater's my only lead."

"I've had Neskahi questioning attendants at gasoline stations in the area, day and night shifts, and we spoke to a few patrons who live in the area. But we have nothing. We tried the bloodhounds, but they couldn't get a scent once we got away from the car, and there were no hits at the medicine hogan, which means that Thomas didn't go inside. I'm now trying to find out if there are any wells nearby or houses with basements in the area. It's a problem because most people don't bother with building permits—they just build what they need," he said. "The long and short of it is that no one's going to get any sleep tonight. Where you headed next, Shorty?"

"I'm going to call the owner of the mortuary at home and wake him up. But we'll need to track down that number from the county's business listings database first. We're on our way to the station now."

"Call the sheriff's office and save yourself some time. One of these days, Shorty, we'll get computers in our units like the big guys."

"I'm not holding my breath, boss," Ella replied, then ended the call.

It was one in the morning when Ella and Justine finally tracked down Jack Krause, the owner of Mesa Vista Mortuary. His soon-to-be ex-wife had gladly given them his new telephone number and address.

Ella let the phone ring ten times before the groggy mortician picked up the telephone and identified himself.

Ella came quickly to the point. "We need to track down one of your employees, Melvin Rainwater."

"I have his address at the office, not here."

"We *have* his address, Mr. Krause, and his phone number, but he's not at his residence. I was hoping you might know where he goes after hours, or be able to give me the name of anyone he hangs out with."

"I don't keep up with the social lives of my employees," came the cold reply.

"This is a matter of vital importance, Mr. Krause. *Think.* Does Mr. Rainwater have any friends at work that he might associate with after hours?"

There was a pause. "There's another driver, Dan Bailey."

"Give me his number," Ella asked.

"He's in the phone book. All I remember is that he lives on Elm Street."

"All right. Thank you very much. Sorry to disturb you so late."

Ella placed the phone down, looked up the address, jotted it down, then glanced at Justine. "Let's roll."

They arrived at Dan's home, a southeast Farmington apartment complex, in less than thirty minutes. No lights were on inside the apartment. "We'll have to wake him up," Ella said.

Justine stood just behind her as Ella rang the doorbell. Moments later they heard the sound of a baby crying, and footsteps. A lamp went on somewhere in the front room, then the porch light.

A man's voice called out from behind the door. "Who the hell are you?" he demanded, ostensibly having looked through the peephole.

Ella held her badge and photo ID. "Are you Dan Bailey?"

The door opened, though a security chain was still in place. The young man standing there was wearing jeans and no shirt.

"Mr. Bailey?" Seeing him nod, she continued. "We're looking for Melvin Rainwater," Ella pressed.

Justine held up her ID and badge, too, folding back her jacket subtly with her arm so her sidearm was visible.

An overweight blond woman in a bathrobe holding a crying baby came to the door and joined Bailey as he half opened the door. "Why would you think he's here?" she asked. "He's just one of the guys my husband works with, that's all."

"We know that, ma'am. And we're sorry about disturbing you at this hour," Ella said, trying not to sound like she felt—grumpy and tired. "But Mr. Rainwater's not at his own residence and we need to talk to him on an urgent matter. Do you have any idea where we might be able to find him?"

"You woke up my baby just for that? How should we know? Go look for yourself!" she said angrily. When the baby cried even louder, Mrs. Bailey immediately began rocking him. "Next time you ring our doorbell at this hour, you're not leaving until you get Kasey back to sleep," she hissed.

As she walked away, singing and rocking the sobbing infant, Ella looked at Dan. "You work with Melvin, Mr. Bailey. Don't you have any idea where he might be?"

"What's he done?"

"Nothing that we know about—yet. We just need to talk to him to verify some information. Tell us where he might be at this hour and we'll get out of your hair. I'm sure you want to go back to bed."

"I really don't know where he is, but I've heard him mention a sports bar called the Double Play several times. It's over in Kirtland just north of the main highway. You can't miss it. A lot of oil workers hang out there."

"Thanks."

As Ella and Justine returned to the SUV, Ella glanced at her partner. "Do you know anything about the place? I've never heard of it."

"It's fairly new, past the turn off where El Paso Gas Company had that small housing area for such a long time. It's a dive already, and a rough one at that. My sister, Jayne, had to actually punch an obnoxious creep who grabbed her by the arm. He didn't want to let go unless she promised to go out to his pickup with him."

"Well, that's where we're going next. I hope you remember where to kick a man if you really need to."

"Sure. And here's a hint for you, via my sister. Never punch a guy in the stomach if he's been drinking all day," Justine said, chuckling.

They arrived a short time later and, to their surprise, the small parking lot was full of pickups and SUVs despite its being nearly two in the morning. One big Harley motorcycle was parked by the door.

"What sports action could there be this time of night, Ella? A soccer match from Germany?"

"Somehow I don't think this will be a soccer crowd, cuz. Remember, we're looking for a guy in his early twenties, short and stocky, Navajo, with slicked-back hair and black markings on him, maybe. Don't flash your badge unless it's absolutely necessary. We're out of our jurisdiction and things could get ugly in a hurry."

"Not a problem," Justine said. "I like the set of teeth I have in my mouth now."

When they entered Ella didn't need to wait long for her eyes to adjust. It was nearly as dark in here as it was outside—the only illumination in the room came from very low wattage lamps recessed in the ceiling. Country music blared from hidden speakers, and the three TVs mounted on the walls around the room were showing some recycled auto race, though the sound was off at the moment.

To the right of the bar there was a cluster of noisy patrons watching two men throwing darts, though in the dim light the contestants would have had to aim by Zen. The bar smelled of cigarette smoke and sweat.

Directly ahead of her was a heavily tattooed man, smoking, and wearing a black leather vest and a red bandanna on his head. His biceps were the size of hams and he could have rented out his shoulders as bookshelves, not that anyone in this crowd was likely to be a heavy reader. He kept looking around, as if challenging anyone who met his gaze to tell him to put out his cigarette. Ella decided to give him a wide berth.

"Let me check out the group watching the darts match. I think there's a Navajo man standing there," Justine said, then moved off.

Hearing the rumble of voices on the left side of the room near the back door, Ella glanced around. A man was hurrying to make it out the exit, his face down and tilted away slightly toward a blank wall to ensure she couldn't see him clearly.

Ella went after him, acting on instinct. Anyone who was so determined not to expose his face had something to hide. But before she could reach the door two men stepped into her path.

"Hey, you just got here, *chica*," a skinny Hispanic man in western garb said. "Come talk to us. Let me buy you a beer."

"You'd be smart getting out of my way," Ella said, meeting his gaze and holding it.

"Now, big girl," the other man, a tall, lanky, pale-eyed cowboy added, grasping her forearm, "don't run off so soon. You've come to the right place if you're looking for some loving."

"Let go of me," Ella said, shaking loose.

"A woman as pretty as you doesn't need to go chasing after any guy. Let them come to you."

"What are *you* talking about?" Ella said, still trying to step around the men and realizing that it wasn't going to happen the easy way.

"Melvin told us you've been stalking him, even at work, begging to get him to go out with you," the Hispanic man said.

"Melvin lied. I'm a police officer," she said, pulling back her jacket and exposing her badge. "Clear out now or you're going to need a lawyer and bail money. Obstruction of justice is a crime."

The Hispanic man stared at her in surprise, and his friend took a quick step back, nearly toppling the chair behind him.

"Hey, I don't want any trouble, Officer," the blond said.

"Me neither," the other one added, seeing Justine coming up, a frown on her face.

"Melvin ducked out," Ella said, opening the door and quickly stepping out onto the parking lot. But they were too late. There was no sign of Melvin anywhere. She couldn't even see any taillights in either direction.

Empty-handed, Ella and Justine returned to their vehicle. "If I ever catch that weasel, it's going to take a surgeon to remove my boot from his backside," Ella growled.

"We're lucky we didn't have to fight our way out of that dive," Justine said. "It could have been worse."

"Yeah, but not for Agent Thomas. So, it looks like we're going back to Rainwater's place and staking it out."

As Justine drove Ella could see that her partner was starting to wind down. Every few minutes she'd yawn and blink her eyes. "We'll keep watch for a few hours," Ella said. "If Melvin doesn't come home by then—and he may not, now that he knows we're looking for him—then we'll turn the surveillance over to Tache until morning. You and I will go home and grab a few hours of sleep."

Fifteen minutes later they were parked off the road in a low spot about fifty yards past the turnoff leading to Rainwater's house. There wasn't much ground cover or vegetation, so it was simple keeping watch. Time dragged, and they kept talking mostly to make sure they remained alert.

"Things still working out between you and Emily?" Ella asked.

"Yeah. I think the fact that we're both officers helps a lot."

Ella had met Sergeant Emily Marquez of the County Sheriff's Department during a case several months ago. Emily had been searching for a roommate, and so had Justine, so she'd brought them together and so far she'd heard no complaints.

"Sharing a house is never easy," Ella said thoughtfully, "particularly for adults."

"It helps that she and I work different shifts for different departments. Emily has nights these days, so we hardly ever meet except when one of us is about to go on duty. And when she's home she spends a lot of time in her little greenhouse. It smells great inside the house now because she's always bringing in fresh flowers. We don't really have a lot in common, though, except for our career choice. Heaven knows I *hate* gardening. But we go our separate ways and things are working out fine."

"It's different when you're living with family," Ella said quietly. "Even though there's only the three of us at home, we still manage to get in each other's way. Dawn's growing up and needs her own space. So does Mom, and I sure could use a bigger office— one that I didn't have to share. Whenever I try to work in there I end up having to move Mom's maps and plant inventory information aside just to make room to sit down. We're practically bursting at the seams."

"It seems to me you need to add on or find a bigger house."

"I know, but Mom has a lot of memories attached to that place. She doesn't even like to rearrange the furniture. Mom's never actually *said* anything, but I know that having Dawn and Dawn's friends around really bugs her sometimes—particularly when she has her group of Plant Watchers over for a meeting. And as Dawn gets older, it's going to get worse," Ella said. "Friends, music, boys. I can't wait," she said sarcastically.

"It *is* a small house," Justine agreed.

Ella nodded. "That's for sure. But what I hate most of all about living at home is seeing the worried look on Mom's face whenever I come home late after a tense shift or a shooting incident. To be honest, I'm not sure I'm helping her much by living in that place. But moving out would mean leaving her all alone and I couldn't do that."

"I think you're underestimating Rose. She can take care of herself. Mind you, she'd absolutely hate it if you moved too far away, but as long as you stayed in the area, I think she might enjoy having her space."

Ella gave some thought to what Justine had said, but no matter how logical, it still didn't *feel* right. As she glanced over at her partner, Ella saw Justine almost nodding off, then shaking her head to stay awake.

"Get Tache and have him come over to relieve us," Ella said. "We need to go home and get a couple of hours of sleep."

Justine picked up her cell phone and made the call. "He'll be here in a half hour," she said.

"Good." Ella opened the window to help them both stay alert and pulled her coat around her more tightly.

"The darkness and the cold will be tough on Agent Thomas, particularly if he's injured," Justine said.

Ella nodded slowly. "We either find him quickly or we can give up any hope of finding him alive."

EIGHT
✖ ✖ ✖

Day two

Justine picked her up at six-thirty the following morning. By seven, they were in Big Ed's office at a briefing. Dark circles rimmed Big Ed's eyes and Ella had a feeling that he'd gotten even less sleep than she had.

The reports were frustrating. No actual progress had been made, despite a massive but low-profile effort. "Officer Tache's going to alternate with Sergeant Neskahi keeping an eye on Rainwater's place, Shorty," Big Ed grumbled, then took a sip of coffee from an enormous mug. "I could really use both of them out in the field with the search parties, so make sure that the instant Rainwater turns up, you pull them off surveillance duty."

"I may need them to run down leads or examine evidence," Ella said slowly.

"Your case has priority, but the second they're free, send them back to me."

"Any news on my old cases—the Twin Lakes hit-and-run?"

"As a matter of fact, the Window Rock officer working that got a break. The woman was picked up at a woman's shelter in

Gallup. She's lawyered up now, and apparently going to claim self-defense," Big Ed said.

"And the ex-husband?"

"Out of intensive care. At least he won't have the strength to beat her up again for a while." Big Ed leaned back in his chair, a disgusted look on his face.

After their meeting ended, Justine and Ella headed to Farmington to question the mortuary's personnel. Since neither of them had eaten breakfast, they agreed to pick up some breakfast burritos from one of the Navajo vendors along the highway before they left the reservation.

They stopped, picked up the food, and were on their way again within three minutes. Justine ate as she drove. "These hand-made tortillas are warm and soft and taste sweet too, almost as if they're cooked in butter."

"*Naniscaadas*—breakfast of the gods. I love Navajo breakfast burritos. No rice or cheese, just lots of eggs, sausage, and bacon," Ella said, taking a big bite. "These are excellent. Remind me to look for that woman again next time I pass this way during the morning."

Ella glanced out the side window, staring at the haze that ran along the river, hating the pollution that the coal-fired power plants brought to the Rez. The newer plants kept their smoke-stacks clean using the latest technology, but one plant in particu-lar had been built prior to 1970, and wasn't subject to the same EPA standards. It was under a grandfather clause that made it ex-empt from new requirements. To add insult to injury, much of the power it provided was sold out of state. But the damage it did re-mained here.

By seven-thirty, they arrived at the Farmington mortuary. Jus-tine grimaced as she parked her unit in the circular parking lot, just a few feet from the white hearse. "Ugh. I'm a Christian and consider myself a modern Navajo, but jeez, I couldn't work here no matter how much they paid me. Can you imagine riding around town with a corpse right behind you?" She shuddered.

"I'd keep looking in the rearview mirror just to make sure the passenger was still dead. Give me something cheerful like police work."

"I think you're suffering from sleep deprivation and too many bad movies," Ella said, laughing. "But, hey, we may be in luck with Melvin. I can't see the plate from here, but there's a Chevy Blazer the right color in the parking lot over there," she said, gesturing.

As they approached the entrance, a brown-haired, pleasant-looking Anglo wearing stylish wire-rimmed glasses and a dark blue or black suit came out of the garage and walked up to them. "Good morning, ladies. Our chapel isn't open at the moment, but perhaps I can be of service? My name's Jack Krause and I'm the director of Mesa Vista Funeral Home."

Ella recognized the voice, friendly in a businesslike way, and tried to evaluate the man from looks alone, though he was hard to read. There was a sympathetic expression on his face, probably worn automatically when conducting business with someone who'd just lost a loved one.

Ella showed Krause her badge and introduced herself and Justine. "I spoke to you last night."

His intelligent eyes turned cool and analytical for a few seconds, as though he were evaluating one of his . . . work assignments. Then he actually smiled. "Officer Clah, yes. You woke me up out of a sound sleep. Were you finally able to interview Melvin?"

"Not yet. That's why we're here. We're hoping you might have heard from him. It looks like his Blazer's over there in the parking lot."

"You're right about that. He's inside the garage, detailing one of our limousines. If you want to speak to him now, that's fine, but please don't keep him from his work. I suspect you're outside your jurisdiction, but I'm always willing to do what I can to cooperate with the police. But in exchange I hope you'll extend me the courtesy of not taking up too much of his time. We need to get ready for funeral services later this morning."

Krause opened the side door leading into a two-bay garage. A long, shining black limousine took up most of the closer bay, and the other was occupied by a black van with a side door. Ella had seen a similar vehicle once or twice in the Shiprock area, as had most officers. That was the vehicle used to pick up bodies when they were slated for the mortuary instead of the morgue.

Ella glanced around and saw a man vacuuming the interior of the limo, unaware of their presence. A radio, just a few feet from where he was, was blaring out "Ain't Going Down Till the Sun Comes Up" by Garth Brooks.

Ella turned to thank Krause but, as she did, saw that he was already stepping inside the other building through the main entrance.

"He seemed pretty normal . . . and that worries me," Justine muttered. "How could you get used to this place?"

Ella motioned to Justine to circle and approach from the other direction, then walked around the limousine from the back and approached the man. When he saw her legs he turned his head slightly and she saw he was Navajo, though any blackening marks on his face had obviously been washed off. "Melvin, we need a second of your time," she shouted over the sound of the music and the vacuum.

Melvin straightened immediately, reaching for the radio, and his eyes widened when he saw who she was. For a moment, Ella was sure he was going bolt, but Justine had come from the front and now blocked his only exit. He had nowhere to go except into the limo itself. With a scowl, he reached over and turned off the vacuum, then the radio.

Ella flipped her badge. "You're a tough man to corner, and I'm in a real bad mood after that stunt you pulled last night. So here's a little word of warning. Don't give me a reason to make you miserable, for, say, the rest of your life."

"Last night? You're crazy. Listen, Officer, I have no idea what you're talking about. And if you and your sidekick are Navajo cops, you have no authority here."

"Well, if you really want Sheriff Taylor in your face, I'll just handcuff you to the door handle of this fancy taxi and we'll wait for him to show up. He's a friend of mine, so I know he'll be glad to accommodate us. But it may be a while. He's a busy man. And what will your boss say when another cop car shows up, lights flashing and maybe a siren? Hard to get a bad reputation clean again, even in the funeral business. What's it going to be, Mr. Rainwater?"

"Chill, will ya? It won't kill you to cut me some slack. I need this job," he said in a low tone. "It's a little strange, working here, but the man pays top dollar, almost union scale."

"Then you don't have a problem. Just cooperate, tell us what we want to know, and we'll leave," Ella said matter-of-factly.

"What *do* you want?"

"Let's start with Agent Thomas. I understand he was at your Sing."

"Not by invitation," he shot back. "That crazy redhead almost ruined everything."

"We know he was on your trail, and that he was getting ready to haul you in," she bluffed, hoping that if he assumed she already knew everything he'd be less guarded about what he said. "But I want to hear *your* explanation of what was going on."

"You've got it all wrong. The FBI guy wanted to ask me more questions about a pickup I made around Beclabito a few weeks ago. One of my jobs here at Mesa Vista is to go onto the Rez and pick up unclaimed bodies. The mortuary has a contract with the tribe. A lot of our people don't want anything to do with a corpse, so nobody comes forward to claim the body. You know what it's like. That's when we get called in. Sometimes I go with another Anglo worker here, Dan Bailey, but not always. I've gone alone too."

"What exactly did Agent Thomas want to know?"

"He was sure that I'd picked up the body of a murder victim by mistake, one that should have been examined by the medical investigator. But I hadn't. I did pick up a body west of Beclabito, but the tribal PD had checked it out and signed off on it. That's why we were called in. I told him that, but Agent Thomas just couldn't let it go. He'd had a report about a murder victim there." He shook his head slowly. "Those guys think that if they ask you the same question fifty-two times, you'll change your story, remember something you're not telling them, or make their day and confess to a crime."

"Wait a minute. The FBI thought that there was a murder victim at Beclabito? That doesn't add up. Our officers, and my office in particular, would have been notified. Are you sure that's the story you want to stick to?"

"That's what the Anglo told me, so that's all I know. After a while I started avoiding him but he wouldn't let up. Then he showed up at the Sing the other night."

"What happened when he was spotted?"

"My cousins ran him off and then we finished the ceremony."

"Who are your cousins?" Ella pressed.

"Jim Joe and Eugene Franklin."

Ella had heard them called the Darwin rejects by some of the officers who insisted the pair was far too stupid to live—a definite contradiction of evolution. They roamed around at night together and seemed to have a knack for causing trouble.

"Where can I find your cousins right now?"

"They're usually still at home this time of day. They don't have day jobs so they sleep till noon or watch cartoons on TV."

Ella glanced at her partner, then focused back on Melvin. "Tell me something. Working here doesn't seem to bother you, obviously. But if you're that much of a modernist, why did you bother getting a Sing?"

Melvin gave her a sheepish look. "My girlfriend is coming back to town. She's been away at college in California. I made the mistake of telling her where I was working and she said she wouldn't get anywhere near me unless I had the Sing done."

"But you've washed off the blackening," Ella said. "The healing can't take place unless you carry out every step of the ceremony."

"Yeah, well, when I got called back to work, the people here were bummed out by my paint job. The boss said that it was bad for business, so I didn't have a choice but to wash it off." He stared at the garage floor and shifted from foot to foot. "But, hey, my girl-friend won't know I didn't leave it on the whole time, and I'm not stupid enough to tell her."

It was a plausible explanation but she had a strong feeling that there was more to it than that. Undoubtedly Melvin had also cleaned up because he hadn't wanted to be associated with a cer-emony that had been punctuated by a confrontation with a federal agent. He obviously was just going through the motions on the Sing anyway for his girlfriend.

Ella handed him one of her cards. "Don't leave the area with-out notifying us first."

"Why? Am I in trouble?" he asked immediately.

"Oh, yeah. I'm just not sure how much yet," Ella replied. "But we'll be seeing you again, I'm certain of that."

As they walked back to Justine's vehicle, Ella glanced over at her partner. "I need my own unit back. We can't keep going out together to question people. We're wasting manpower and time. Which reminds me, I also need to call Big Ed and tell him we've found Rainwater and he can reassign whoever's watching Melvin's home."

Just then a pickup the size of a tour bus pulled up beside them, making it impossible for Justine to pull out from the curb. Justine tensed up immediately, but Ella placed a hand on her arm before she could reach for her weapon.

"It's Bruce Little. He's okay."

"*Okay?*" She gave her an incredulous look. "He's as big as a bear and just as strong. Are you sure he's not still pissed about get-ting cut from the force?" Justine asked in a harsh whisper as Teeny rolled down the passenger's window and called out to them.

"Ella, I need to talk to you. Wait up," he said, then maneu-vered his monster vehicle toward a parking space.

Justine glanced at Teeny's truck, then back at Ella. "I've heard some officers say that if they weren't cops, they'd probably be bad guys. They're addicted to the danger and the rush. Are you *sure* this guy's still on our side?"

"Of course he is. In fact, my guess is that he's probably getting paid a lot more now doing his computer consulting and security work than he ever did on the force. But make sure you don't call him Teeny. Sergeant Begay, who'd gone to elementary school with him, made the mistake of doing that once."

"I never heard about it. What happened?"

"Nobody said a word later, but I saw the tail end of it when I was passing by the squad room. Teeny picked Begay up by his belt and spun him around like a pinwheel. Begay almost fell over when Teeny finally set him back down on his feet again," Ella answered. "I think I'm the only one who gets away with calling him Teeny but, even so, I try never to do that in front of anyone else."

"Wow. Begay must easily weigh a hundred and fifty pounds." Justine shook her head. "Thanks for the heads-up."

"There's one thing you have to remember about Teeny. He uses his size every once in a while, but he's not a bully. He just wants respect and gets testy when he doesn't think he's getting it. He and I are friends and that cuts me a lot of slack. He's nothing if not loyal, and he's always looked out for me, for some reason. He and Clifford."

"And Wilson," Justine shrugged, a hint of sarcasm in her voice. Justine had broken up with Wilson Joe just last year, but knew Ella had always been special to him as well.

Teeny came over to Ella's side of the car and leaned in the window, grinning. "Hey, ladies. Looks like you beat me to the punch, at least by a few minutes. About an hour ago I discovered that Rainwater had made a lot of calls to this place, so I thought I'd come by and check it out. Imagine—a Navajo working at a funeral home."

Hacking into the phone company's records was illegal, but Teeny hadn't volunteered how he'd obtained the information, and Ella wasn't planning to ask. At the moment she had more pressing matters on her mind.

"Hey, since you're here, can you give me a ride?" she asked him.

"Sure. Where do you want to go?"

Ella glanced over at Justine. "Which one of the cousins do you want?"

"I'll take Jim Joe. I know him. He'll behave around me because one of my brothers beat the crap out of him once for giving me a hard time. But Eugene Franklin is a real hard case, so watch your back. Last year, he pulled a gun on Joe Neskahi when Joe went to question him about a hit-and-run. Gene spent some time in jail for that, but he's a real slow learner."

"Ah, the Darwins. I can help you there," Teeny said. "Eugene and I get along just fine."

"Great." It would save time—one commodity that was in short supply for Agent Thomas. "Drive me over so I can talk to Mr. Franklin." Ella glanced back at Justine. "Give me the address."

Justine did, but gave her a worried look. "What if Big Ed . . ." Her words trailed off softly.

"Bruce is already getting paid by the tribe, at least until I no longer need his services. Why don't you call the chief and tell him about us finding Rainwater?" she asked as she got out of Justine's unit. "And look for a report on a murder victim or suspicious death that corresponds with what Melvin told us. If he's lying, we need to know ASAP."

"I'll take care of it."

As Justine drove away, Ella looked up at Teeny. "This is a *police* investigation, so you've got to play it by the book. Clear?"

"Sure. Like I said, Eugene and I go back a ways. He'll be a pussycat. There'll be no need to take him for a spin."

Ella smiled but didn't comment.

It was eight-thirty when they got under way. Her stomach ached from the tension, but she wasn't tired—too much adrenaline coursing through her system. "How well do you know Eugene?"

"Well enough. What do you need to know?" he asked over the deep-throated rumble of the souped-up engine. Teeny was heading south toward the truck bypass, a route she'd often taken when trying to avoid Farmington downtown traffic.

"For starters, do you think he pitched Agent Thomas down a hole somewhere? Is he capable of that?"

"Physically capable, sure. He outweighs Andy Thomas by fifty pounds, at least. But Gene's a spineless wonder. If you looked up bully in the dictionary, you'd find his photo. He likes to throw his weight around 'cause he thinks he's big and bad. But when he meets someone who stands up to him, or is even meaner and tougher—not to mention larger—he's a real sweetheart," Teeny said, then paused before continuing. "But the bottom line is that assaulting a fed is bad trouble and I really don't think Eugene has it in him to do something like that. Andy Thomas isn't a big guy, but the gold badge adds to his weight and stature, if you know what I mean."

"I hear you," she said with a nod. "Now let's see what Mr. Franklin has to tell us."

Teeny looked over at her. "You've always had guts, Ella—but I'd hate to see them on the floor if he panics and grabs a gun. I should back you up when you go in there."

"I don't need a bodyguard," she warned, "but avoiding a confrontation will save me time, so you're on."

After twenty-five minutes, they arrived at a small residential area dating back to the 1950s—former housing for uranium and, later, vanadium plant workers. The search for the house number took them to a house on a dead-end street.

"Ironic, don't you think?"

Ella laughed. "Reminds me of a truck stop down South called The Terminal Café."

Teeny parked across the street and then walked with Ella to the front door of the house, an old white frame building with a pitched roof and tiny porch. As before, he circled around to cover the back while Ella paused a few seconds, then knocked. "Police, Mr. Franklin."

Hearing the sound of running footsteps inside, Ella tried the knob immediately and found that it was open.

Ella ran through the simply furnished living room toward the kitchen, quickly verifying that nobody was going out the back door. Turning, she headed into the hall and heard the sound of a window opening. Ella pushed open a bedroom door and spotted Eugene halfway out the window, staring at Teeny, who was shaking his head slowly. Franklin turned his head and saw her standing in the doorway.

"There's nowhere for you to go, Eugene, so come back in here," Ella said. "Let's not make this ugly and messy."

Moving slowly and grudgingly, Eugene crawled back inside. "Okay, Clah, so now what?"

"Let's go back into your living room and have a little chat," Ella said, her tone making it clear that it wasn't really a request.

Ella stepped back as Eugene passed through the doorway, keeping her distance and watching his hands. He was barefoot and had no apparent weapon. From what she could see, his jeans and sports jersey didn't seem to contain anything at all except himself.

She followed him back into the living room and motioned him toward the couch. As Eugene sat down, Teeny came inside.

"Does *he* have to be here?" Eugene asked, his face an ashen color.

"You don't *like* me?" Teeny asked in almost a purr.

"Never mind. It's cool." Eugene looked back at Ella. "What's going on, Officer? Did you come here to arrest me?"

"That'll depend on how honest you are with me. I understand that you ran Special Agent Thomas off when he showed up at your cousin's Sing the night before last. Why don't you tell me all about that."

"That guy is one dumb Anglo, you know that? He insulted all of us and the tribe, too, by spying on a ceremony. Me and Jim went to ask him to leave, but Mr. FBI waved his badge around and said he wasn't going anywhere until he talked to our cousin. That's when we told him he could either leave or we'd kick his sorry ass all the way back to Shiprock. He was disrespecting the People and we weren't going to put up with that. Redheaded city boy thought about it for a while, and when he realized it was either back down, draw his gun, or take us both on, he decided to leave. We never saw him after that, but we did keep a close eye out for him."

"Did you actually see Agent Thomas drive off?"

Eugene hesitated. "Well, we followed him until he reached his car and got in. Then we hurried back to the medicine hogan to let the others know that everything was okay."

"Did you actually hear the car drive off?" Ella pressed. Instinct told her that he was holding out on her. She knew that Agent Thomas's car hadn't left the area, so if he answered with a yes, she'd know for sure that he was lying.

"Not really, but the chanting would have drowned it out."

"So it's that simple, huh?" Ella challenged. "You were so sure you'd scared him off that you never even bothered to check."

Before Eugene could reply, Teeny cleared his throat and gave him a hard look.

"We *did* scare him off," he protested, then seeing Ella's skeptical look, added, "Okay, okay, so it didn't go down exactly the way I said. We didn't really threaten to kick his ass. I kind of had my thirty-thirty rifle across my arm, and I told him he should have worn red. He was starting to look more and more like a deer every second."

"So when Agent Thomas walked off, you just figured that he wasn't coming right back?"

"I didn't say that," Eugene muttered. "Someone else was driving up. We could see headlights and figured he might have called for backup before we got there so we decided not to stick around. I was carrying my Winchester, and I already know what happens to any Rez Indians stupid enough to show a gun to a half dozen jumpy FBI agents."

"What kind of vehicle was coming up? A big SUV? A car? A Jeep? You can tell sometimes by the sound of the engine."

"Hey, it was dark, and all I saw were the headlights. The thing was in low gear and the only thing I can tell you is that it didn't sound like a little car with a dinky engine. But like I said, we didn't stick around. I got to thinking that they might have those night goggles and be able to see us in the dark." He looked directly at her, and added, "That's all of it, I swear."

"I'm sure it is," Teeny said. "I'd hate to think you wasted my time . . . and hers."

"It is, man, really."

"Do you know why Agent Thomas wanted to talk to your cousin?" Ella pressed.

"Something about picking up the wrong body." Melvin grimaced. "Man, talk about a crazy job for a Navajo. But sometimes you do what you got to do. We all have to eat."

"Now tell me one more thing. Why did you run when I identified myself?" Ella demanded.

"Yesterday my cousin called and said there were some Navajo cops looking for him, and that they might come looking for him here. I didn't want to have to rat him out, saying where he worked and lived and stuff." Eugene looked at Teeny as if hoping for approval.

"What time did your cousin call?"

"Like four in the morning," he said. "So I guess that really makes it today, not yesterday."

Ella held his gaze and watched him squirm, knowing that there had been plenty of time for Rainwater and the cousins to come up with a cover story. It was possible he was still holding out on her. "Stay out of trouble," she said, then walked to the door with Teeny.

"Where to now?" he asked, as they climbed up into his truck.

"Back to the station. I need to pick up my own unit."

"Ten-four. And just so you know, I'll be coming back here later to confirm he didn't leave anything out."

"I never heard that," Ella said, checking her watch, then looking down the highway in both directions as they left the neighborhood. "Can you step on it? Don't worry about a ticket," she added with a smile.

She regretted her request almost instantly. Teeny stomped on the accelerator hard and the sudden burst of speed pushed her back into the seat like a space shuttle launch. Mercifully, he was a good driver with pursuit-driving training on his résumé.

"Slow down when we get into traffic," she asked, gritting her teeth and seeing an intersection ahead.

Teeny complied, but was still driving close to the edge, weaving in and out between cars like a slalom skier at the Olympics. The high-profile vehicle rolled like a rowboat in a hurricane, but Teeny seemed used to the motion. When they pulled up to the station five minutes later, Ella sighed. "Like a Disneyland ride. Remind me to keep my mouth shut next time."

"Anything else I can do to help?" Teeny asked. "I like working for the department without a keyboard in front of me. It's like old times, before I became the department's techno geek."

Ella considered the offer. They didn't have the manpower to keep an eye on Melvin Rainwater, but her gut instinct was telling her that he'd bear watching. Opening the door, she climbed down out of the vehicle as she spoke. "You're still on the payroll, so keep an eye on Rainwater for me, will you? I have a feeling he might bolt again."

"Okay." He gave her a twisted smile. "I'm glad we're working together, Ella, even if it's just temporary."

Ella nodded and, as she stepped back, Teeny drove out of the parking lot onto the street, tires squealing just loud enough to be heard.

As Ella crossed the parking lot, she noticed the oversized tire was still on her unit. Muttering an oath, she strode inside. She'd check to see if Justine was back and if she'd made any progress, then call Larry Jim, the mechanic, as soon as she reached her desk. As she passed the lab, Ella ducked in, knocking as she opened the door a crack and found Justine sitting at her computer.

"How did it go?" Ella asked.

"I found out a few interesting things. Jim Joe says that Melvin was in serious trouble with Agent Thomas, that Melvin had screwed up one of his cases and he was out for blood. Melvin was ducking him because he was sure he'd end up in jail even though he didn't think he'd done anything wrong. I don't know how much truth to place on secondhand accounts like this, but it made interesting listening."

"What bothers me about this is that I never heard anything about a murder victim in Beclabito," Ella said. "Did you check into their alibi?"

"Yeah, and as far as I can tell, there are no homicide reports that coincide with what they saw. Either Melvin's lying and his cousin's backing up the phony story or Agent Thomas was seriously misinformed."

"I couldn't find any paperwork in his office pertaining to the case he was working on, but if Thomas was investigating a murder, Simmons must have known about it. I'm going to call again and press him on this."

Ella went to her office, dialed, and after a moment got Simmons. She updated him first, then brought up what Melvin Rainwater and Jim Joe had said. "That's what I've got so far, but I need you to fill me in on everything you know. Was Agent Thomas investigating a murder near Beclabito or not?"

"Hang on," Simmons said, then listened to an announcement coming over a loudspeaker. "Sorry. I'm in D.C. trying to get an early flight back, but some jackass apparently left a note about a bomb and now nothing's moving," he added. "To answer your question, there *was* a glitch in some paperwork filed with the county. I don't have my notes, but I do recall the problem came from some confusion with the names of the deceased. Daniel Yarborough was a homicide victim in Farmington, Daniel Yellowhorse died of natural causes on the reservation. If the folder on that isn't in Blalock's office, then I have no idea where it is. There's more documentation in my Albuquerque office, but it basically amounts to what I've just told you."

"There was nothing in Thomas's office or in his vehicle. My team and I did a thorough search," Ella said.

Simmons grunted skeptically, then told her he had to hang up, and warned her that when he finally got into the air, his cell phone would have to be switched off during his flight. "I'll get in touch with you as soon as I can."

As Ella placed the phone down, Justine walked in. "Did Simmons have any answers?"

Ella filled her partner in on what Thomas's supervisor had said. "So as it stands now, a dead Navajo named Yellowhorse is our last connection to Thomas. Maybe Simmons is the one who's been misdirected, and Yellowhorse was the one murdered after all. Thomas may be missing because of what he learned. Let's check the computer for background information and get an address for Daniel Yellowhorse and his next of kin." She paused. "Come to think of it, Justine, why don't you take care of that while I call Larry Jim and find out why my unit isn't ready."

"No problem."

Ella called the motor pool and got Larry, the PD's chief—and only—mechanic at the Shiprock station. "I really need to have that vehicle running right. I'm on a priority case," she explained.

"I still have to get a purchase order signed and no one's around to do it. One of the tires could be repaired, but the other was too badly damaged to use. I was sent a retread as a replacement, but that would be dangerous because it's not rated for higher-speed operation. I do have some tires, but they've already been allotted to another patrol officer."

"Put the tire you repaired back on my vehicle and I'll use the retread as a spare. I'll pick up a better tire whenever. This case is time-sensitive."

"Yeah, okay, just try not to get another flat," he said. "Your unit'll be ready in ten minutes."

"Oh, and the oversized tire that's on the rear is my brother's. Just stick it in the back when you're done."

Ella remembered that she hadn't told Big Ed about her continued use of Teeny. But he hadn't been in his office when she'd passed by earlier, so in order to save time she scribbled a quick note and left it with his secretary.

Twenty-five minutes later, after Justine had tracked down the address of Daniel Yellowhorse's widow, they left for Kirtland.

"Daniel Yellowhorse died alone in his home outside Beclabito while waiting for a heart transplant. A neighbor saw him on the floor and called nine-one-one. Apparently one of the EMTs made the declaration, and Yellowhorse's physician signed off on the cause of death," Justine said. "But I suppose it's entirely possible the paperwork got screwed up along the way."

"A lot of crimes are committed because of mistakes and misunderstandings," Ella said, picking up the cell phone. "I'm going to check in with Sheriff Taylor. I know there are Bureau agents working his turf, and I want to find out if there's any information he can pass along."

Ella got through to Sheriff Taylor quickly and gave him a progress report. "I'll be in your jurisdiction talking to a Navajo family, but it's mostly routine at this point," she said. "That's all from my end, but I understand there are FBI agents in the county sniffing around. Have they turned up anything useful?"

"They're looking into Agent Thomas's personal life. Thomas's Farmington apartment is under a microscope, practically, but I don't think they've found anything significant—or, if they have, they're being really closed mouthed about it. All I know is that they've been ordered not to interfere with the investigation that's taking place on the reservation, but I wouldn't count on Agents Newberry, Marquez, and Edwards staying out of your hair for long. These three guys are young, eager, and determined to be The Ones who find Agent Thomas."

"Thanks for the heads-up." Ella hung up and explained to Justine what was going on.

"Hopefully we won't end up looking for four agents instead of just one," Justine said, rolling her eyes. "Of course if Simmons ever makes it back, that could make it five."

NINE
✖ ✖ ✖

They were in Farmington, heading east in the direction of Kirtland, when her cell phone rang. Ella picked it up and recognized Teeny's gravelly voice immediately.

"I've got bad news," he said.

"What's up?" she asked, bracing herself.

"Rainwater did a jackrabbit on us before I could get back to him."

"Damn. That means he knows a lot more than he's been telling us." Knowing that Teeny would be on his trail even as they spoke, she added, "What else can you tell me, Bruce?"

"Melvin told his employer at Mesa Vista that he had an emergency, and left, but he didn't say what kind of emergency and he didn't go home or to either of his cousins's—according to everyone I've spoken to. But don't worry. I'll track him down again."

"Good. When you get a lead, let me know."

"All right," he said, and without saying good-bye, hung up.

Justine looked over at her. "Let me guess. Melvin has disappeared, and Bruce is going to try and find him?" Justine asked, putting things together after hearing Ella's side of the conversation.

"Yeah. Something must have changed and spooked him, or else he thinks we're about to uncover evidence that shows he lied to us."

"Teeny is an ex-cop so he knows what to do. Best of all he has a lot of old contacts. He'll probably track Melvin down before too long, unless he's left the state."

"Teeny is, was, a good cop. I wish he were still on the force," Ella said.

"There's something I've *just* got to ask you, Ella. Is there something between you and Teeny? Or was there at one time?"

Ella looked at her in surprise, then burst out laughing. "No! We've just always got along well."

"Then I've got news for you partner. You may not realize it, but that guy's crazy about you."

Ella shook her head. "Teeny knows what our relationship was—and is. He's helping us now because we're short of manpower and we need to find Agent Thomas fast. That's all there is to it."

Justine gave her a skeptical look but didn't pursue it. "How long do you think Big Ed will be able to pay for his services? Our budget is almost nonexistent."

"Hopefully long enough for him to track down and hang on to Melvin Rainwater. Teeny's perfect for the job, Justine. He can work on and off the Rez without a problem. And as far as Big Ed is concerned, he and Teeny go back a ways. You know the story, don't you?"

"What story?"

"I'll take that as a no," Ella said with a grin. "Before Big Ed became police chief, he and Teeny were providing security at a Chapter House meeting where tensions were high and trouble was expected. Big Ed broke up a big fight, sending the two ringleaders on their way. Later, after the meeting ended, someone tried to crack Big Ed on the head with a bat, but Teeny put his arm up and deflected the blow. His arm was broken, and two more guys jumped in, but even with a broken arm, Teeny and Big Ed were able to fight off them off. Big Ed might have been killed if Teeny hadn't spotted the bat and intervened. That's one of the reasons why when budget cuts came down, and Big Ed was ordered to lay Teeny off as nonessential personnel, he held firm and refused to do it. But Teeny had enemies and some tribal leaders went over the chief's head and forced it to happen anyway. Teeny was angry about losing his job so abruptly, mind you, but the two men still have a lot of respect for each other."

"He shouldn't have been let go. Our department needed him—and he needed us. I've heard stories of how Teeny handles troublemakers when he's working security these days. He's really physical, throwing people over cars and stuff like that. To me, it sounds like Teeny's become a grenade without the pin. He should stick to his computer tech work before he ends up killing someone, even by accident."

"You're wrong about him," Ella answered quietly. "He likes intimidating people who mouth off to him, sure, and he's got the physical tools to do it. But he's really bright, with good instincts, and streetwise as well. But in any case, what he's doing for us now is strictly a one-shot deal. He's on this because we have to move fast and we can't turn away qualified help. Agent Thomas is fighting for his life. We've got to do all we can to find him."

"I hear you," Justine said.

Ella checked her watch. It was now ten, midmorning, and another hour had passed without any new answers or leads. The call they believed had come from Thomas would soon be twenty-four hours old, and he'd been missing for nearly twice that time. "Step on it, partner."

They arrived at Yellowhorse's address in Kirtland about fifteen minutes later. The semirural neighborhood was filled with inexpensive ranch-style homes, some of them thirty years old, others almost new.

Ella and Justine were walking up to the front door of an older one-story stucco house with peeling trim when an elderly Navajo woman came around the corner, a handful of bulbs in her hands. Her hair, which was tied back in a knot against the nape of her neck, was almost completely white. Her dark eyes, in contrast, were bright and shone with awareness and intelligence.

"I see badges and guns, so you must be the police. Are you here about my husband's death benefit?"

Ella identified herself by name, seeing the small crucifix the old woman wore around her neck and assuming that she wasn't a traditionalist. "Are you Lorena Yellowhorse?"

"Yes. Are you sure you're not here about my check?"

Ella nodded. "But we do need to talk to you. Could we go inside?"

Lorena nodded, then led the way through the front door into the small, brightly decorated kitchen. Fresh flowers were everywhere, and the cabinets were yellow with blue trim. "If this isn't about my social security check, why are you here?"

Ella and Justine sat down at the small wooden table and accepted glasses of iced herbal tea. As they waited for Lorena to take a seat, Ella looked around the homey kitchen. The appliances and countertops were old, but attention to decorating details had given the room a facelift.

"I know this must be a difficult time for you," Ella said. She was trying to look sympathetic, but it was difficult because the herb tea was so tart she felt like puckering up instead. "The death of a loved one is never easy. . . ."

Lorena held up her hand. "My husband, Daniel, was sickly for many years. His death wasn't unexpected," she said. "But it's strange how life works. My husband was very organized and he worked hard to make sure that all the paperwork was ready for me once he passed on. All I'd have to do was sign a few things and go on with my life. But despite all he did, I've had nothing but trouble."

"What do you mean?" Ella asked.

"I counted on his death benefit to pay off some medical bills, and was supposed to get his social security instead of mine, which is a lot smaller because I didn't work nearly as long as he did. But everything went wrong. After my husband died, I sent in all the right forms like he'd told me to, but his check suddenly stopped coming. I called the local office, and they sent me to Agent Blalock, an Anglo FBI agent with an office in Shiprock. He found out that the checks were going to some other address and called to tell me that Agent Thomas, an associate of his, would find out why and put a stop to it. But I haven't heard from either of them since then."

"How long ago was that?" Ella took another sip of tea. It was still dreadful.

"Well, the younger man, Andrew Thomas, called me just four days ago. He said he needed to verify some things before he could give me any more details, including where the checks were going. But I haven't heard from him or Agent Blalock since then," she said, then paused thoughtfully. "Maybe the reason for all my bad luck is that God's punishing me because I left my husband and came here. I moved in with my daughter a few months ago because my husband didn't want me at home where I'd see him dying bit by bit. He was a proud man who wanted no pity from anyone. He chose to die alone." There was a hitch in her voice, a hint of an overpowering grief held at bay only with effort. Mr. Yellowhorse wasn't the only proud member of his family.

It was several minutes before the old woman spoke again, but patience, despite the urgency of the current situation, could pay high dividends.

"But everything's going wrong. Recently someone started stealing my mail from the box outside. I called the post office, and spoke to Agent Thomas about that as well. I was thinking that maybe it's connected to the people who are getting the social security checks that should be coming to me. Agent Thomas was going to come by yesterday and talk to me about that, but he never showed up."

"He's been sidetracked with a missing-person's case," Ella said, figuring it wasn't a complete lie. "But for the time being, I'm going to ask that a county deputy be sent to keep an eye on things here for you."

"You mean so they can catch whoever's stealing my mail?" Her expression brightened hopefully.

Ella hesitated, not wanting to alarm her. The truth was she was worried that Mrs. Yellowhorse could be in serious trouble. It was starting to look like Blalock and Thomas had uncovered some kind of social security scam just before Thomas disappeared. If

the perps were trying to cover their tracks and get rid of witnesses, Mrs. Yellowhorse might be in danger, too. It also meant
that perhaps Blalock was on an enemies list. She'd have to try
harder to track him down and warn him.

"People will be helping protect your mail, ma'am, and also
making sure you don't have any more problems," Ella said, not
wanting to get any more specific than that for now.

"I appreciate anything you can do. Today he didn't stop, but
my mailman usually comes at around nine every morning. You
might want to tell the deputy."

Ella gave Justine a nod. Seeing it, her partner walked off,
phone in hand. Moments later, she returned. "It's being handled.
A deputy will be in the area shortly," Justine told Ella.

"Did you talk to Sheriff Taylor?" Ella asked.

"Just for a moment. Emily's the one making the arrangements."

Ella nodded, and accepted the refill of tea Mrs. Yellowhorse
was offering her, though she would have much rather walked
barefooted through a cactus patch.

A full ten minutes later, a county sheriff's deputy arrived out
front and Ella and Justine stood, thanking the widow for the tea
and saying good-bye. Nodding to the deputy they continued to
the SUV. As soon as they were out of earshot, Justine looked over
at her. "I've got a water bottle in the seat. You want to share?"

"Oh, yeah. *What* was in that drink?"

"It tasted vaguely like peppermint—and alum."

Sitting in their unit, they traded the water bottle back and
forth until they'd each had several swallows of water. "Were you
thinking that Thomas uncovered a scam, and now the thieves are
trying to cover their tracks—starting with the investigating officer?" Justine asked.

"In my opinion here's the way it went down. Melvin picked
up the body, which was released because he'd obviously died a
natural death. At the same time he learned that Yellowhorse lived
alone. So he and possibly Krause, who owns the mortuary,
changed the name on the paperwork and rerouted Yellowhorse's
social security to themselves or an accomplice. But they never

counted on a widow somewhere else raising the alarm when her benefits stopped coming. Plain and simple, we got lucky 'cause they screwed up. I have a feeling they've been pulling this con for a while," Ella said. "It's a brilliant plan and a veritable gold mine because no Navajo likes to talk about the dead."

"Of course they could only try this with people who'd died of natural causes since then there would be no need for further investigation," Justine commented thoughtfully. "But where's our evidence? We can't prove any of it, even if it's one hundred percent true."

"We'll start by checking to see if there's a death certificate for Daniel Yellowhorse," Ella said. "We can then—" Ella stopped in midsentence as she glanced back in the side mirror. "There's a gold SUV parked halfway down the street. It's been there since we went in and there's a driver behind the wheel. He may just be waiting for someone, but let's go check him out."

Justine started to turn the vehicle around but, as if guided by a sixth sense, the SUV wheeled around quickly in the street and raced south down a narrow, tree-lined residential street.

"Close in on him so I can get a look at his plates," Ella said, reaching for the radio. "I'll call for county backup."

Justine shot after the fleeing vehicle, siren on and emergency lights flashing. She quickly narrowed the distance between them as they raced past fenced-in yards in the old neighborhood closer to the river.

"New Mexico tag, but I still can't make out the letters and numbers," Ella said.

"Is that Melvin's Chevy?" Justine asked.

"No, it's a Ford, probably the same Excursion that flashed Herman and me," Ella said.

"Huh? Oh, right. The mirror."

The SUV ran the stop sign at the end of the street, sliding out into the old Shiprock highway, then accelerating away with smoking tires toward the west. An oncoming pickup swerved and went off onto the shoulder as the suspect came across the centerline.

The three teens inside were cursing and flipping off the driver of the SUV as Justine and Ella shot by after him.

"He's driving like a wild man, Ella," Justine said, her voice a half octave higher. Her expression was taut as she focused on controlling their unit over the wavy, cracked pavement that had been patched hundreds of times by now. "Man, this old road is a piece of crap."

Ella looked over at their speed. In a shrinking old farm and orchard area where the speed limit was thirty-five, they were approaching sixty. She watched ahead, hoping to help Justine spot any road hazards. The worse thing in the world now would be to meet up with a farmer pulling his tractor out onto the street.

The big SUV disappeared around a curve, then Ella caught a flash of gold. "He turned left, Justine."

"I'm on it, boss."

Justine took the corner well, but a chunk of old pavement must have broken loose from the strain because there was a loud clunk and the left rear tire slid just a little. Ella hung on, not saying a word, and reached up toward the stone badger fetish on her neck. She wrapped her hand around it, noting that it wasn't hot, a sign of great danger, but it was definitely warmer than usual.

The high vegetation lining the fields along the side road reflected back some of the engine noise, making it sound as though they were racing down a tunnel. Within a half mile they were back in the same residential area they'd been five minutes ago.

Justine was approaching an intersection when a small rubber ball came bouncing out a driveway into the street.

"Hit the brakes!" Ella yelled.

TEN

✖ ✖ ✖

Justine responded instantly and something slippery in the road, perhaps leaves from an overhead branch, caused them to skid wide to the left. She corrected, and the unit screeched to a stop in the oncoming traffic lane.

Out of the corner of her eye Ella saw a toddler and a small black-and-white terrier come running out into the street in pursuit of the ball. A scream was already fading as a woman wearing leotards and a sweatband came rushing off the porch of the house adjacent to them. The fair-haired woman raced into the street, scooped up the frightened child, then glared at them accusingly.

"You're going too fast!" she screamed. "You could have killed my baby!"

"Sorry. But your child wouldn't have had the opportunity to run out into the street *if* you'd been keeping a better eye on her," Ella answered firmly although her hand was shaking as she held up her badge. "Didn't you hear the siren?" Ella looked down and saw an MP3 player hooked to the woman's waistband, and headphones dangling down. "Never mind."

The woman turned sharply and stalked back into the yard, still clutching her child. The little dog followed, barking.

Justine's hands were clenched around the wheel in a death grip, and she was cursing softly to herself. "I can't believe this!

That kid came out of nowhere. How did you know? You told me to brake *before* the kid and dog came out."

"The ball," Ella said, her voice still shaky. "Rule of thumb—if you see a ball, a kid isn't far behind."

"I saw the ball, but I didn't see anyone around, and we were running code three—with siren and lights. If you hadn't yelled . . ."

"No one was hurt. That's what's important. Now let's go. Maybe we can still spot where that gold SUV went." Ella called in another report, relating the incident with the child as well as the fugitive, then asked for an APB on the gold vehicle.

Emergency gear off now, Justine and Ella searched for over twenty-five minutes, looking down long driveways, beside farmhouses, and even in the parking lots of the area schools. They found a lot of SUVs, some gold, but none that matched the right make and model. It was as if that particular vehicle had vanished into thin air.

"We've lost him," Justine said at last.

"Yeah," she admitted through clenched teeth. "Let's go talk to Sheriff Taylor. We need to get more on Jack Krause, the funeral home director. Maybe he's got priors. We also need to find out if the county has a death certificate on file for Daniel Yellowhorse. If not, then somebody else along the document chain is also involved in this social security scheme."

"If you ask me, this case centers on Melvin Rainwater. Despite his alibi covering the time when Agent Thomas went off the radar—being the patient at the Sing—he's still the one who's dropped out of sight again. Melvin could be the key to finding Agent Thomas."

"You may be right," Ella answered. "We'll come down hard on Melvin once Teeny finds him—and I have no doubt that he will."

Sheriff Taylor, a lean-looking cowboy in his late fifties with pale blue eyes, sat behind his desk and regarded Ella thoughtfully as she filled him in on recent events.

"I'm glad you reported that near accident over in Kirtland. But we haven't received a call from the mother—which means she's either willing to accept the fact that she should have been watching her kid better or she's getting ready to file a complaint."

Justine groaned. "I hope not."

A young man holding three paper sacks came in just then, and placed them on the desk. Ella reached for her wallet, but Sheriff Taylor shook his head. "Lunch is on me today," he said.

"Thanks. I wish we didn't have to make it a working one but I really need some leverage to use on Krause. And the sooner the better. I think we're onto something here."

"If you're right, it's a freakin' foolproof scam," Taylor said. "His chances of getting caught were almost zip. I'll have one of my people run over to county records and check for a death certificate on that Yellowhorse fellow. It'll save you some legwork."

"Thanks."

Taylor made a quick call, putting the records check into motion, then took a bite out of his sandwich while punching keys on his computer keyboard with his other hand. A couple of beeps and a mouse click or two later, he looked up at them. "Krause is squeaky clean. He's got two parking tickets, one outstanding. That's it. I'll run him through the feds next."

There was another beep from the computer. "Wait a second. Talk about coincidences. We just got a stolen vehicle report. Mrs. Krause, Jack's wife, just reported that one of her vehicles has been stolen."

"Let me guess. A gold Ford Excursion?"

"Bingo. And she just noticed it missing, though she can't really say how long it's been gone," Taylor answered.

"Krause's wife's car. Too much of a coincidence for me, too, Sheriff. Will you have a deputy do spot checks on Krause?"

"Sure, Ella. You don't think his wife is involved, then?"

"I got the idea she was about to become his ex-wife, but the husband may have kept a key to the gold SUV."

"Yeah, okay."

"Thanks for helping us out," Ella said standing up. "I'm

going to concentrate on Rainwater next. If I can get something to nail him on, I may be able to pressure him into talking once we find him. If he's involved in some kind of dead-body switch or social security fraud, I doubt he'll roll over on his partners easily, so I'll need to have something solid to use against him."

"I'll stay on Krause, follow through on the check for Yellowhorse, then get back to you."

As they walked out, Justine glanced over at Ella. "I hate to put a damper on things, but getting something on Melvin might be like putting the cart before the horse. He might have gone underground for good."

"Teeny'll find him."

Justine smiled. "That sure of him, are you?"

"Yeah. It's a matter of pride to him to be able to carry it through, and he doesn't have all the restrictions we have as cops. We're under public scrutiny much more than he is."

"His new job does have its perks, doesn't it? I mean, being able to charge lots of money to use his police training on cases and not having to stick to the book?"

"I'm not sure that's really a perk in the long run. Truth is, I like the black and white of police work. We know what we can and should do to bring a criminal down. Working within the system is a pain in the butt, but it maintains order. Without all the regulations, we'd be working in gray areas and, if you stay there long enough, the line separating the good guys from the bad can become real blurry."

As they climbed into the department vehicle, Justine glanced at Ella. "Where to?"

"Back to the station. I want to study all the photos we took of the area where Agent Thomas's car was found."

"I've already done that and included what I found in my report."

"Let's go over it again."

As they got under way, Justine glanced over at Ella. "You know I've been thinking of how Teeny—Bruce—was forced to leave, then started his own company. And then there's Sam Pete and Harry Ute. Both of them left our department and ended up with new careers that suited them perfectly."

"Don't tell me, cuz. You're thinking of leaving too?" Ella asked, hoping she was wrong. Justine was her right arm, and they'd really learned to work together well.

"No—not yet, anyway. But a while back I did consider working for a private security firm who offered to pay me double what I'm getting now. I turned them down because it felt like I was selling out. But I've been thinking about my job here lately and . . ." She shook her head and grew quiet.

"What?" Ella pressed.

"Don't take this the wrong way, Ella, but most of my life I've lived in your shadow—like little sisters sometimes do. Since I admire you and what you've done with your life, following in your footsteps wasn't a bad thing as far as I was concerned. But the truth is that I don't want my accomplishments weighed against yours for the rest of my career and I'm afraid that's exactly what'll happen if I don't leave. And, let's face it, I have no chance for advancement here unless you retire or I start lobbying for a desk job."

Ella knew Justine was right. "So what have you decided?" Ella asked, dreading the answer.

"Well, like Harry and Sam, I gave some thought to other PDs or joining one of the federal agencies. But what I'd really like is to work for a crime lab somewhere."

"You could probably get a job in a forensic lab anywhere you chose. Those places are usually short of qualified people, like the state lab in Santa Fe. But our department really needs you here, Justine. With your qualifications you'd be almost impossible to replace."

"I know. That's why I haven't done anything about it," she said, then shaking her head, continued, "Well, there's more to it than that. The fact is I'd miss my family and my life here terribly," she said, then paused before adding, "And off the Rez I'll always be marked as different. Here, I'm just one of the many. I fit in, you know?"

Ella nodded, remembering her own experience in the FBI, where Indians of any tribe were almost nonexistent. "When I joined the Bureau I didn't think that would bother me, but after a while it did. For one, I got trapped in what's unofficially called the taco circuit. Because of the way I look, I only got sent to places with a large Spanish population. Never mind that my Spanish stinks. The career-making high profile cases usually went to the guys with light skin."

"Yeah, some things never change."

"But tell me, do you really think you're in my shadow?" Ella asked. "I honestly don't think people compare us."

"They do, but you don't hear it because you're not the *clone*. It followed me through all my classes at the police academy because we're cousins. By then, you were well-known around here as a successful FBI agent so people began to think of me as the generic Rez version of you. Now that we're both here, it's worse."

"I never knew that."

"The thing is that we're not all that alike. True, we're both detectives who love what we do, but that's where the similarity ends. I really don't want to spend the rest of my career out in the field," she said. "I'm sure that I'd excel in a lab with the latest equipment and state-of-the-art technology."

Ella didn't reply right away. "You love lab work, like Teeny with his computers, and that's fine. But give yourself time to think things over first. Don't set yourself up for regrets later on in your life."

Justine nodded slowly.

Ella thought of all the years she'd spent in the field. Every case stayed with her, much more vividly than it would have if she'd been investigating from the relative security of a lab or from behind a desk. And with those memories came nightmares. The faces of those she'd killed in the line of duty always came back to haunt her. Whenever she awakened from one of those dreams, she'd lie awake for hours staring at the ceiling, or maybe sit at her computer and surf the Internet the remainder of the night. "We all pay a price for our choices, cousin. Or, as my brother would say, everything has two sides."

When Ella's cell phone rang, she answered it and recognized Special Agent Dwayne Blalock's voice immediately.

"What the hell's going on, Ella?" he asked. "My sister said you'd called and that it was an emergency. This better be good. Even though I was pressured into it, I'm having a good time. This is my first vacation in ages."

"I wouldn't have called unless it was important, Dwayne. Listen, Andy Thomas disappeared after interrupting a Navajo ceremony. He managed to send a cell phone message that he was trapped in some dark place, injured, but lost contact before we could get anything more. Nobody's been able to call him back either. A search is under way, and we're trying to figure out what happened and where he is right now."

"That idiot kid. I should have known he'd pull something like this. I tried to warn him that on the reservation things were done differently, but I just couldn't get past his ego and his thick head. Andy thinks he's invincible with that badge in his pocket."

"I should have made time to brief him, too," Ella said. "Maybe hearing it from me would have brought the point home. I could have used your early years on the Rez as a lesson in stupidity, you know."

"Yeah, yeah, I used to be a jerk. But okay, enough what-ifs and second guesses. What's going on now?"

She told him about Simmons and her inability to find any paperwork pertaining to Thomas's cases.

"There's a reason why Andy kept that to a minimum. His reports to Simmons were sketchy because Thomas was hoping not to have that a-hole breathing down his neck like he does mine," Blalock said.

"What exactly was Agent Thomas investigating? Our best guess so far involves some social security check problems."

"Then you already know almost as much as I do. The case I started—that I turned over to Thomas—suggested possible social security fraud. A widow, Lorena Yellowhorse called me, saying she hadn't received her husband's benefit check or his social security after he died, like she was supposed to."

"I've talked to her about that already. Is there anything else you can tell me?"

"Just one more thing. Her checks weren't getting to her because someone had filed for a change of address—Mr. Yellowhorse ostensibly. But the EMTs made a positive ID and swore the man was dead. That's as far as I got when I had to turn the case over to Thomas. Simmons got pissed at me for not filing reports on time so he told me to give the case, and any others I was working on, to Agent Thomas until I caught up with my paperwork. I advised Simmons strongly against that course of action. I explained that I didn't think Agent Thomas was qualified to work a case on the reservation yet and mentioned the cultural factors, but he wasn't listening.

"I had no choice," Blalock said, then in a somber voice added, "I was real close to losing it with Simmons, Ella. Before I could say something that would have undoubtedly ruined what's left of my career, I took his suggestion to take my annual leave and went on vacation."

"If you started the case, then handed it to Thomas, there's got to be a file or notes on this somewhere," Ella said.

"Yeah, there is. I know because I started the file myself and passed it on to Andy. It should be in our office."

"Yeah? I haven't been able to find it."

"It's probably on his desk somewhere. His filing system sucks worse than mine."

"It's not there. Simmons, Officer Tache, and I all searched your office."

"I'm coming back today, Ella. I'll find the file."

"Is it possible Agent Thomas took it home?" Ella asked.

"No way. He wouldn't even take his computer files with him."

"Somebody must have. The case file is missing."

"I'll look through my desk and his file cabinet. Maybe you all overlooked it or it was mislabeled or relabeled," Blalock replied, undaunted. "Did you check every folder?"

"No. That would have taken time we didn't have. And I couldn't turn it over to a clerk, considering the nature of the job. We weren't supposed to be going through those files in the first place."

"Yeah. Simmons would be facing the mother of all reprimands if his boss found out you'd been given access to Bureau files," Blalock replied. "Looks like you need me, Clah."

"Not as much as Andy Thomas does."

"You got that right. What are the chances he's still alive?"

"It's been over a day and a half since he made the call. But if he's in a mine shaft, and could still speak and get a signal out, he's probably got air available. It all depends on what his injuries are, I guess."

"Right. Fingers crossed here. He's an idiot, but nobody deserves to die alone like that."

"Tell me about it," she muttered. "I guess I'll see you when you get here. Give me a call as soon as you get back, or if you think of anything before then."

"Count on it."

"One more thing before you hang up. Did you ever talk to anyone at the Social Security Administration office?" Ella asked.

"No, but I think Andy did," Blalock said.

"I'll follow it up and see what I can uncover."

"Good. And, Ella, a word of advice about dealing with Simmons. He's got a chip on his shoulder about minorities and women in the Bureau, if you haven't noticed already. Passed over too many times for promotion, I think. Don't let it get to you, okay?"

"You mean I can't shoot him?"

"Better not. But you have my permission to beat the crap out of him," Blalock asserted, then ended the call.

It was 1:00 P.M. by the time they arrived at the station in Shiprock. Ella was happy to see that her vehicle had been repaired. Once inside the building, Justine brought out the file with all the photos of the area where Thomas's car had been found and set them down on Ella's desk.

Ella studied each photo carefully, especially the close-ups. "Check these tracks against the ones made by Rainwater's vehicle or any he might have driven at work—except a hearse, of course. I want to know if they're a match. And if we ever find Mrs. Krause's stolen vehicle, it should get the treatment as well. Meanwhile, I've got a phone call to make to the social security office in Farmington."

Ella was put on hold three times. She was getting impatient and close to losing her temper when a cold, disinterested voice answered.

"This is Jerry Hathaway. What can I do for you, Mrs . . ."

"*Investigator* Clah of the Navajo tribal police. I'm working on a case in conjunction with the FBI. A resident FBI agent named Andrew Thomas was making inquiries into a suspected social security fraud case and called your office to get some information."

"Agent Thomas, you said? From the FBI?"

"Yes. Do you remember speaking to him?"

"Yes, as a matter of fact, I do. A Navajo woman had reported that she'd never received her husband's death benefits or had his monthly survivor-benefit checks sent to her at her new address. We looked into the matter and learned that the man had supposedly filled out a notification for a change of address on-line. His social security checks were being mailed to the new address as requested but, according to Agent Thomas, he was deceased and couldn't have made that request on the date we had on record. We take fraud very seriously and cooperated fully with Agent Thomas. To give you an idea, it would normally have taken us weeks to get the information he wanted, but I phoned him with the names he needed in less than four days."

"Names, you said?"

"Agent Thomas asked me for a list of other social security recipients on the reservation who'd filed a change of address during the last six months. He was particularly interested in people whose checks were going to a post office box number off the reservation."

"Can you give me those names?"

"Yes. I have them in a folder. Hold please."

Once again Ella was subjected to the drone of the elevator music. She was drumming her fingers on the table impatiently when Justine came in. Ella looked up at her, scowling.

"What did I do?" Justine protested.

"It's not you, it's the bureaucratic runaround phone tag that's got me annoyed."

Justine nodded. "While you're in limbo, I have some bad news. No match on the tire tracks on site and Rainwater's vehicle. I also checked with the mortuary. They have a van there, but the tire size would be wrong. Were you thinking someone at the Sing went after Thomas after Jim and Eugene left?"

"It was a possibility I wanted to check into since the Darwin rejects told us they'd seen someone driving up," she said, then switched her attention to Jerry Hathaway. "Yes, I'm still here."

"Here are the three names I gave him—Daniel Yellowhorse, Billy Tom, and Roy Blackhat," he said, then proceeded to give her the addresses of the latter two.

"Did he ever call you back and update you on what he'd found?"

"No, he didn't."

After thanking Hathaway, Ella ended the call and glanced at Justine. "We've got to do some serious digging," she said, and passed on what she'd learned. "We know Yellowhorse is dead, but let's go to the addresses Hathaway gave me. We need to see who's living in those homes now and talk to someone face-to-face."

"You want to split up?"

"No. I have a feeling we may have to canvas their neighborhoods and two can work that faster than one," she said. "But let me call the sheriff's department again. Taylor was going to have somebody check on the status of Daniel Yellowhorse's death certificate. You didn't take the call, did you?"

When Justine shook her head, Ella called Sheriff Taylor. Three minutes later, she hung up, shaking her head. "The deputy is trying to locate a supervisor. The clerk that runs that part of county records closed up for lunch and still isn't back. But we should be getting an answer within a half hour—tops."

"Right. And the choppers are coming—and the check's in the mail. Count me as a pessimist. Just when we need to know this stuff yesterday, another roadblock appears in our way. I sure hope Andy Thomas is still hanging on."

"Me, too," Ella nodded.

As they walked out to the parking lot, Ella glanced at her now repaired unit, spotting Clifford's spare in the back. She'd drop it by next time she went home, or in that direction. "My wheels are good to go, but I need time to think, so we'll take your cruiser and you drive. Go to Billy Tom's house first."

Silence stretched out between them as they drove across the river and past an old residential area on the southwestern side of Shiprock. The houses there had been demolished, hauled away, and buried years ago because they'd been constructed with materials contaminated with uranium tailings—a legacy of the old uranium mill across the highway. The land there was still uninhabitable in the eyes of some, so the former neighborhood of fifty or more houses was no more. A few houses adjacent to the three run-down streets had cropped up but the area, for the most part, was an eyesore where memories of lost innocence lingered.

"That place gives me the creeps," Justine said. "Like it's haunted or something."

Ella nodded slowly. "People didn't know any better back then, so they lived in the houses the Bureau of Mines provided for them, trusting they were safe. The workers at the helium plant had children and raised them there for twenty or more years. Then, when it was too late, they found out that their homes had been built using concrete and mortar contaminated with radioactive materials. And politicians wonder why the People don't trust the federal government."

They circled toward the north to a neighborhood of single- and double-wide mobile homes, each separated by a quarter of an acre, closer to the river. Sheep and goats grazed on the meager pickings the small parcels provided, supplemented by alfalfa and whatever other feed was available.

Billy Tom's house was positioned perpendicular to a ditch about fifty feet away, having apparently just been backed into place. Seeing no vehicles or livestock, Ella glanced around, walked up the rickety wooden steps to the door, and knocked. No one answered.

"He's not there," a boy about eight years old called out from across the road where he was playing with a toy truck.

Ella walked over to question him, but before she could get there, an obviously pregnant Navajo woman in her late twenties came out.

"Go inside, son," she said. "And get your toy." The boy picked up the red dump truck and went inside without a word. Without so much as glancing at Ella, the woman turned to follow him inside.

"Wait, ma'am. We're trying to locate your neighbor," Ella called out.

"He's gone." The woman half turned to look at them, a scowl on her face.

"Do you know where he's gone?"

She shook her head, and hurried inside the trailer before Ella could ask another question.

Justine sighed. "My guess, judging from that response, is that Billy Tom died."

"We need to know for sure. Then we have to find out where he died and who buried him."

"Our best shot is getting that information from records. This isn't a traditionalist area exactly, but from the looks of it, no one's going to rush right out and talk to us about a dead man," Justine said. "They probably figure that they have enough bad luck without risking calling a *chindi*."

Ella nodded slowly, taking a look around. There was no local trash service here, and garbage was piled in barrels or plastic bags, ready to be burned or taken to the closest dump. Beer bottles and cardboard boxes were scattered all over.

"I don't know if it's bad luck or just loss of hope," Ella commented softly, her gaze taking in the area. "There's never enough money, just kids that have to be fed and clothed. A lot of our people can't make a living from the land anymore and many of them just don't know how to do anything else. The ones that get a good education have to move away to use what they've learned since there are so few opportunities here."

"It's a wonder we don't have more crime considering how many people live below poverty level," Justine said. "I read an article Jaime at the *Times* wrote last week saying that more than half the Navajo homes still burn wood for heating, but a lot of families can't afford woodstoves so they're making their own using whatever they can get, like empty metal containers. Deaths inevitably follow."

Ella looked down the street. "Come on. Let's start knocking on doors. We're bound to meet a Christian or a modernist who won't mind talking about the dead."

ELEVEN
✖ ✖ ✖

It was a long process. Justine finally caught up with Ella as they reached the opposite end of the row of mobile homes. "Most people aren't home right now, cuz," Justine said. "But I found an elderly man who told me that his neighbor went out and never came back. Unfortunately, I couldn't get him to clarify so I don't know if the body was carried out, or if the man just drove away."

Ella knocked on the door of the last mobile home in her section and a teenager wearing a Britney Spears T-shirt and baggy jeans answered. Ella figured that she should have been in school, like the boy at the other trailer with the truck, but decided to let it pass.

After introducing herself Ella learned the girl's name. "Roxanne, I'd like to ask you some questions about one of your neighbors—Billy Tom."

"Oh, the old man down by the ditch?" Seeing Ella nod, she continued. "What about him? He's gone now, you know. His trailer's filled with some good stuff, but no one wants it. The family across the street is really upset about the whole thing and they're going to be moving their trailer away from here."

"So he's dead?" Ella asked.

"Worse than roadkill. Mrs. Begay, the pregnant woman next door, smelled something rotting in the trailer and called the cops.

It turned out to be Mr. Tom. They found him sitting in front of his TV, watching *Jeopardy*. Well, not really watching, I guess. He'd been dead for weeks. So now no one wants to talk about him, but I've got to tell you, I sure thought about getting his TV set. If it works that well after being on all that time, and no one else wants it, why not?"

Ella didn't comment. "Did you see who picked up the body?"

"I don't know. The sergeant called someone, I guess."

"Sergeant? Who was the officer, do you know?"

Roxanne grinned, standing up straight and accentuating the front of her blouse. "The cute guy with the cool hair—you know, real short. He's built like a wrestler."

"Joseph," Ella and Justine both said at the same time, glancing at each other and trying hard not to burst out laughing.

"Sergeant Neskahi?" Ella asked, looking at the girl.

"That's him. He patrols this area sometimes when he's not helping out the tribe's murder squad," she said.

"Murder squad?" Justine whispered to Ella, who just grinned.

Ella thanked Roxanne, got her last name, then walked out with Justine to the unit. "Call the station and have the desk sergeant check through records. I want to know if there's a mention of the pickup by Mesa Vista."

Justine used her cell phone, and a moment later nodded. "It was them, all right." Justine then listened to the person on the other end of the phone again, frowned, then disconnected the call.

"What was the second thing?"

"Sheriff Taylor's office called because they couldn't get through to us on the radio. You know the deputy that was checking to see if there was a death certificate for Daniel Yellowhorse?"

"Yeah. Let me guess, there wasn't one." Ella shrugged.

"Wrong. There *was* a death certificate for him." Justine said. "Which leaves us nowhere. Who do you think arranged for a change of address then?"

"Either the social security people are screwing things up and covering for it, or the county records people are responsible and changing the information now that they know it's being searched. We need to confirm what kind of checks are being rerouted—survivor benefits to the spouse or retirement benefits for the guys who just happen to be dead. But either way, someone is getting these checks, and we've got to figure out who that is. I'm convinced these answers are the key to finding Andy."

"But in order to make someone appear to be still living, on paper at least, wouldn't their death certificate have to disappear?"

"Yeah, or have them filed under another name. Let's see what happened to Roy Blackhat. If he's dead, too, we'll ask the county to find out if there's a death certificate on file for him and Billy Tom. If the county has a record of the deaths, and the checks are just the result of a clerical error, we've gone around in a circle and nothing makes sense. But my instincts tell me some kind of fraud is going on, and Thomas was about to confront those responsible."

As they walked Ella looked down at the address they'd be going to next. "What I still don't have a handle on is exactly what happened to Agent Thomas. Did he fall into one of the mines while being pursued and the perps decided to leave him there, or did Thomas hide and become injured later? What really worries me is that if the bad guys know where he's at and we tip our hand, they may just go back and finish the job."

"Good point."

As they reached the car, Ella handed Justine the second address. After a drive through Shiprock they reached a modern housing area on the bluff north of the river valley. Judging from the late-model cars, this was an area of Navajo professionals. They located the house number quickly, but a look through the parted curtains as they walked to the porch revealed that the house was empty.

A middle-aged Navajo woman wearing jeans and a sweatshirt and sweeping her front porch watched them peek through the windows, then came over. "Are you looking for Mr. Blackhat?" she asked.

"Yes, we are," Ella said, and flashed her badge.

"You're a little late, I'm afraid. I think he's dead."

"But you're not sure?" Ella pressed.

"Well, I do know that he was diagnosed with a brain tumor and didn't have long to live. He gave away all his things. Then, one day, right in the middle of winter, he just got into his car and drove off."

"To where, do you know?"

"He said he was going to have a Sing done, then die in the old way. But I'm not sure if he meant in a hogan somewhere or if he was saying that he intended to just walk off into the desert. If he did, he would have frozen to death for sure. It was January."

"Do you know who was going to do the Sing?"

"I don't know, but I suppose it would have had to have been someone who lived close by. That car of his wouldn't have taken him far. It was a good thirty years old, and the tires were so bald you could almost see air through them."

"What type and make?" Ella asked.

"An old VW van, probably from the sixties. Faded blue—well, closer to tan now—the blue is almost completely gone."

Ella nodded to Justine, who called it in. Minutes later as they were walking back to Justine's unit, Neskahi called them back.

"A vehicle that fits that description is parked in the impound yard. It was towed in late last winter, March eighteenth. It was found abandoned in a ravine south of Big Gap," he told Ella. "Isn't that in the same area as your brother's hogan?"

"Yes, it is. I'll be going there next, Joseph. Anything on Rainwater yet?"

"No, but we've got his house staked out."

"Who's watching it now?"

"Philip Cloud. Between him and his brother, Michael, we've got it covered round the clock."

"Good job."

Ella placed the phone back in her jacket pocket. "Drop me off at the station. Then I need you to go back out to the place where we found Agent Thomas's car and take another look around. After that, go search Blalock's office, and look through every single file if necessary. It'll be hours before he's here and I don't want to wait. Blalock says that there's a case file for the social security investigation in there someplace. Search behind the file cabinet, desks, and any place where it might have fallen during a previous search. Here's a key I 'borrowed' from his desk."

"Sneaky, aren't you?" Justine said, smiling. "If there's anything there, I'll find it, Ella."

After Justine dropped Ella off near her vehicle, Ella took a moment to decompress. Her stomach hurt round the clock these days. It was tension. Some people got headaches—she got stomachaches. Pushing the pain back into a dark corner of her mind, Ella drove to her brother's hogan south of Shiprock, parked, then unloaded Clifford's spare tire and rolled it over to his truck while she waited to be invited in. Seeing her lifting the tire into the bed of the pickup, Clifford's wife, Loretta, called out to her from the porch of their home. "Your brother's not here."

"Where is he?" Ella asked. "I need to talk to him."

"Picking herbs again. This time he's in the field on the far side of the irrigation ditch."

"Thanks." There was no time to walk. Instead, Ella took the unit and drove straight to the area, which she knew well from previous visits. First, she'd find out if her brother knew anything about what had happened to Roy Blackhat and then figure out what part, if any, the mortuary had played in Thomas's disappearance. Agent Thomas's future hung by a delicate thread and instinct and logic told her that she was somehow missing a big piece of the puzzle. She still hadn't made the connection that would link motive and crime.

Ella parked beside the empty irrigation ditch, took a look around, then got out of her unit. She scrambled down to the dry, sandy bottom of the four-foot-deep ditch, knowing that this was the shortest route to where she was going. Driving alongside the ditch in her vehicle to a crossing point would cost her half an hour. Here a five-minute walk would pay off.

Ella climbed out the other side, then jogged down the track that lined a field, which had been allowed to go fallow. It now contained native plants instead of melons, corn, or alfalfa. Once she'd gone about fifty yards, she saw her brother squatting down beside a plant.

Seeing her, Clifford smiled and stood up. "What brings you all the way over here?"

"I put your spare tire in the bed of the truck, but that wasn't the only reason I came. I have a question for you," she said. "Did you do a Sing for an elderly patient who'd been diagnosed with a brain tumor?" she asked, doing her best to avoid mentioning him by name. "He has a house on the mesa at the east end of Shiprock. I understand he had a Sing done, and I'm hoping that he came to you."

"Thank you for not mentioning his name," Clifford replied. "I don't know why you're interested in him, but my guess is that he's dead by now."

"That's what I've been led to believe. He drove one of those old VW vans, and it was found abandoned not too far from here last March," she said. "Can you tell me what happened after you saw him?"

"He came to me late January asking for prayers to protect him on his final journey. He'd made up his mind not to live out his last few months in a hospital surrounded by the *chindi* of those who had died there. He was in his eighties, had no family left, so he planned to abandon his car and then start walking into the desert. His grandfather had died that way and, as he said, it was an honorable death."

Ella said nothing for several long moments, then gave him a hard look. "You knew he was going to commit suicide, so why did you let him go?"

Clifford shook his head, disapproval shining clearly in his eyes as he gazed back at her. "You're a part of our tribe, yet sometimes I'd swear that you understand nothing. He was going to *die*. The doctors knew it, he knew it, and so did I. All he was asking was to go his own way. He wanted to die in the desert he loved, not tucked away out of sight in a little hospital room where he couldn't even see the sacred mountains," Clifford said, searching her eyes to see if she understood now. Apparently not satisfied with what he saw there, he added, "The last words he spoke to me say it best. He told me he wasn't taking his life—that he was going out to enjoy what he had left of it. Then he'd sit down and rest."

Clifford crouched down, inspecting a plant for a moment, then glanced back up at her and regarded her thoughtfully. "He died honorably—in the tradition of his ancestors. That's worthy of your respect."

"There *are* simpler and more comfortable ways to go."

"Maybe in *your* opinion."

Ella heard the tone in his voice and knew that an argument would get them nowhere. Clifford's mind was made up. "So, for the record, you believe he's dead."

"Absolutely. You could see his end was near just by looking at him. If you need to verify it, check your records and see if a body was found in the desert around here sometime after January."

"I will." She started back toward the ditch and Clifford joined her.

"You don't look so good and your feet are dragging. Is it the case you're working on?"

"Yeah. I'm exhausted. There's an FBI agent out here on the Rez somewhere, lost and maybe dying, but I can't get a fix on him at all. His time may be running out, and I'm still spinning my wheels and getting no place."

Clifford studied her expression, then lapsed into a lengthy silence. At long last he spoke. "The problem is that you're torn between going by the book so you can make a case against the guilty and doing whatever's necessary to find this agent while there's still hope. But by trying to cover all the bases at once, it's impossible for you to make progress."

Ella considered it. "There's some truth in what you've said but you're not entirely right. I want whoever did this. And if they get away with it because of something I did or left undone, it'll haunt me for the rest of my life. But I'm also doing everything I can to find Agent Thomas quickly. He's at the heart of this case. Both aspects balance each other."

"You've defined yourself as a cop for a long time. You like being ruled by Anglo laws, because they give you structure and let you find harmony. But the structure you need is part of who you are. Listen to your inner voice and stop letting only what you can see and prove direct you."

"My instincts are pretty reliable . . . but not in this case. I don't know the missing man, but I can taste his fear," she said softly. "I've been to that place where everything looks hopeless. I *know* what he's thinking. I can *feel* the waves of panic that hit him."

"You're taking too much on yourself. His rescue doesn't depend solely on you. There are others at play in this."

"I'm the head of the Special Investigations team. If we fail, it'll probably be because I made the wrong decisions." She took a deep breath. "But I *won't* fail."

When they reached the irrigation ditch, Ella saw two boys farther down, kicking a soccer ball back and forth. She was about to warn them about playing in the ditch when she heard a strange bubbling noise. The kids froze and looked upstream, surprised.

A heartbeat later one of the boys pointed toward a curve in the ditch farther uphill. "Water!"

Before they could get halfway up the sides, the dirty, churning rush of water slammed against them and they lost their grip on the banks.

"Get a large branch we can use to pull them out," Ella yelled to Clifford as she raced down the side of the ditch, trying to keep pace with the boys, who were being swept downstream by the raging stream.

Fear sliced through her. She hated water. And she hated *rushing* water even more. But one way or another, she and Clifford would have to get the boys out of there before they drowned.

TWELVE

——— ✖ ✖ ✖ ———

Ella raced along the side of the ditch, catching up to the taller boy, who'd managed to take hold of some roots extending out from the side of the embankment and was clinging to them desperately. Ella stopped, reached down, and grabbed his wrist.

Just then Clifford came up. "Pull him out," Ella told him quickly. "I've got to go after the other one."

"Go. I've got things here," Clifford said, reaching out for the kid.

As Clifford took over Ella shot after the second boy. He was being swept down the ditch at an alarming speed, rolling along, unable to right himself. Carrying the branch her brother had brought, Ella sprinted down the bank. She had to catch up to him before he reached one of the irrigation gates. Once there, he could easily get sucked down a culvert and end up trapped in a pool at the bottom.

The ditch continued in a wide curve, making almost a ninety-degree change in direction. Hearing a yell somewhere ahead, she managed to get a fix on his position. Ella cut across the field, running so fast that she almost fell into the ditch herself before she could stop. Dropping to her knees she held out the branch as the boy drew closer.

"Grab on!" she yelled, but the current was still spinning the boy and he couldn't bring his arm around in time.

"Help!" he cried.

Ella saw the desperation in his eyes as the current swept him past her. Like too many kids on the Rez, he didn't know how to swim. In a panic, he was fighting the water instead of bobbing up and down and taking advantage of the fact that bodies floated naturally. At this rate he'd tire soon, so she had to do something fast.

Ella sprinted to catch up again and saw the closed diversion gate ahead. It was designed to direct water into the field to her right. Running as fast as she could, she managed to overtake and pass the boy, arriving at the gate a few seconds ahead of him.

Lying down, she looped her legs around the sturdy metal post where the water wheel was attached, then looked upstream. The boy was almost there. Hanging on to solid ground only by her legs, she pushed off the bank with her arms, held her breath and lunged out into the water. The cold current was a shock.

As she reached out, the boy slammed into her right arm at the inside of her elbow. Grabbing on to him, she held on tightly. Their combined mass in the water swept her around, and her head kept going under as she clung to the boy, bringing her left arm around to encircle him completely.

Ella struggled to keep her ankles locked around the only anchor, the threaded steel post that operated the irrigation gate. Her lungs about to burst, she noticed that the boy wasn't struggling now, even though his head was below the surface as well.

Just as she was about to run out of air, she felt a firm grip on her ankle, then on her other leg. Concentrating on holding on to the boy, Ella felt herself being pulled out onto the bank. When her head finally came out of the water, she gasped for air.

"I've got you," Clifford said, dragging her onto dry ground.

Ella raised her head and looked at the boy, who had her arm in a death grip. His eyes were wild and his breathing ragged.

"You're safe now. Just rest for a moment and catch your breath."

Terror, cold and dark, lit up his eyes and shivers racked his body. In her gut Ella understood and knew that he was as incapable of unclenching his fingers from around her arm as he was of flapping his arms and flying to the moon.

Clifford crouched beside her. "The other kid's safe. Are you both okay?"

"I am. Our boy here just needs a few moments to get over the shock." She was incredibly cold, and the slight breeze felt like ice cubes on her skin.

Ella reached over with her free hand and placed it on the boy's shoulder. "Just relax."

The boy nodded.

Ella watched his eyes, and saw him break through his fear to find bits and pieces of sanity. He was probably ten, and this had undoubtedly been the worst experience of his life. "You're all right. It's over now."

She could see exhaustion taking over as his fear retreated and his breathing evened. Finally, he let go of her arm and sat up. "Thanks for pulling me out," he said, then seeing her pistol and the handcuffs on her belt added, "Officer."

Ella glanced at Clifford and saw him nod in approval. The boy's companion, an older brother judging from their resemblance, was there now too, standing and watching, his arms wrapped around himself for warmth.

"You going to arrest us?" the boy managed, looking at her, then Clifford.

Ella shook her head. "Just stay out of the ditches this time of year."

The boys looked at each other. "Okay," the younger brother said quickly and his brother nodded and added, "Yeah, okay."

"Then get home and out of those wet clothes," Clifford motioned toward a house in the distance. "Hurry."

The older boy reached down, grabbed his brother's arm, and pulled him up to his feet. "Let's go before they change their minds!"

The two kids ran off.

"Remind me to tell my son about this," Clifford said, shaking his head slowly.

"I will," Ella nodded, climbing to her feet and reaching down to confirm that she still had her weapon and phone. The pistol would need to be dried out and cleaned but she had no idea whether her cell phone would still work.

"I know who they are. I'll mention this incident to their father, too," Clifford replied. "But something's bothering me. The ditches are dry this time of year unless someone is irrigating and everyone does that real early in the morning because of evaporation loss. This shouldn't have happened."

"I know. Let's go to the main gate and find out what's going on." Ella looked around, verifying that she hadn't dropped anything, then started walking back upstream with Clifford.

"The closest bridge is this way," he said cocking his head. "But first I've got to pick up the plants."

"If there's no indication that the gate came open on its own, then I'm going to assume that this was done to slow me down. After everything that has happened recently I'm getting the distinct impression that some people just don't want Agent Thomas found, at least not anytime soon. Maybe they're hoping he'll die on his own and save them the trouble of getting to him themselves," she said. "These people are really pissing me off."

"That's pride and frustration talking. You're going to have to put all that aside if you're going to find the Anglo man in time. Concentrate on what you know. On some level all the pieces have to make sense and come together. Find the pattern and then you'll be able to restore harmony." He paused for several moments. "There's something else I can do for you. I'll call on the powers of Thunder to help. Do you remember the stories?"

She nodded. "Thunders have the ability to find things, but not all were good, right?"

"I know you're a modernist, but I'm glad that you've held on to some of what you were taught," he said, pleased. "And you're right. Winter Thunder is not used in sandpaintings because he's unreliable and can cause problems, and White Thunder isn't just a troublemaker—he's evil."

When they reached the irrigation ditch's main gate directing flow from the river, Ella crouched down and studied the wheel and control mechanism. It was intact and there was no sign of tampering. "No fields are being irrigated. That means someone deliberately opened this. There's no other explanation."

As she examined fresh vehicle tracks nearby, she noted that the soil had a high clay content here. The only thing she could tell from the tracks themselves was that they'd come from an SUV or a large truck, and one of its tires had a small gash across the tread.

"Let's get going. We have a long hike, and I'm freezing," Ella said.

They jogged this time, cutting another five minutes off the journey and slowing down only long enough for Clifford to pick up the plants he'd set down when they'd found the boys trapped by the water. But by the time they reached Ella's SUV, arrows of pain were shooting into her legs and her muscles felt tied into knots. "Remind me not to jog that fast when I'm freezing to the bone."

Her brother looked at her and grinned. "Don't blame it on the cold. You just haven't been jogging enough lately and you're a little out of shape and cramping up. That's why you're tired."

She looked over at him and realized he wasn't even winded. "You're so irritating."

"You're still competing with me. After all these years you should have realized how useless that is."

"Excuse me?"

"Since junior high you've always tried to do everything better than me. But it never worked. I'm just bigger and stronger."

"You're hallucinating. Bigger ego and stronger under the arms, maybe."

Clifford laughed.

Ella drove him back to his hogan without another word. No one could annoy her more than Clifford. They were blood and she loved him, but she could have cheerfully strangled him at times.

"You know I'm right. So why bother to get angry?" he said as he got out of the car.

"I'm not angry," she called out the window to him. "And you're *not* right. I was better running long distances in track than you ever were, and *our* girls' basketball team went to state, not the boys'. Your memory's faulty. Maybe you've been inhaling too much piñon smoke lately."

"If it makes you feel better, I'll concede the argument."

She wanted to run him over. Instead, she put the vehicle in gear and drove off, making sure she stirred up a large cloud of dust during her departure.

When she reached the main road leading toward the highway, Ella pulled over and checked her cell phone. It had been in her jacket pocket, and with the flip top cover closed had remained dry except on the outside. She decided to risk it and punched in Teeny's number. Surprisingly, it worked. "Have you gotten any leads on Rainwater at all?"

"All I have at the moment is hearsay. I spoke to one of the vendors over across from the high school."

The words 'over across' were used frequently, but they could mean almost anything—across the street, or across the river.

"Which vendor?" she asked.

"He didn't want me to say."

"Fair enough. What did he tell you?"

"Not enough for you to follow up on, not yet. Let me work on this a while longer. I'll contact you when I've got something. But since I've got you on the phone, I want to give you a heads-up. They're starting to sell kneel-down bread again near the hospital. That used to be your favorite."

"Still is," she said, smiling and surprised that he'd remembered.

"Okay, then, that's it."

"Wait—" she started, but he'd already hung up.

Teeny's memory of their high school days was surprisingly good. Kneel-down bread was made from freshly ground corn, a process done while kneeling, thus the name. It was cooked in pits dug into the ground and was a little smaller than a tamale. It was especially delicious with ground beef and chile. Kneel-down bread was a staple in autumn on the reservation and just thinking about it made her mouth water.

Unfortunately, there was no time to stop for food now. It was late afternoon and she wanted to talk to Krause, the funeral home owner, but she would need some serious leverage to get anything from him.

Ella called Justine next as she headed home to change clothes. "What have you found?"

"I'm still at Blalock's office going through Agent Thomas's case files. But the only thing here that has any reference to the Mesa Vista Mortuary is a sheet from a memo pad that somehow missed the trash. It was behind the filing cabinet next to the baseboard."

"In your opinion, could someone have broken in and stolen the file?"

"The window latch could be slipped loose, I guess, so it wouldn't have taken an expert locksmith to get in," she said after a pause. "Or the lock could have been picked. It's not impossible, but if someone managed that, then we're not dealing with an ordinary burglar."

"The more we get into it, the more I know there's nothing ordinary at all about this case, partner," Ella said. "Someone's been holding us up every step of the way, and pulling our strings." She told Justine what had happened when she'd gone to see Clifford. "Send Tache to the irrigation ditch to take photos of the tracks left by the vehicle that pulled up there."

"Okay. Where are you off to now?"

"I'm wet—or at least my blouse and sleeves are. Thankfully, my cell phone didn't fall into the drink. But I'll need to get dry clothes, so I'm stopping by the house. After that, I've some things to do on my own."

"What are you up to?" Justine said immediately.

"Nothing you want to get involved in," Ella answered flatly.

"I'll meet you at your mother's house."

Ella was about to say no, not wanting to let her partner in on what she was planning, but Justine beat her to the punch by hanging up.

When Ella reached the lane leading to her house and looked up ahead, she groaned. There were about ten cars parked around the house. Her mother must be hosting one of the Plant Watchers meetings.

As Ella pulled up, she saw Dawn running in her direction. She turned off the engine and stepped out just in time. Long black ponytail flying behind her, Dawn raced up and grabbed her, knocking her back on her heels as she squeezed a massive hug.

"Yuk, Mom, you smell like ditch water, and you're all wet. You didn't find that guy in the river, did you?" Dawn stepped back, shaking her head. She was tall and lean for six and a half, and the older adults were constantly commenting on how much she looked like Ella at that age.

"No, but I did get a rinse in the ditch." Ella smiled. "Did you know *you* smell like a horse?"

"Duh, Mom, I rode Wind for, like, two hours today."

"That figures. What's your father doing here?" Ella had noticed Kevin walking in their direction.

"He came for me. Mom, I'm going to spend the night at Dad's. *Shimasání* said I could. It's okay, right?"

"Yes, Mom, how about it?" Kevin strolled up, looking as handsome as ever in his steel blue western suit, minus the striped tie and jacket at the moment. He was even taller than Ella, edging six feet, and had an ever-present sparkle in his eyes that few women were able to resist.

Ella looked down at her daughter, and realized once again that Dawn had Kevin's intense gaze and many of his personality quirks already. These past few months they'd grown closer, too. Lately Dawn had been spending more time with her father, though those visits were always limited to how long Dawn could bear to be away from Wind, her pony.

"It's fine," she said, looking at Kevin, then back at Dawn. "But you're still going to make sure Wind's taken care of, right?" Ella tried to look stern, but Dawn was already ahead of her.

"Dad promised Grandmother that he'd bring me by every morning and evening to feed *both* Wind and Chieftain. And if he gets called away to work, Boots will come and stay with me."

Dawn gave Kevin a special crinkly-nose grin she saved exclusively for him, and he winked back.

"It's all part of my deal with Rose, Ella. I'm a lawyer, remember? I have to figure every angle to get your mother's approval. We just finished with the horses. You got time to drive over to my house with us?"

Ella shook her head. "Sorry, but I promise to call when I get the chance, or maybe even stop by. It's this missing-persons case, but I can't really discuss it at the moment."

Kevin nodded. "Dawn told me something about that. But it's our secret, right, Bright Eyes?" He reached down and put his hands on Dawn's shoulders, and she leaned back into his chest, looking up and grinning.

"Right, Dad."

Ella thought about how much she would have enjoyed going somewhere with them for a quiet family dinner, but it wasn't to be. On the other hand, maybe that was for the best. Dawn still wanted her and Kevin to live together and she didn't want to do anything that might get her hopes up. "I've got to change clothes and get back to work. You two be good, okay?"

"You know me, Mom." Dawn grinned, grabbing Kevin's hand and pulling him in the direction of his pickup.

Ella caught Kevin's eye. "You two watch out for each other, okay?" She still remembered the all-too-recent incident involving an attempt to kill Kevin and kidnap Dawn—an event that still triggered her nightmares.

Kevin recognized the look. "You can count on that, Ella." He reached over and touched her arm, and she enjoyed the gesture for a second.

"Good." Ella broke contact. Kevin was too attractive for her to let the touch linger, and they both knew where that could lead. She took a step toward the house, turning her head as she walked. " 'Bye, pumpkin."

" 'Bye, Mom. You'll find that guy." Dawn pulled Kevin toward the truck impatiently.

"I hope," Ella said quietly to herself as the two climbed into his pickup.

As Ella walked up to the door, she saw her horse, Chieftain, in the corral, his head down in the feeder, munching alfalfa. They'd constructed a stall area with an adjoining pen, but Chieftain, as they'd learned the hard way when he'd tried to kick his way out, wasn't used to such amenities. Enclosed places bothered him and it would take time to train him. Wind, on the other hand, loved the stall, so that was his new home, while Chieftain took the corral.

Spotting her, Chieftain whinnied, then went back to his feed. Ella smiled. Boots exercised him regularly, so he didn't need to be ridden at the moment, but there was no time now to even stop and pet him. "Hello, boy. Not today, but soon, I hope."

Ella tried to sneak in through the kitchen, but the living room was adjacent to it, and most of the women turned to look when she came into the house. Several were dressed traditionally with long skirts and brightly colored blouses adorned with squash-blossom necklaces.

Although they greeted her cordially, Ella could sense that a very volatile discussion had been under way and Rose's icy cold glare confirmed it.

With a wave, Ella quickly passed through the living room into the hallway. Once inside her bedroom, she dried herself off and reached for warm, dry clothing. She'd just pulled on a shirt when Rose walked in. "Do you need anything from the living room or kitchen? This meeting is going to take a long time."

"No, I'm going right back out. I'm just here to change clothes."

"Shoes too. You tracked mud in everywhere."

"Sorry, Mom. I didn't even notice. I was trying to rush through there without interrupting your meeting."

Rose nodded slowly. "The Plant Watchers need to settle some important issues today, so I called your daughter's father and suggested that she might want to visit for a while. He invited her to stay over for a few days."

Ella nodded. "I managed to speak with them before they left. It's a good idea, Mother."

"Do you need anything—maybe something to eat?"

"No, I'm fine," she said, reaching for a clean pair of boots. "I've really got to get going." With luck, she'd be able to leave before Justine arrived. She didn't want her to interfere with what she had planned and Rose didn't need another interruption.

Ella stopped and turned to face her. "Mom, I've been thinking. With all the meetings you're hosting here at the house these days, and my need to come and go at all hours, maybe the time's come for me to find a house of my own. We're starting to get in each other's way and things will get worse as Dawn grows up." Ella watched her mother's reaction carefully.

Rose said nothing and stared at an indeterminate spot across the room for several moments. "We could add on, I suppose. But the construction's bound to create even more chaos. There's another option, though. Your daughter's father has a nice, big, new house. Plenty of room for three or four people and a home office."

Her mother's casual tone didn't fool Ella. Dawn had been pushing for Ella and Kevin to move in together and weaving that into every possible conversation the past few months. Knowing that Ella wouldn't even consider it, Rose was now trying to start an argument that would derail their conversation. Rose knew as well as she did that although the attraction between Kevin and her remained strong, it took more than that to make a marriage work. The truth was that, in the things that mattered, Kevin and she were poles apart.

There was only one possible counter. "You're absolutely right, Mom. Kevin's house is huge," she said seriously. "That's certainly something to consider. . . ." Ella responded, turning her face away so she wouldn't be caught grinning when her mother's jaw dropped halfway to the floor. It was no secret that Kevin had never been Rose's first, or even second choice as a husband for Ella, though Rose had finally begun to respect the man as a loving father to Dawn.

"Let's not rush this, daughter," Rose said after a short,

stunned silence. "Nothing has to be done right away. My grand-daughter is still very young and, for now, things are working out just fine. Like Bizaadii likes to say, 'if it ain't broke, don't fix it'."

Hearing two women arguing, and probably anxious for an excuse to end their conversation, Rose stood up quickly and hurried down the hall.

Ella finished getting dressed, lost in thought. She'd managed to call Rose's bluff—this time—but the problem lack of space posed for them wasn't likely to just go away. As it was, whenever she had a visitor, even if it was Justine or Carolyn and not a date, Rose would have to discreetly vanish into the kitchen so as not to be underfoot, just as Ella did when Bizaadii came over.

The simple fact was that they had no real privacy because someone was always in the next room. But it wasn't just about their personal lives. With both of them working actively for the tribe—Rose with her consultant job concerning environmental issues and traditional herbs and Ella as a police officer—they both needed more workspace at home.

Ella was checking her pistol when she heard footsteps at her door. Looking up, she saw Justine standing there.

"*Wherever* you're going, you're taking your partner," Justine said flatly.

Ella shook her head. "I don't think that's such a good idea."

Justine simply stared back at her.

"Oh, crap," Ella muttered. "Okay, okay. Just remember you insisted."

Ella looked through her notes to make sure she had Jack Krause's address, then called Sheriff Taylor to see if he'd found out any information they could use as leverage against the funeral director.

"I've got nothing. He was brought up on charges way back in 1972 for writing some bad checks. He got off by making restitution and apparently has been clean since. He has a black SUV registered to him, there are a couple of parking tickets on it. And that missing gold Ford Excursion was transferred to his wife's name, so he's not legally connected to it anymore. Apparently the two live apart."

Ella remembered the big vehicle tracks by the irrigation gate. They might have been made by an SUV. If a social security check scam was going on, Krause could turn out to be her direct route to Agent Thomas.

Ella thanked Sheriff Taylor, then, after hanging up, turned her attention back to Justine. "I have no leverage and I'll need it before I question Krause, Justine. We can't wait around for a paper trail of circumstantial evidence that may eventually point to him for forging documents and scamming social security. We need to dig up something *now* that'll force him into a corner."

"How about getting a sneak-and-peek warrant? This is a federal crime we're checking into," Justine said.

"Our probable cause is pretty shaky, but maybe Simmons has the juice to make it happen," Ella said. "The problem is that I can't get hold of him. He's flying back as we speak and cell phones have to be turned off during a flight. But let me give him a call anyway and see what happens."

Ella brought out her cell phone, but after three minutes of trying, all she could get was a message that the number was unavailable. Ella closed the phone in disgust. "Forget it. For now, he's out of touch."

"So what do we do? Wait or try to get a warrant from someone else?" Justine asked.

Ella looked at her watch. "See if you can get your grandfather." Justine's grandfather was a judge and could issue a warrant, Ella knew.

Five minutes later, Justine hung up her phone in frustration. "He'll have to call back. He's in court."

"We can't wait any longer, cuz," Ella said flatly.

"I agree. What do you want to do?"

"What I have to—and I'd rather do it alone."

Justine looked at Ella and held her gaze. "I think I know what you've got in mind, Ella, but think carefully about this. If you're planning to break into his home and check through his stuff without a warrant, you won't be able to use anything you find as evidence. Is that really worth your career?"

"I'm going to be looking for leads, not evidence—anything that'll tell me where to look for Agent Thomas. A secondary goal is to find evidence that will hold up in court so I can go back later and grab it legally." Ella took a deep, steadying breath. "I've thought this out. If going by the book means more to me than a man's life, I've lost the essence of who I am and what I'm trying to do. I signed up to protect and serve people—not the rule book."

"All right. Then I'll go and watch your back."

"I wish you wouldn't. I've got to do this, but that doesn't mean *you* have to put everything on the line too."

"All true, but I'm going with you anyway."

Ella chuckled. "Okay. Let's get moving," she said, then added quickly, "But we can't take my unit—or yours. Mom's truck is kind of unreliable, and I don't want her involved even inadvertently. Any ideas on transport?"

"We can go to my place and take my little pickup. It's about as generic as they come—tan, and no distinguishing marks. It'll do."

Ella nodded. "We can muddy up your license plate, just in case, and the entire tailgate area, too, so it won't look so obvious."

On the way over, Ella telephoned the mortuary and waited until Krause's secretary put him on the line. "Good evening, Mr. Krause. Has Mr. Rainwater come back to work?"

"No, and I've got to tell you, I'm none too happy about that. I've been thinking that it probably has something to do with that black face paint I asked him to wash off. He must be more religious than I thought. But, in either case, unless he's got an amazing explanation, he's going to find himself back on the job market tomorrow."

"We may need to talk to you within an hour or two. Can you tell us if you'll be at home?"

"Not until later this evening. I'm stuck here at the office, drowning in paperwork. But I may step out for dinner, so call first unless you want to take a chance on missing me."

"Will do. Thanks a lot," Ella said, then hung up.

"That was smooth," Justine said.

"Just covering all the bases," Ella murmured, then shook her head. "I *hate* having to do this, Justine. But if I wade through channels on my own to get a court order, Krause might get wind of what I'm doing, know we're onto him, and cover his tracks—and if he knows where Thomas is, he may just kill him. Or he may just keep stalling. Either way, Agent Thomas is a dead man."

"Then, in this particular case, we're obeying a higher law and doing what's necessary," Justine said quietly.

Ella nodded. "What worries me is that I know that this type of thinking is dangerous," Ella said somberly. "Once a person starts believing that the law isn't enough, a vigilante is born."

"You and I both know that if your back wasn't to the wall, you—we—would have never taken this route. Simmons will send a troop of agents onto the Rez if we don't get answers soon."

She nodded. "And blame us all for being incompetent, if my impression of him is correct. Simmons will be here later tonight or tomorrow morning, depending on how long it takes him to drive to the Rez after he talks to his people in Albuquerque. It's now or never."

They arrived in Farmington about forty minutes later. Krause's house was in a new residential neighborhood on the north side, filled with the kind of fancy houses Ella knew she'd never be able to afford. Krause's two-story house, with wrought-iron scroll-work and clay tile roof, was at the end of a cul-de-sac.

"So what's your plan?" Justine said, parking about half a block down.

"I'm going into his garage first. I want to check out his second vehicle. Then I'm going to take a look around the house."

"The best way in will be through the garage window on the right side," Justine said, pointing. "You have maximum cover there because of the partition that screens the trash cans from view."

"Agreed. At least the sun is setting now and it'll be dark soon. Keep a sharp lookout, but if something goes wrong, just drive away."

Justine exhaled softly. "I don't see any sign of an alarm system. Just don't get caught."

"I meant it, Justine. If things go sour, cut and run."

Justine didn't answer directly. "What's the signal if I spot trouble?"

"Call me. I'll set my cell phone to vibrate," Ella said, reaching down and pushing the button that changed the mode. She stuck the phone on her belt, then opened the pickup door.

Her long hair tucked inside a baseball cap and wearing a blue windbreaker, Ella got out of the pickup. She had a clipboard and a pen in hand and walked quickly across the driveway, looking up at the house and pretending to write something down, as if she were some kind of inspector, taking notes.

Heading down the side of the house, she wasn't visible to anyone in the house next door due to a six-foot-high stucco wall. Once she stepped past the trash cans hidden behind the partition, she went over to the garage window and peered inside, putting on a pair of disposable latex gloves.

The window was locked tight, but between the garage and the neighbor's wall was a wide gate in the wooden fence that closed off the backyard. The gate was fastened, but she was able to reach over and unlatch it easily. The yard was tastefully landscaped with roses and a lawn so green they must have had a regular gardening service. From here she could see a back door leading into the garage.

The lock was so simple all it took was a twist of her pocket knife into the mechanism to open it and slip inside. The garage held a blend of new-car smell and motor oil. Taking a flashlight from her jacket pocket, she looked around. An enormous luxury-model SUV—a Ford Excursion—took up half of the garage, and had a real chance of scraping the top of the garage door if the two-hundred-dollar tires were accidentally overinflated. The black—naturally—vehicle was spotless, making Ella suspect that the mortuary's owner spent a part of every day making sure no dust marred the beautiful finish.

Ella crouched down to examine the oversized tires and studied the treads. This was the only area where dirt had accumulated. A twig just big enough to lodge between the treads was jammed in firmly, held by dried clay that resembled the color and texture she'd noticed up by the irrigation ditch.

The tread patterns she'd seen in the tracks by the ditch were either identical or very similar to these tires, but only a photo comparison would prove it. If she had time, and the damaged section wasn't on the bottom, she might be able to find that thin slice she'd noticed in the track left back on the Rez.

Seeing some seeds stuck inside the tread, she took out her pocket knife and worked them out into the palm of her hand. Ella had no idea what plant they came from, but Rose or Clifford probably would. She placed the seeds and the twig into a plastic self-seal bag along with a scraping of the clay, then stuck the bag into her pocket.

Ella started to look for the cut in the tread of a right side tire when her cell phone began to vibrate. Headlights shining through the garage window traveled along the opposite wall and told her a vehicle had come around the corner and was close. Staying low, Ella slipped out the back door of the garage, closed it gently, then ducked behind one of the rosebushes. It was dark now, and with the wooden fence blocking her from the street, she was safe for the moment.

Seeing the emergency lights of a patrol car through small gaps in the cedar pickets of the fence, she moved toward the back wall of the house, screening herself by staying in line with the rosebush as much as possible. Someone, probably a neighbor, had seen or heard her and had called the police—unless, of course, there was a silent alarm in the garage she hadn't noticed.

Ella reached the back wall and pulled herself up high enough to look over. There was an easement, really an alley, and another wall on the other side. Seeing no dogs or people in either direction, she clambered over and dropped quietly to the ground, crouching low.

Chances were there was only one police car responding to the call, so she'd have a clear run if she moved out quickly. She raced down the easement, stopped at the street and checked for cars, then turned left and ran down the sidewalk until she reached another alley. Ducking inside, she removed her cap, placed it into her pocket, and allowed her hair to fall around her shoulders. Ella turned her jacket inside out—it was reversible to another color—and put it back on as she stepped back out onto the sidewalk.

Dialing as she walked briskly away from the area, she gave Justine her location. A few blocks later, she saw Justine parked at the curb, waiting. Ella got in quickly and, before she'd even closed the door, Justine was driving off.

"Good timing," Ella said.

"I just saw the one police car. Was it worth it?" Justine asked through clenched teeth.

"Yes, I think it was." Ella told her what she'd found as she labeled the bag with the time and place—for her own use, not as evidence that could be considered in a trial. "The black Excursion was in pristine condition, Justine. That's not his everyday car, it's his baby. It was so clean I have a feeling that he doesn't drive it too often. That makes the clay, the seeds, and the twig interesting pieces of evidence. The clay may match the soil by the irrigation ditch. If the twig and the seeds aren't from the same location, maybe they'll lead us to Agent Thomas."

"I can test the clay, but don't count on anything conclusive because the sample may have been contaminated with road debris from his trip back. But how about asking your mom about the plant material? She knows more about that than even Clifford."

"That's who I was thinking of, too."

It took another hour for them to drive back to Justine's, pick up Ella's unit and return to Ella's house. Several cars were still parked there and Ella sighed as she pulled up, looking for a place to park.

"I'm glad Dawn's with Kevin right now. Mom's probably in a foul mood if her meeting's taken this long. Let's slip through the living room as quickly as possible, okay?"

Ella led the way inside, entering through the kitchen door.

"Grab whatever you can from the fridge," she whispered. "It's going to be a long night."

Rose came in to see who was in the kitchen, apparently, and hearing what Ella had said, shook her head. "No, let me fix you both a proper dinner."

"No, Mom. We don't have that much time."

"I'll make you a *naniscaada* sandwich. Fried Spam, some onions and a tomato. Making two will only take a few moments."

Ella had heard that the big grocery store in Shiprock sold more Spam and Pepsi than any other merchant in the state. These types of sandwiches were common to the Rez, but none were as good as her mom's. Her special touches made her sandwiches delicious. Today she was putting in just a hint of homemade green chile salsa on top of the fried Spam.

Ella got her mother's attention again as soon as the sandwiches were done. "Mom, I need you to look at something for me," she said, turning around in her chair after taking a few quick bites of her sandwich. "Can you tell me where these seeds and the twig come from?" Ella fished the plastic bag out of her pocket and handed it to her. "Take them out if you like, but don't spill the clay. I'll need to save that."

While Ella and Justine ate, Rose studied the evidence carefully, taking one seed out to sniff it and feel the texture in her hand before answering. "I think this is from the gray greasewood plant. It's used for skin irritations and for the Evil Way and Navajo Wind Way. It grows in alkaline soil."

"Okay. So where, exactly, could I find this plant?" Ella asked. Cramming the last bite of sandwich in her mouth, she walked to the counter and began spooning instant coffee granules into a thermos.

"Right now, you mean?" Seeing Ella nod, she shook her head. "I usually find it while looking for something else, but let me ask the other Plant Watchers. Maybe one of them will know offhand."

"Go ahead," Ella said, noting that Justine had turned on the teakettle.

Rose returned a few moments later. "Nobody's really sure. I could check my maps and tell you where some has been in the past, then get back to you. But if you need to know right away, I think you should talk to your brother. He's more likely to know because he uses it more than I do."

Ella grabbed the thermos and hurried outside with Justine. Soon they were on their way to Clifford's hogan in Ella's unit, Justine at the wheel.

"Do you think those seeds will really help us pinpoint Agent Thomas's location?"

"That's too much to hope for, but if we narrow it down to a smaller area than we've been searching, or even several areas, and then factor in what we already know, I think things will fall into place. Or as my brother would say, we'll see the pattern."

Seeing the skepticism on Justine's face, Ella added, "We're close to finding Agent Thomas, Justine. I can feel it. All we need now is a break."

THIRTEEN
——— ✖ ✖ ✖ ———

There was no full moon tonight and navigating the narrow dirt road to Clifford's was always a bumpy proposition. Ella hung on as Justine skirted a hole that was as big around as a washtub and nearly as deep.

"Cuz, I've never interrupted my brother when he's in his hogan with a patient, but this is a case for firsts. If he doesn't come out right away, I won't cool my heels. I'm just going to go right up to the door. That'll really piss him off, so if that's what I end up having to do, let me go in alone."

"You've got it."

As they pulled up and parked, Ella saw a familiar truck near the blanketed entrance. Herman Cloud, her mother's friend, was there. Ella got out of the unit slowly. Herman wouldn't have come to see Clifford if he hadn't been having a problem . . . maybe something to do with the accident. He'd had a rough ride after being forced off the highway. Before she could give it much thought, Herman and Clifford came out of the hogan together. Herman waved at her then got into his truck, and drove off. Clifford cocked his head toward the hogan, inviting her in.

As Ella hurried to the hogan she motioned for Justine to come and join them.

"You both look like you're in a hurry, so I'm assuming you still haven't found the missing man. What's going on, ladies?"

Clifford asked as soon as they were both inside. Several small piñon branches were burning warmly in the center fire pit. During colder months Clifford used a woodstove in his medicine hogan.

Ella brought out the plastic bag containing the evidence she'd collected from the vehicle in Krause's garage and held them close to the kerosene lantern so Clifford could see. "I need to know where these seeds can be found, narrowing it down to somewhere between here and Gallup. Mom said that they and the twig come from the gray greasewood plant and recommended I come talk to you."

He studied them for a moment, then handed the bag back to Ella. "They're from the plant Mom mentioned, but gray greasewood grows in a lot of places this side of the mountains."

"Let me put this another way. Could these seeds have come from an area where there are mine shafts? Coal or uranium or other mines?"

"Sure. I actually collect cuttings of that plant in an area much like what you just described," he said, and mentioned a spot south of Beautiful Mountain not far from where Melvin Rainwater's Sing had been conducted.

"That area's been searched thoroughly," Ella said.

"There's an easy way to tell if those seeds came from an area with uranium mines," Justine said suddenly. "I should have thought of this before. I could use a Geiger counter on them, and on the clay you collected. The dried mud and the seeds themselves might show the radiation to be at higher levels than normal. That'll suggest whether the plant grew near a uranium mine or processing plant, and positively rule out coal mines. But, unfortunately, it won't tell us exactly *where* to search. Uranium mines are up and down the mountain ranges, and on both sides, east and west."

As they got under way, Justine glanced over at her. "I know that someone's trying to slow down the investigation, but have you figured out why? Do you think they're buying time so they can wrap things up and leave town before we can make our move, or are they trying to keep us from finding Thomas alive because he knows something that will lead us to them? But wait, if that were the case, they'd just kill him right now."

"There are things about this case that still don't add up right. But if Rainwater and Krause are both involved in slowing us down, it would explain why we had the problem in Kirtland and with the ditches, even when Melvin was being shadowed. It's not all fuzzy anymore. I think we're getting closer to finding Agent Thomas and maybe when we do, if he's still alive, he can fill us in."

Justine nodded, knowing that Ella's instincts were usually accurate.

"Let's say we find him alive, but we still can't arrest the perps because we don't have enough evidence," Justine asked, her voice dying out as if the thought pained her. "What then?"

"At least we'd have him back, and that's our primary objective right now. As my brother reminded me earlier today, saving this man's life is the most important thing. Anything else we'll worry about later."

"It's always worse when it's a fellow officer—or agent in this case—isn't it?" she asked, not expecting an answer. "The usual agency rivalries don't matter much in a situation like this."

"No, they don't, even if it means we have to deal with a dinosaur like Simmons. The thing that gets to all of us is that we can easily see ourselves in his shoes. Plus it's a matter of honor. That's an old-fashioned word, but it still means something to most law-enforcement officers. We take care of our brothers and sisters who carry a badge and we count on our peers to watch our backs if we're ever down. Right now Andy Thomas is betting his life on us."

They were in Shiprock, heading north and still west of the bridges across the San Juan, when Ella's cell phone rang. She identified herself and heard Teeny's satisfied voice on the other end.

"I've tracked down Melvin's mangy butt. He's at what I suspect is his girlfriend's house. Do you want me to grab and haul him over to you?"

"No, just watch and listen and don't let him out of your sight. I need to get some other information first, then we'll move in on him together."

Ella brought Justine up to speed on Teeny's call. "After we try the Geiger counter on the seeds, we'll take Rainwater. We'll use what we learned about the seeds, pretend we know far more than we do, and try to pressure him into implicating his boss or at least giving us Agent Thomas's location in exchange for reduced charges."

They arrived at the station five minutes later and Ella and Justine hurried into the small forensics lab. They'd just walked in when Ella's cell phone rang again.

"It's Tache," the familiar voice said. "One of the people we questioned about Rainwater's whereabouts told us that, on his way back from Gallup a few days ago, he saw Melvin just off the highway near the turnoff to Red Rock. It wasn't much of a lead, but it was all I had, so I decided to check things out. I walked around the area between there and Cactus Peak and, down in a low spot not far from the road, I discovered the dismembered body of an Anglo man. Some of the body parts are missing, like the head and hands, but I found a wallet with an FBI shield and ID in the man's jacket pocket. There was no money, but there was a credit card. That and the ID belonged to Agent Thomas."

Ella felt the contents of her stomach burning the back of her throat. Anger choked the air out of her lungs and she felt like slamming her fist into something.

"Oh, crap. What's wrong?" Justine asked, glancing over.

"We need to go to the scene of a new crime," Ella managed, her voice strained.

"Not Agent Thomas?" she replied in a taut voice.

"Looks like it," she said, giving Justine directions to the site.

The trip took about twenty minutes, but neither of them spoke. As they walked down from the dirt road running west from the highway, using their flashlights to guide the way, Ella could see Ralph Tache standing down the slope. His body was silhouetted by quick flashes of light as he took photos of the scene.

As they approached, he turned to them and gave them a quick nod. All expression was gone from his face, a sure sign that he was trying hard to keep it together. As Ella looked down at the body dressed in a short-sleeved shirt and slacks, she suddenly understood why. He was chest down—facedown didn't apply, not with the head gone. There was jagged tissue and dried blood and bone exposed where someone had sawed or hacked off his head. A strong wave of nausea washed over her.

"Has the ME been called?"

He nodded, then handed her a clear plastic bag containing an opened wallet. She could see the gold badge and the young redhaired agent's photo ID.

Ella's gaze remained on the photo of Andrew L. Thomas. The hope she'd felt just a half hour ago crumbled into sharp splinters that, like glass, cut into her insides filling her with pain, sorrow, and regret. Then, slowly, the part of her brain that never stopped questioning began to work overtime. Why decapitate him and take his hands supposedly so he couldn't be identified, yet leave his wallet, photo ID, and badge? Something wasn't right.

"Anything else in his pockets?" Ella asked Tache.

"All I pulled out was the wallet. Once the ME gets here we can move the body and see if something's beneath it . . . him."

"The body belongs to a redheaded man, judging from the hair on his arms," Justine commented softly.

"I know, but it still isn't adding up right. Somehow, we need to start seeing what's going on through the eyes of the perp. That's the only way we'll find the pattern," she said softly.

"It could be that they want us to suspect a deception and cling to the hope that this isn't really Agent Thomas, so we'll stay focused on the search instead of going all out to find them," Justine said. "But, to me, it looks like it's over."

"Maybe they dumped him in one of the mines, came back to make sure he was dead, found him alive, then finished him off. But he wasn't killed or dismembered here, or there would have been a lot more blood," Tache said.

"Let's get some more lights and process the scene *very*

carefully," Ella said. "They might have left more behind than they intended." Dividing the scene into sections, Ella helped put up floodlights, then searched for evidence with Justine while Tache continued taking photos.

Carolyn Roanhorse-Lavery, the only medical examiner operating outside the state Office of the Medical Investigator because of the Navajo's cultural traditions involving death, arrived a short time later. Giving Ella a nod, she crouched beside the body. "There's not enough blood, barely any at all, considering what's missing, so this isn't the primary crime scene. Whoever removed the head and hands used a sharp power saw, judging from the clean cuts across bone. Like a butcher. And the victim wasn't dismembered until long *after* he died."

"I need a positive ID as soon as you can get it to me," Ella said, then left Carolyn to her work, and joined Justine. "We need to expand our search perimeter. Maybe the spot where he was actually killed is around here."

"There are vehicle tracks over there," Justine said, pointing to her right, "about twenty yards from where the body was. That's how they transported him here. But the footprints were rubbed out, and there are no drag marks. Probably two or more people, or one very strong guy hauled the body out of the vehicle, carried him over here, then just dumped him."

Ella and Justine combed the area, but there was no sign of the missing body parts. After a half hour they were forced to conclude that the original theory had been right and John Doe's body had simply been left there.

Seeing the ME bringing out the body bag, and noting that Tache was putting distance between them, and Justine was busy scouring the ground, Ella went down into the arroyo to help her. But lifting the heavy body out of the low spot ended up requiring everyone's help, and Carolyn was forced to enlist them all. Working together, the SI team got the body onto a stretcher and carried it out of the arroyo and back to the van.

"I'll start on this as soon as I get back," Carolyn assured Ella while the other officers got back to work. "All I can tell you at this point is that the body belongs to someone who's been dead at least a day or two, maybe longer. Based upon the relative absence of flies and other carrion feeders, it has only been at this location a few hours. I'll have something more conclusive once I run tests, but it'll be closer to morning by the time I've got a preliminary report. You want me to fax it to your home or to the office?"

"Both. That way I'll be sure to get it. I probably won't be catching much sleep tonight, not after seeing this," she said, cocking her head toward the bag.

As she slammed the van doors shut, Ella's old friend looked back at her. "You better figure out a way to unwind or you won't be any good to anyone."

Ella nodded but didn't answer.

As the ME's body bus disappeared from view, Ella joined Tache and Justine and continued searching the area. The lights, placed in key locations for maximum illumination, helped, but the perimeter was sizable, particularly now that they'd decided to expand their search. Ella took a flashlight and tried for the second time to find footprints, but it was fruitless.

"There was a pretty good cleanup crew at work here," Justine said, looking up. "Even some of the vehicle tracks are brushed out, probably because a footprint was over them."

"They didn't want to be found, and made sure nothing remained that would help us to do that," Ella said.

"All that stealth, yet they dump the body here, not fifty feet from the road, where it could be seen easily," Justine said. "It makes no sense . . . unless it was to make an example of the victim."

"You mean to let everyone know that they'll kill whoever threatens their operation?" Tache asked, and saw Justine nod. "Or maybe it's one of our own people who's trying to warn Anglos away from our ceremonies."

"If Krause and Rainwater wanted to make an example of the agent, why would they decapitate him and saw off both of his hands?" Ella countered, shaking her head. "Or wait this long to dump the body when they had to know we'd be checking them out? It also doesn't add up if we take it from the other angle and say that one of the Dineh did this. Dismemberment of this type isn't part of any Navajo ritual. And Melvin Rainwater couldn't have done this two or three days ago when your witness spotted him. The body hasn't been here that long."

"Well, there is a possible explanation for at least one of our questions. The corpse may have been mutilated just to unnerve us," Justine said. "But I have no reasonable answer as to why the killers took so long to get rid of the body. No Navajo would keep one around, not unless they were seriously disturbed."

Ella joined Justine, who was searching through the sand near the body. "What's this?" Ella asked, picking up a flint arrowhead that appeared to be smeared with ashes. Holding it in her gloved hand, she studied the artifact. "And what the heck is it doing here?"

"I can answer the first question," Justine said. "I think it's something used by the participants of a one-day Evil-Chasing Sing. I attended a ceremony of that type back in high school and I remember the *hataalii* passing those out," she said, then paused. "Or I think I do. It's been a long, long time since my high school days."

"I'll ask my brother," Ella said, placing it in an evidence pouch, then labeling the outside with time, date, location, and her initials. "This means something, I'm sure."

"Well, we know for sure that the body was dumped here, so I suspect that the arrowhead was also planted here for us to find," Justine said. "There are no other signs of artifacts or pot shards, like you'd find around old Indian campsites. But why are they doing all this *now?* Do you think they somehow found out that the agent called us on his cell phone? And where is his cell phone anyway? Why not leave it behind along with the badge?"

Ella shrugged. She couldn't help but notice how Justine avoided mentioning Agent Thomas by name just in case the body they'd found *was* his. Even modernists were reluctant to break tradition and speak the name of the dead, particularly at a crime scene. Some things were so deeply ingrained that they became almost instinctual.

"There's only a very short list of people, almost all of them on our team, who know about the missing agent's call to Dispatch. We've deliberately kept a lid on that in order to protect him," Ella said.

"Then do you suppose one of us inadvertently tipped someone off as we questioned them?" Justine asked.

"The trail begins—and maybe ends—at the mortuary and the goings on there with Krause and Rainwater." Ella considered her next move. "I want you to stay and continue helping Ralph process the scene. Maybe the cell phone will turn up. While you're taking care of this business, I'll call Simmons, then go deal with Rainwater."

Ella tried to raise Simmons again on his cell phone, but had to settle for leaving him a message to call back immediately. Then she spoke to Big Ed, telling him what they'd found, and suggesting he contact the Albuquerque office and tell them about the body, and the physical evidence. She stressed that they didn't know for certain it was Thomas, though it was a possibility.

Discouraged but knowing the investigation had to continue, Ella met up with Teeny in a low-income neighborhood among the cottonwoods and close to the river on Shiprock's east side. It was very dark, and the only lights came from a few porches down the dusty street. As she pulled up behind him, Teeny came out of his massive truck and they met in the gap between vehicles. He nodded as a greeting, then handed her a pair of low-light binoculars.

"Nice." She pressed the top button, and could see the house in shades of green. Even from fifty yards, she could tell that the windows were all open a bit to cool the house. "But I don't see Melvin's vehicle."

"It's either not here or he's managed to hide it within walking distance. But he's inside," Teeny whispered, "and probably asleep. I have a cheap parabolic device that can pick up most conversations, but haven't heard a peep for hours."

"Before that, did he say anything we can use?"

Teeny shook his head. "No, he's been talking a lot of garbage about taking a big trip to Vegas. Sounds like he's trying to convince his girlfriend not to dump him. They argue so much, you'd think they were married," he said with a scowl.

It took Ella a moment to realize that it had been a grin. "Let me bring you up to speed," she said, telling him about the body they'd found.

"But you don't think it's him," he observed, reading her accurately.

"I'm not convinced, but there aren't that many missing red-haired men around here at the moment," Ella said, then clearing her throat, added, "Let's go wake up Melvin and his lady."

Again, Teeny walked around back to keep Melvin from bolting. Ella knocked loudly on the front door and identified herself, stepping back to avoid becoming a target in a doorway. Her hand was resting on the butt of her weapon as the lights came on inside, and slow footsteps could be heard approaching the door.

Then the porch light came on and a woman in her late twenties wearing a long T-shirt, pajama shorts, and fuzzy slippers opened the door about six inches and peered out through heavy-lidded eyes. "Police? What do you want?"

"Where's Melvin?" Ella held up her badge in the light.

"Who?"

"Got him!" Teeny yelled before Ella could answer. A moment later Teeny came around the corner, holding Rainwater by the back of his shirt. His toes were all that touched the ground, and he was gagging from the collar gathered under his chin.

"Put me . . . ack . . . down!" Melvin sputtered, wriggling to get free. He reached back, trying ineffectively to grab Teeny, who now held him almost at arm's length.

"Shall we talk while he holds you up so you won't make like a jackrabbit on us?" Ella asked Melvin, glaring at him. Out of the corner of her eye she kept an eye on his girlfriend just in case she tried something stupid.

"I'm cho . . . king," Melvin said, making more gagging noises.

"Not nearly enough," Ella said calmly, then nodded to Teeny who eased his hold slightly.

"Let's go inside. We can talk there like civilized people," Melvin said in a whiny voice.

"Not into *my* house, you loser!" The woman came out onto the porch and glowered at him. "You just can't stay out of trouble. What were you going to do, sneak off and leave me here to cover for you? You're such a snake!" She turned and looked at Ella. "He thinks I don't know about his other girlfriend. Can you imagine that? Take him wherever you want—jail, the dump, anywhere you like. But he's not coming into my house again, not ever."

"But Mona!" Melvin called out. "You're the only woman in my life."

"Do I look that stupid, you cockroach? You really blew it to-night. We're through, Melvin." She gestured for them to leave. "Go away. You can have him."

"We may need to talk to you, too," Ella said. "You're Mona? . . ."

"Etcitty. You know where I live, obviously," she said. Then, glaring at Melvin, she added, "And where he'll never be again."

The second they turned away, she slammed the door on all of them.

Ella smiled at Melvin. "Well, it looks like you're running out of women *and* places to hide. How about jail? You'll love the carrot suits."

"Jail? Not me. I haven't done anything!"

"Then why did you run?" Ella countered. "For the second time, as a matter of fact."

"I wasn't running," he said, still struggling to get away from Teeny's iron grip. He reminded her of a fat catfish on a short stringer, wiggling to get back into the water.

"Melvin, here's the way it shapes up," Ella said. "Teeny's go-ing to shove you into the back of my unit. No door handles there, but there's a nice wire partition so we can drive around and talk for as long as we need. If your answers start to put me to sleep, then I'm hauling you in."

"Okay, just let go! You're ruining my shirt!"

Teeny set him down, but kept his hand on his arm, urging him along the gravel road to Ella's unit. Once there, Teeny shoved him inside hard and closed the door while she climbed in and rolled down the window. Ella sat sideways so she could make eye contact with the prisoner. "Okay, Melvin. Let's start at the beginning. Why did you suddenly disappear from your job at the mortuary?"

"I didn't disappear. I left. I took some time off," he said, casting a nervous glance at Teeny who was crouched down low just outside the car, watching him.

"Why didn't you mention this little detail to your boss?" She gave him a skeptical look. "I believe he wants to fire you."

"He can't fire *me*," Melvin shot back, then stopped speaking and looked down at his feet.

"As interesting as your shoes might be to you, Melvin, I'm going to need some more information," she said, then in a firm voice ordered, "*Talk to me.*"

"It's the Sing. I washed off all that stuff from my face and hands, and I got afraid that I'd start having real bad luck, you know?" he said.

"And you were absolutely right," Ella said, smiling. "Your luck has taken a definite turn for the worse. And it'll continue to go downhill unless you start giving me some real answers for a change. Again, why are you running and trying to avoid the police?"

"I *told* you. I had second thoughts about washing the stuff off so I went to talk to the *hataalii*. He told me that I'd have to have another Sing. But I can't afford one right now."

Ella sighed, then shifted. "Wrong answer to the wrong question. I guess I better make myself comfortable because it looks like we're going to be here long past sunup."

"What do you want from me?"

"I want the truth about the real issues here. What's spooking you? What happened to that redhaired Anglo agent the evening of your Sing?"

"I don't *know*. I never saw him. I've been telling you the truth about that."

Ella smiled. "And what are you keeping back or lying about?" she pressed.

"Hey, Ella, let's speed this up," Teeny said, opening the back door just enough to lean inside and get eyeball to eyeball with Melvin. "Why don't you go buy yourself a cup of coffee at the Totah Café and let me have some time alone to motivate our reluctant citizen. By the time you get back, I bet he'll be eager to tell you all he knows."

Melvin's eyes grew wide as he looked over at Ella. "No, don't do that. Don't go."

"You're not giving me much of a choice here, Melvin. Why don't you try to help me out a little more?" Ella said, hopefully convincingly, though she would have never turned Teeny loose on him.

"I can't tell you what I don't know. But no one at that Sing went after him—not in the way you're thinking. Of course if, say, someone else happened to follow him there . . . it's possible that person might have taken advantage of the situation."

"Who else confronted the agent?" Ella remembered the vehicle the Darwin rejects had said they'd seen coming up as they were leaving.

"How many times do I have to tell you? I never saw him so I don't know what happened." He looked her directly in the eyes and held her gaze. "Do you want me to start making stuff up?"

"You realize that you're now implicated in a murder, right?" Ella countered. "Agent Thomas is dead."

His eyes became as big as saucers. Then he began moving back and forth in a barely perceptible rocking motion. "That's not true. You're just saying that to scare me."

He had to be putting on an act. "No, I'm not. It *is* the truth. We found his body not far from Sheep Springs."

"If I knew anything more about what's going on, believe me, I'd tell you," he said seriously. "I never bargained for something like this."

"Bargained with whom? About what?"

"Look, I work two jobs and I do my best to earn an extra buck here and there. Sometimes families on the Rez call me personally to pick up a body for them. They might be wanting to get it out of the house before anyone finds out that a death occurred there, or maybe they want to get rid of it before the *chindi* shows up. When that happens, I pick up the body, haul it away in my pickup in a trash bag, then dump it in the county landfill. I pocket however much the family is willing to pay me. That FBI man found out what I was doing and was convinced I'd buried a murder victim."

"Who? I need a name."

"He didn't tell me. What he wanted was the name of everyone I'd buried off the books in the past six months and the addresses where I'd picked up the bodies. But there was only one—old man Pinto."

Ella nodded. Rose had helped Ray Pinto a few times so she knew who he meant. He'd been dying of lung cancer last she'd heard.

"I was straight with that agent but he just wouldn't let it go." Melvin looked directly at her. "And that's absolutely all I know about Agent . . . the agent, and what he was doing."

"Okay, Melvin. But *don't* run away again. I want to be able to find you, night or day. I won't be as nice next time. You get me?"

"Yeah, yeah." Melvin gestured over at the house. "She's not going to let me back in. Can you give me a ride to my cousin's? He lives about two miles from here."

"Two miles? Aw, come on, Melvin! You can walk that far."

"Hey, it's cold outside! It's got to be forty something and I don't even have a jacket."

"Then be ready to do a little shivering, Melvin. Now get out."

"But—"

Teeny reached over, grabbed him by the shoulder, and hauled him out onto the street. "You heard the officer. Now get going."

"Melvin," Ella added, "where is your Blazer anyway?"

"Not here, or I wouldn't be walking, would I?" Melvin set out, muttering under his breath. He looked back at them, raising his hand as if he were about to flip them off, then changed his mind and disappeared quickly into the dark.

"Now what?" Teeny asked with a chuckle.

"I'm going to ask Joseph Neskahi to keep an eye on him while you and I catch a few hours of sleep. I noticed you stifling a yawn a few times, and I'm beat."

"You know Melvin hasn't told you everything, right?" Teeny asked.

"Sure I do. But we aren't going to get anything else from him right now without breaking all of his . . . civil rights." An intense weariness swept over her and she blinked twice to ease the burning in her eyes. "I'm going home, Teeny, and I suggest you do the same."

Teeny looked at her and expelled his breath slowly. "If that body you found really is Agent Thomas, that means the race is over and we lost."

She didn't argue, she didn't have the energy, but something was telling her that the worst was yet to come.

FOURTEEN
——— ✖ ✖ ✖ ———

Day three

Ella stood at her bedroom window, staring outside as the predawn light fell softly over the rocks and sandy earth that comprised the backyard. It was around five-thirty, but she'd gotten all the sleep she could already.

First had come the nightmare. She'd been driving around the desert, car window open, when she heard Andy Thomas calling out for help. She'd stopped her unit and, as she walked toward the sound, she'd discovered his headless body, his voice coming out of the raw opening at his neck. Terrified, she'd become frozen to the spot, but suddenly the headless man sat bolt upright and reached out to her with his handless arms. That's when she'd woken up covered in sweat, a scream dying at the back of her throat.

Her heart rate had returned to normal afterward, but with all the questions circling in her brain her attempt to go back to sleep had proved futile. Her eyes open now for good, Ella noticed the faint glow on the horizon. Somewhere close, a solitary bird was chirping in her mother's garden.

Tossing the covers aside, she swung her legs over the side of the bed and stood, stretching sore muscles tightened from what little rest she'd managed to salvage from the night.

Getting dressed quickly, she grabbed a banana on the way through the kitchen, then crept out of the house. Two, their old mutt, was curled up on the porch atop a worn-out quilt, but he just lifted his head and watched as she climbed into her unit. A minute later she was driving down the dirt road toward Clifford's place. He'd be up, offering his prayers to the dawn.

It was a little past daybreak when Ella arrived at her brother's hogan, parked, and looked around. The sky was clear and clean, and everything was quiet. The beauty of the stark land and the relative absence of modern civilization soothed her.

She thought about her past, working in the FBI and being assigned to cities where the only discernible change between night and day, besides the obvious, was finding a different crowd walking along the streets. She remembered being surrounded by lush vegetation, too, in San Juan, Puerto Rico, and parts of northern California, but as undeniably beautiful as those places had been, theirs was a flashy kind of beauty that didn't seem real to a Navajo woman with her background.

In comparison, the desert's subtle charm called out to her soul in red dawns and dusty orange sunsets that draped the land in a mantle the color of life. The distant peaks that rose up from the arid landscape spoke of endurance and power. The Dinetah, the land of the Navajos, whispered to hearts wounded by poverty and trials, imparting serenity and quiet inspiration.

Ella was glad she'd chosen to return to her homeland. Although it had taken her many years, she finally understood why many Navajos chose to stay on the reservation despite the hardships. To those who understood the Way, there was beauty and harmony in the land between the sacred mountains.

Spotting Clifford climbing down a low hill carrying an armful of firewood, Ella waved and went over to help him. Clifford entered the hogan with his load but Ella remained outside.

Turning his head, Clifford gave her a curious look and went

back to take the piñon branches from her arms so he could place them with the rest. "What's up?"

Ella gestured for him to join her outside. "I'd like to show you something," she said. Ella retrieved the plastic bag that contained the flint arrowhead from her jacket pocket and showed it to him. "Can you tell me what this is?" Since she'd found it near a body, she hadn't wanted to take it into the hogan out of respect for his belief in the *chindi.*

Suspecting that something wasn't right, he looked at it, but made no attempt to touch the plastic bag. "It's from a one-day Evil-Chasing Sing. The arrowheads are given to the participants and covered in gray ashes from the fire. Then the ashes are blown toward the smoke hole to chase away the *chindi.*"

"Thanks," she said, putting it away. "That fits in with what I already know."

"Should I ask where you got that?"

"No," she said quietly.

"Be careful."

"I will."

As Ella drove away, she considered stopping by home for breakfast, but it was six-fifteen and still too early for Rose to be waking up. And stopping by Kevin's to see Dawn was also a waste. Kevin wasn't an early riser either, and Dawn often took advantage and slept later than usual herself. Typically, according to Dawn's amused accounts, Kevin would barely get her to school on time.

Ella continued past the house and arrived at the highway within minutes. From there, she drove north to Shiprock.

On the strip downhill from the hospital, like on the opposite side of Shiprock toward Farmington, local vendors usually gathered selling breakfast burritos, Navajo style, for people on the way to work. Problem was, she was still about fifteen minutes too early, despite the travel time. The vendors, who sold from the tailgates of their pickups for the most part, didn't normally set up shop until around seven. But the food was always good and worth the wait, as was the gossip she picked up there from time to time. In the past, she'd been able to turn that information into some very promising leads.

Luckily Ella discovered a vendor just starting to set up—a friend of Rose's. Raylene Curtis wasn't a member of the Plant Watchers, but her youngest daughter, Dulce, had dated Clifford years ago, and, as far as Rose and Ella were concerned, Dulce would have made a far better match for Clifford than Loretta.

These days, Raylene raised cash to supplement her social security by selling breakfast burritos. Ella ordered four—two intended for Justine, unless, of course, she ate them first.

"And how are your mother and daughter?" Raylene asked her as she took the money Ella handed her.

"Both are doing great. Thanks for asking."

Raylene started to say something, then stopped. Moving slowly, she sat down on the folding chair she'd brought along and began her wait for customers.

"Something on your mind?" Ella asked, taking a large bite. The burrito was delicious, filled with soft fried potatoes, fresh eggs and bacon, and the aroma was particularly enticing on this cool morning.

"Did you know that the police aren't the only ones interested in where that Anglo agent is?" Raylene asked.

Ella swallowed quickly, barely avoiding choking. "You heard about that?" Seeing Raylene nod, she quickly added, "Who else has been asking questions?"

"The patient from that Sing. You know the man I'm talking about?"

The news that Melvin had been searching for Agent Thomas, too, came as a complete surprise. Was that because he wanted to avoid being blamed, or because he wanted to try to finish him off?

"I understand that the police think that the red-haired Anglo disappeared after the Sing because of something the patient's cousins did. But, from what I've heard, the FBI man had someone else come after him—another Anglo."

Hearsay wasn't evidence, it had to be sifted and evaluated carefully. But often tales like this led to the truth. "Have you heard who the other Anglo was?"

She shook her head. "No one's said. But there are other Anglos—people not with the FBI—looking for the agent, too. No one seems to know where he is, but everyone wants to find him."

Knowing how strapped Raylene was for money, Ella tipped her ten dollars because twenty might have been considered an insult, then thanked her for the information and continued on down the highway.

Ella's thoughts were racing. Maybe those people Raylene had mentioned had already found Agent Thomas and killed him. But who were *they*, and why would they mutilate the body in a way that would slow down the identification process? Why not just bury him someplace where he'd never be found? She'd need more pieces before the puzzle made sense.

A short time later Ella walked in through the station's side door, carrying her paper bag containing the burritos, and discovered Justine standing by the coffee machine. Joining her, Ella reached into the bag.

She gave Justine a sheepish smile as she brought out the one remaining burrito, double wrapped in foil. "I bought two extras but I guess I ate one of them on the way here."

Justine grabbed it immediately. "Double wrapped?"

"Yeah. Raylene's trademark," Ella nodded.

Her cousin smiled. "I'm surprised you resisted temptation and left any at all, Ella. I can down four in one sitting easily. Thanks, partner."

Ella nodded.

"Can I buy you coffee?" Justine offered.

Ella shook her head, still feeling guilty about being such a pig and leaving only one for Justine. Maybe they could buy another one or two later this morning if the opportunity arose.

Leaving Justine to retrieve the coffee, Ella continued down the hall. The minute she stepped inside her office, the phone began to ring. Ella picked it up and heard Carolyn Roanhorse-Lavery's voice.

"I've got some interesting news, Ella. We don't need finger-prints or a face. That body *isn't* Agent Thomas. The blood type doesn't match."

"Whose body is it, then?" Ella asked quickly.

"I don't know. I'm having to wait until I can access local rec-ords. There are no hits with any of the missing-persons files I've checked. Maybe the victim is from out of state."

"You might compare the body with the description of those picked up by Mesa Vista Mortuary. They're contracted by most of the area police departments, the county coroner's office, and one of the area hospitals. But don't call the funeral home itself and try to get that information, okay? They're on my suspect list."

"All right. I'll start making calls, and get back to you if I iden-tify the victim."

Ella hung up and hurried down the hall, meeting Justine, who was headed in her direction.

"Good news—the body doesn't belong to Agent Thomas," Ella said, taking one of the cups of coffee. "The hunt's still on. Go call Tache and Neskahi and let them know. I'm on my way to Big Ed's office."

Ella, seeing the chief's door was wide open, knocked and went inside immediately. "The body we found *isn't* Agent Thomas's. Someone just tried to make it look that way."

"So we'd stop looking? That puts a new spin on things," he said.

Ella filled him in on what she'd learned from Raylene. "I think that after Melvin's cousins told Andy to leave—and this corroborates their story—someone else came in that vehicle they claimed to have seen, and confronted Thomas. There must have been a struggle, or he was momentarily under someone else's con-trol, because Thomas obviously lost his badge and ID. After that it gets a little fuzzy."

Big Ed leaned back in his chair, his eyes narrowing as he con-sidered possible scenarios. "He was able to use his cell phone, but said he was trapped in some dark place. . . ." Big Ed rocked back and forth in his chair as he spoke.

"Maybe he lost control of his weapon and ID, but managed to break away and run for it," Ella said. "Later on, he either fell or was pushed into a place where they couldn't get to him. And he either was knocked unconscious for several hours, or lost his cell phone and it took that long for him to find it again. All we know for sure right now is that they didn't have him at the time he called." She took a sip of coffee from the foam cup. It was still hot.

"And they don't have him now, either, or they wouldn't be trying to interfere with the search. If Raylene's information is right, and they're trying to find him too, then we better get to Andy Thomas first," Big Ed concluded.

"Do you think they've found out that he managed to get a call through to us, and either know, or can guess, what he told us? If we knew one way or the other we might be able to use that to our advantage."

"Since we have no way of knowing, that's not a card you can afford to play. It could backfire badly."

"His time is running out, Chief. It's been nearly three days now."

"Get Neskahi to round up the search team and send them back out there twenty-four/seven. You and Justine keep working Agent Thomas's last case and see where it leads you."

Ella nodded. "I'm going to ask for Sheriff Taylor's help again. Social Security Administration gave me the names of two people who'd requested a change of address and I've verified that both are deceased. Since social security checks will come out in a day or two, I'm going to request a stakeout on the post office boxes those checks are being mailed to so we can see who shows."

"Taylor's a good man. He'll put his best people on it."

"It's also time for me to follow up another hunch," she said, re-calling the seeds she'd extracted from the SUV in Krause's garage.

"Care to share?" he asked pointedly.

"Actually, Chief, no. Give me a chance to work things out in my own head first."

"All right, but you should know that Agent Simmons called me earlier this morning. He finally got into Albuquerque late last night on the red-eye, and is going to—get this—take a quick hop to Flagstaff and 'motivate those slugs' searching the Arizona side of the Rez. He plans on returning to Albuquerque later today, then catch an evening flight into Farmington. Simmons should be in Shiprock by nightfall. If we don't have this thing wrapped up, or close to wrapped up, by then, he swears he'll dig up every fed he can and blanket the Four Corners. Simmons probably knows that it won't make much difference, and may make things worse, but my guess is that he's been reamed out by his own superiors and is trying to save his own butt. So go out there and get the job done, Shorty, before he adds to our problems," Big Ed ordered.

"We're getting close, I can feel it."

After a nod from Big Ed, Ella hurried back down the hall to Justine's office. "I want a workup on those seeds and the clay."

"Already on it," she said.

Ella returned to her own office. Cross-jurisdictional requests usually had to be worded just right, but she'd known Sheriff Taylor for nearly a decade and they were past that. She didn't expect any trouble, particularly because of the nature of the case and the fact that he'd already taken part in the search.

Ella dialed and, as soon as Taylor answered, got right to the point and filled him in on the latest.

"So basically, you're at square one again," he said dourly.

"No, not quite. Whoever picks up the checks may have answers that would otherwise take me weeks to find. I need to hold somebody's feet to the fire in order to find Thomas, and to do that, I need strong leverage."

"I'll post plainclothes officers to watch the mailboxes. You're covered. But the bad guy may not show up if he knows the heat's on. Right now, time's on their side."

"I know, but we've got to try."

After getting Neskahi back on the job, Ella returned to Justine's office and saw her partner working with the computer. "Do you have anything for me?"

"I took readings on the clay-soil mixture and got nothing conclusive, but the radioactivity level on those seeds is pretty high. I'm checking in the geological database trying to find areas where that level of radiation is still present. Then I'm hoping to narrow it down some more by overlapping the places where those seeds will grow with the active sites."

"Okay. That's something. I'll tell Neskahi to concentrate on uranium mining and processing sites where this plant might be found. We're looking for a hole, tunnel, or mine shaft Thomas could have fallen or been pushed into. That would explain the FBI's inability to track his cell phone before it went completely dead."

"Even narrowing it down that way, there're still a lot of square miles to search," Justine said. "We're looking for a pretty small needle, considering the size of the potential haystack."

"Keep working. Concentrate on sites within walking or running distance from where the Sing took place but still far from civilization. We're assuming he didn't make it to help," Ella said. "Meanwhile, I'm off to pay Carolyn a visit."

Ella drove to the hospital, then walked downstairs to the basement where the morgue was located. Although the dead didn't scare her—she worried far more about the living—she still got a bit uneasy whenever she came down here.

Ella stepped into the ME's office. Carolyn was behind the plexiglass, working on the body they'd found and initially assumed was Agent Thomas.

Ella watched her friend for a moment. Carolyn had paid a high price for serving as the tribe's ME. She had few friends, and even bore the nickname of Dr. Death, though she was called that mostly behind her back. Since her job required her to work with the dead, she was ostracized by too many—some who believed in the *chindi* and others who were simply repulsed by the nature of her work. Loneliness had been a constant in her life until she'd married Michael Lavery, a retired county ME. But even then happiness had eluded her. Carolyn's marriage was in serious trouble. Michael and she had too many conflicting goals.

As Carolyn moved around the body, she glanced up and saw Ella. Stepping back, she stripped off her latex gloves, washed up, and came into her office.

"You wasted a trip, girl. I'm still waiting for a list of names from my sources. Things move slow, and most of the office people with access to the records work day shifts. I don't have any more to tell you now than I did an hour ago."

"That's okay. I wanted to talk to you about protocols. I know that, generally, a body is pronounced dead by an officer or a paramedic at the scene. If the cause of death is believed to be from a chronic illness, or an obvious accident, nothing further is done and the body is sent to a funeral home."

"That's right," Carolyn replied.

"But who does the paperwork?"

"It eventually ends up at the county coroner's office. He has to issue an official death certificate. For the most part, all the mortuary is required to do is take care of the body and bill the tribe, if that's what you're asking."

"And what about the people at the scene? Is that the extent of their involvement?"

She nodded. "As long as the paperwork is completed properly, they're out of the picture—that is, unless a relative files a complaint or wants to talk to them—but, on the reservation, that's beyond rare," Carolyn said. "Of course murder or suspicious deaths follow their own set of rules, but you already know the protocols for a sudden unexpected death following trauma, or sudden unexpected death without obvious trauma. That's your area."

Ella gave Carolyn the highlights of what she'd learned so far. "The way I figure it, someone has to be tampering with the paperwork before it can get to the social security office. Either an officer or paramedic is deliberately putting down the wrong name on the records or it's being changed by someone at county level so the social security checks can be rerouted without problems."

"It's not likely to be the officers or EMTs, since they vary from scene to scene," Carolyn said, reaching into the bottom drawer, and pulling out a sandwich.

"Smells good. What is it?"

"A pork chop wrapped in a *naniscaada*," she said with a smile. "They're *good*. I have two more. Want one?"

Ella shook her head. She normally didn't turn down food, but the body in the next room was enough to put a damper on her appetite. "How can you eat here?"

"Oh, you mean 'cause of him?" she asked, tilting her head to the right. "Don't worry. He won't mooch." Seeing Ella smile ruefully, she shrugged and continued. "Why should I walk all the way upstairs, where everyone is afraid of me anyway, just to eat?" Carolyn sighed, then gave Ella a sympathetic smile. "In med school, I used to react the same way you do. But you build up an immunity after a while."

After saying good-bye, Ella headed back to her unit. The second she stepped out of the hospital doors, she took a long, deep breath. There was one peculiarity about the morgue—a lingering, sometimes strong scent that she'd never encountered anywhere else. The odor was hard to describe, but the closest comparison was the smell of meat stored too long in the refrigerator. Then again, maybe that description was more appropriate than she'd realized.

Unfortunately, like smoke, the odor seemed to cling to her clothing long after she'd left. But she was willing to concede that it may have been partly her imagination because no one else had ever commented on it—or run away from her screaming.

By the time she reached her car, Ella had decided what her next step would be. She would concentrate on whoever had custody of the paperwork just before, and right after, it arrived at the county offices. And the best place for her to start would be with Melvin Rainwater. She had a plan.

Ella called Justine and got her on the first ring. "Are you still at the station?"

"Yes, I'm still running tests on these seeds."

"I need you to do something else for me."

"Name it."

"Remember that surveillance gear that Blalock gave us a few

months ago? One was a mike that could be hidden almost anywhere. His example was a pen."

"Yeah, I remember."

"Place one of those mikes inside one of our generic department pens as soon as possible and meet me in the east parking lot of the Totah Café. I'll need the device before I make my next stop."

"I remember all the pens at Melvin's house. It looked like he'd stolen one from every place he'd ever been. What are you up to now?"

"I'll tell you later. Just get me that pen, ready to activate."

Ella contacted Teeny. "Where's Rainwater now?"

"With a woman, as always. This time he's at the home of the mortuary's secretary, over in Fruitland. She's at work, but Melvin's watching TV. I can see him sitting there from where I'm at."

"I need to speak to him again. I'll be there in thirty," she said. That would give her all the time she needed to meet with Justine and get what she needed.

Ella spotted Teeny's truck almost immediately. Parking half a block from his location, she walked up quickly and slipped into the passenger's side.

"What have we got?" she asked. Teeny had a powerful set of binoculars on the console between them, and a small parabolic antenna device she knew allowed him to pick up conversations a considerable distance away without bugging anything.

"He's alone and he's had at least three beers, so I would imagine he's in the process of getting wasted."

Ella filled him in on her plan, and he nodded. "Okay, Teeny, then let's go. You cover the back. I've called Sheriff Taylor and I'm free to question the suspect."

"Wait. Take one of these. Hold down the button when you want to speak." Teeny handed her one of two small walkie-talkies, inexpensive-looking devices but very practical at the moment. "I'll beep you when I'm in position."

Ella went to the front door of the small wood-frame house, and heard a slight beep from her pocket. She knocked and, this time, didn't identify herself.

Melvin opened the door, saw her, turned, and shot out of the living room. He'd only reached the kitchen when he suddenly stopped and glanced back at her. "This is getting old. I give up. Godzilla's back there waiting, isn't he?"

"If I were you, I wouldn't let him hear you calling him that."

Crestfallen, Melvin walked back to the living room and Ella gave Teeny the all-clear on the walkie-talkie. Just as Ella sat down across the couch from Melvin, Teeny came in the front door.

"I've got some serious questions for you, Melvin, and I don't want to play any more games." Ella said. "Got it?"

"Sure, but you can't pin a murder on me. I had nothing to do with that."

"You're looking at conspiracy *and* murder, Melvin. And you're withholding evidence, so that's another federal charge. You're going down so deep you'll never see daylight again."

Melvin leaped to his feet and bolted across the room toward the kitchen. Reacting in a heartbeat, Ella dove, catching Melvin in a shoestring tackle, and he went down hard, bumping his head on the kitchen floor. Melvin rolled over and tried to throw a punch, but Ella blocked the effort, grabbing his head and thumping it hard against the wooden floor.

"Wake up, stupid. You've just assaulted a police officer. You can count on six months in Sheriff Taylor's jail, for starters," she said, then in a slow, purposeful voice added, "Or, if you play your cards right, you might be able to save your own skin and keep from sharing a cell on death row with your accomplices. Which will it be?"

"I've told you all I know."

"Wrong answer," Ella said, and brought him to his feet by the front of his shirt. As she reached for her cuffs, Teeny placed his arm across the entrance into the kitchen, standing beside Melvin like a stone sentinel straight from Easter Island.

"I want to speak to an attorney," Melvin said.

"You're not being charged," Ella said. "At least not yet. Believe it or not, I'm trying to give you a break. Think about this. *If* I arrest and book you, the second you make bail your partner Krause will do everything in his power to make sure you turn up dead. But, if we keep this informal, say, just between the three of us, you've got a shot at staying alive. Remember that although there's no death penalty on the Rez, this *is* a federal crime. But what the hell, you'll probably never survive jail anyway." She met his gaze and held it. "You're at the end of the line here, so decide."

Ella saw the fear in his eyes, this time not just part of an act, and knew Melvin finally understood. His life, like that of Agent Thomas's, was hanging by a very slim thread.

FIFTEEN

✖ ✖ ✖

Melvin sagged down onto the sofa and Ella sat across from him on a chair. Teeny stood just to his right, his massive shadow, cast by a lamp in the corner, falling over the smaller man's face. Whenever Teeny moved slightly, as he seemed to be doing constantly, the light would flicker in Melvin's eyes, making him squint. Ella knew Teeny was probably doing that as a reminder to Melvin that he was there and in control.

The next step would be tricky. One way or another, she had to get Rainwater to steal her pen. She'd filled Teeny in on her plan, so now it would all be a matter of luck and timing. Planting a bug officially would have required legal paperwork and, Andy Thomas, if he'd managed to stay alive, didn't have the luxury of time.

"Start talking and play it straight, Melvin. I'm all out of patience."

"What I've *told* you is the truth," he said. "I didn't lie to you. I just didn't mention a few extra details."

Ella toyed with her pen, occasionally taking notes on her small notebook. Then, in a gesture of annoyance, she tossed both down onto the coffee table between them, leaned back in her chair, and stared at him. "Now's the time to protect whatever future you have left. Stop trying my patience and start talking."

Ella watched him stare at his hands, and knew exactly what

he was thinking. On one hand, he'd be branded a rat and prison wasn't kind to those who bore that label. On the other hand, if he played his cards right, he might get by with a minor sentence.

Finally, Melvin looked up at her. "You've got me between a rock and a hard place."

"Krause will kill you. I'm giving you a chance to live. My deal's better," Ella replied.

He nodded slowly, took a deep breath, and began. "You're right about Jack Krause being dirty. He came up with a great scam that's been making us a good, steady income. He pays a data-processing clerk at the county office to change the names on the death certificates when they arrive at her desk. Then Jack sends a change of address request to the social security office for the dead guy, using a forged signature. In a matter of weeks, the benefit checks start rolling in. We've only picked on people from the Rez because the chances of getting caught are pretty close to nothing. Nobody likes to talk about the dead, you know that. And, as an added precaution, we only targeted people with no next of kin," he said. "That way no one would be asking about survivor benefits. But I screwed up with Yellowhorse," he said, and scowled. "I spoke to several people and all of them told me that he was living there alone, so I figured he was a perfect candidate. What I didn't know was that he was separated from his wife, and she was eligible to get his checks."

"How long have you guys been doing this?" Ella asked.

"I've only been with them for a year, but Krause has been working it for years. It's a foolproof scam because Krause has been paying off an FBI agent to misdirect anyone who has a question about the dead people or the checks being sent."

Ella, trying not to show her surprise, picked up her notebook and pen, wrote down what he'd just said, then pocketed the notebook and stood, walking away from the table. The pen was still sitting there. "And that's all you know? I was hoping you'd want to avoid the death penalty by giving me Agent Thomas's location. You know that the body we found wasn't his. Wrong blood type, even without the face and fingerprints."

"Yeah, that was a spur-of-the-moment idea anyway," he muttered. "Murder's out of our league, even if we'd been able to find a guy who looked just like him, so Krause and I used what was available at the mortuary."

"So where's Agent Thomas?" Ella pressed.

"I don't know. He was grabbed beside his car after getting run off from the Sing, then later got away for a while. I wasn't there, it was Krause and his FBI partner. Finally Thomas was put out of action—I was told that, anyway. How and where, I didn't want to know."

"You've *got* to do better than that," Ella said firmly. "Give me something. Do they have him or not?"

Melvin stood, glanced at his shoes, then scratched his head and looked around the room, stalling. He had the look of a trapped animal searching desperately for a way out. "I don't know anything more, but there may be a way for you to find out. A few months ago, I overheard Krause on his cell phone talking to the FBI dude. They arranged a meet, so I decided to tail him. He had a lot on me, laws I'd broken, but I had nothing on him, and that wasn't very balanced, you know?"

Ella stared at Rainwater, who was wandering around the room aimlessly, shuffling his feet. Now she'd heard it all. The lowlife was worried about balance so he could walk in beauty as he committed crimes? As she looked at Melvin's expression, she realized that he had no idea how preposterous that concept was.

"I wish I hadn't gotten involved in this crap. But it was so tempting. I mean *legally* it might be considered a crime, but it really wasn't," Melvin argued.

"How do you figure that?" Ella asked.

"They were *dead*. We weren't taking anything from them."

"You were stealing from the government."

"Yeah, the same people who get campaign funds from contractors, then buy their four-hundred-dollar hammers with our money? Or the ones who borrow money we'll have to pay back to give the rich a bigger tax cut? That's the government I'm thinking about. We were tired of waiting for the trickle-down. We figured we'd take back our fair share now."

She looked over at Teeny, who gave her a why-not shrug, suggesting that his thoughts ran along the same line as Melvin's. The one big difference was that Teeny played it straight.

Unfortunately, Melvin was convinced he was in the right and that *he* was the injured party. She could see it in his eyes. Most criminals she'd encountered had an amazing ability to rationalize their actions.

"Okay, enough excuses. Get back to your story," she said. "So you followed Krause when he went to meet his FBI contact?"

Melvin continued to pace around the room nervously as he spoke. "Yeah. He went to an apartment in Farmington, one of those buildings off Twentieth Street. I never saw the FBI guy, but I got a look at the woman who lives there. If they've got Thomas, I'll bet that's where they took him."

Ella considered what he'd said, but it didn't match up with what Thomas had said when he'd called for help—that he was in a dark place and couldn't get out—unless Thomas was in a basement and didn't know it, of course.

As she stood up, she saw that the pen had disappeared from the coffee table. He'd taken the bait, probably when he'd first left the sofa. "This better be on the level, Melvin, or I'm coming back." She turned to look at Teeny. "Or maybe Bruce will do that for me. How about it?"

"Okay by me," Teeny replied. "But if I show up on my own, Melvin and I are going somewhere private first—way out in the desert where nobody will be able to see or hear us . . . talk. But having to take a long drive will probably just piss me off even more. I don't like people who waste my time," Teeny growled.

"I'm on the level, honest!" Melvin was licking his lips nervously, looking in Teeny's direction but not making eye contact.

Ella knew Rainwater was still angling, holding back, and playing games. It wasn't in his nature to be totally forthcoming. But she had all she was going to get for now.

Once they reached Teeny's truck, Ella remained standing

beside the door while Teeny climbed into the driver's seat. "I need you to monitor him using that pen's frequency," Ella said, giving him the small receiver that would pick up the transmissions.

"I'll record everything, but the game's changing if we have dirty FBI in the mix, Ella. Any thoughts on who it could be?"

"Payestewa transferred out months ago, so the obvious candidate would be Blalock, the senior resident agent. But I've known him too long to believe he's dirty." Even as she said it, Ella realized how little she really knew about Dwayne Blalock's personal life. Did he ever date? Did he have kids from a previous marriage? The truth was she'd never met with him socially except over coffee, after they'd wrapped up a case. She'd never even been to his home, apartment, or wherever he lived. Yet, despite all that, she was absolutely certain he wasn't guilty. They'd risked their lives together more than once, and Blalock had a scar on his leg where he'd once taken a bullet meant for her.

"Your gut feelings are legendary, Ella, but the hard truth is that, without evidence, you've got zip. You can't rule FB-Eyes out."

"Maybe not, but I've also got a good idea who's really behind this game and, if I'm right, we're going to be facing a world of problems."

"Let me guess. The suit who came to visit?" he asked, reading her mind.

"Yeah, Simmons. It fits once you put the pieces in the right order. His job requires him to come up into the area from time to time. It would explain why he has been keeping such a low profile recently, deliberately finding reasons to get out of the area and build an alibi, meanwhile getting all the news on the progress of the search. The attempts to slow me down didn't begin until *after* we got that phone call proving Thomas was still alive. Only a few people know about that, and I trust everyone who got that information—except Simmons."

"He must have told Krause about the call right after I told him," Ella continued. "And they gave Melvin and maybe someone else the job of distracting me. But one thing at a time. First, I want to go to the address Melvin gave us. I need confirmation, and the neighbors must have seen somebody besides the woman come and go. We need to link Simmons physically with the other suspects."

"I hope for Thomas's sake that he's being kept there. If we don't find him soon . . ." He let his words trail off knowing Ella would be able to fill in the blanks.

"Don't count him out yet," Ella said. "It's far from hopeless. My guess is that they don't have him yet—that he's still out there down a mine shaft. You often hear about people being found alive after being buried in earthquakes for up to a week, sometimes longer," Ella snapped.

"Be careful, Ella. This case is really getting under your skin."

Ella nodded. "I know what it's like to be trapped in a dark place. I was buried alive, Teeny. My memories are all the motivation I need to keep me going."

Ella drove back to Shiprock, met with Justine less than thirty minutes later at the station, and told her about Melvin Rainwater's latest revelations.

"That's scary, having to add an FBI agent to our list of suspects. I sure hope Blalock isn't involved," Justine said.

"Me too, and it's hard not thinking about that, but we really need to focus on finding the missing agent. We've got to check every lead."

"But Ella, Agent Thomas said he was in a *dark place*," Justine reminded. "How could that be an apartment?"

"His cell phone cut out. Maybe they locked him a closet or someplace like a basement or crawl space where his signal was blocked, and he just didn't get a chance to tell us exactly what he meant. Or maybe his injuries are affecting his thinking."

"But why would they keep him alive?"

"Maybe in case they needed leverage to make their getaway," Ella suggested. "In the long run he'd be a liability, so if they do have him, I doubt they'd keep him alive indefinitely. But considering what our other sources have said, and the possibility that Simmons is involved, I tend to believe that they don't have him at all.

He may have escaped, then gone into hiding and be unable to move or contact anyone. He's been neutralized in one sense, but is still a danger to them as long as he's still alive. That would fit in with the roadblocks they keep putting in our way. Simmons, Krause, Rainwater . . . they want to find him first. But that's not going to happen. Let's get going and check out that apartment."

"And what about FB-Eyes—Blalock?" Justine asked. "What if he's the one that's dirty?"

"Justine, you've known him almost as long as I have. No way he's dirty. He's a straight arrow, bending only enough to work around our culture. If he were the resident agent anywhere else but the Rez, he'd play it by the book all the way," Ella said. "He's just being set up to take the fall."

"By whom?"

"The only one with the clout to deliver the protection Krause is paying for is Simmons. He's got the power and the know-how, and by remaining a discreet distance away from the situation he covers his own back very effectively. Think about it—it's brilliant. Should the scam burst open and the fact that an FBI agent is involved come to light, Blalock would go down for the crime while Simmons walks away smelling like a rose. Simmons not only gets to keep the money but he also eliminates Blalock, who's been a thorn in his side. Thomas, though, who may have gotten too close to the truth, had to be taken out of the picture permanently."

"The pattern comes together. It fits."

"This theory would also explain why Simmons didn't get directly involved in the search for Thomas even though he obviously doesn't think much of the tribal police department's capabilities. He didn't want Thomas to be found alive. He *could* have backed out of his trip to Washington and stayed on the case, but instead he gave it to someone he believes is inept—me. He's convinced I've been promoted well beyond my own abilities, he made that clear already."

"His attitude could be his downfall, then. Simmons keeps underestimating us. But he's coming back now, right?"

"Yeah, but he's certainly taking his time getting here. There was no need to run off to Flagstaff except to give himself an alibi while Melvin and Krause do his dirty work. If Simmons was really interested in finding Thomas, he'd be here. My guess is when he finally arrives, he'll probably do his best to make sure his agent stays lost."

"It's a good theory, Ella, and the timing fits, but without real physical evidence that's all it is—a theory. We've got nothing to point specifically to anyone except Rainwater and Krause, and even so, we have to establish the social security scam with solid physical evidence."

"So let's get busy. I'm going to the apartment Melvin told me about and see who really lives there. Maybe I'll take a look around, too. If Melvin's lying again, it won't take long to prove it. But I could use your help."

"Of course. But we'll need a sneak-and-peek warrant. Didn't Simmons say he had a magistrate advised that we might be needing a quick search warrant?"

"Yeah, but Simmons told me I had to go through him, and I don't want to tip him off. Once we give him more details he'll know how close we are. How about I call your grandfather instead? We didn't give him the specifics on our earlier request, so we can say this was it. And if I can get Sheriff Taylor's cooperation, it'll take care of jurisdictional problems. Also call Tache and talk him through whatever steps he needs to take to get us the name and background of the person renting the corner apartment," Ella said. "It'll help fill more lines on that warrant."

"Good idea."

"I'll ask Sheriff Taylor to get one of his deputies to do the paperwork and drop it by. We don't have to bring it with us. All we'll need is confirmation," Justine said.

While they were en route to Farmington, they made the calls on their cell phones. By the time Ella hung up, the deputy was on the way to the judge's office.

"Things have changed a lot for us recently in law enforcement," Justine said slowly, her eyes on traffic. "Before the Patriot

Act we couldn't have made a covert entry like this. We would have been forced to wait for more evidence and probable cause."

"I wouldn't have waited, not in a situation like this," Ella said quietly. "If a life's at stake, particularly if it's someone in law enforcement, I'm willing to do whatever has to be done. When you were missing I took some shortcuts—had the whole police force questioning my judgement, in fact." After a brief pause she continued. "Since my accident, it's even more so. I don't even hesitate because I know how fragile human life is."

"After what you went through, I expected you to become more detached and less involved in police work. I mean, if you honestly don't think death is the end, then why worry about things here? You *know* you're just passing through."

Ella considered her answer carefully, trying to find a way to make Justine understand. "We live *here* and *now* and this is the place where we can make a real difference—to do something that'll make everyone else's life better. As detectives, we play our part by restoring harmony. At the moment we're the counterbalance to those who are trying to rob Agent Thomas of his life. Even though we may not win, by fighting we stand against evil with the good we manage to do. That's what it's all about."

SIXTEEN
✖ ✖ ✖

They parked in front of a small one-story complex containing eight apartments. The unit Melvin had told them about was nearly thirty yards away and occupied one corner of the building. Although it had two more windows than most of the others, all the curtains were drawn.

"Someone might be inside," Justine said. "It's impossible to see or hear anything from here."

"Right, so here's the plan. Since it's possible that someone who'll recognize me is in there, I'm going to go next door and talk to the neighbor first and see what I can learn." Ella gestured toward a woman getting out of a car parked in front of the adjacent apartment. "From her age and all the papers and books she's juggling, she's either a college student or a teacher."

"Okay, I'll keep an eye on the target apartment."

"If anyone comes out or arrives while I'm checking the neighbor, let me know right away."

"You've got it."

Ella walked up to the door the young Anglo woman had just entered, and knocked. A tired-looking brunette in her midtwenties answered. Her brown hair fell to her shoulders and she wore little or no makeup. Her only jewelry was a pair of small pearl earrings, and her modest-length skirt and loose-fitting sweater were consistent with a school or small business setting.

Ella flipped her badge quickly, and identified herself as a police detective, leaving out the fact that she was a tribal officer. "I need to ask you a few questions about your neighbor," Ella said, cocking her head to the left. "May I come in?"

The woman opened the door wider, motioning for Ella to enter. The apartment wasn't particularly messy, just dusty and cluttered, as though it belonged to someone who was seldom home except to change clothes. "Is Betsy in some kind of trouble?" the woman asked.

"That's what I'm trying to determine. But before we go on, I'd like to ask that you keep my visit confidential," Ella said.

"Sure," she said, gesturing for Ella to take a seat. "How can I help you?" The books the woman had brought in were at one end of the couch, so Ella sat on the other side. Glancing down, she could see they were college-level textbooks. One had a "used" sticker on the front cover.

"Why don't you start by telling me your name and how long you've lived here?"

"My name is Margo, Margo Lowry Stewart. I've been here for a little less than six months. I'm a student at the community college."

"Was Betsy already living here when you moved in?" Ella would ask for Betsy's last name later, if she got the chance. For now she'd get further if the woman assumed that she already knew more about Betsy.

"She and I hardly talk. To be perfectly honest, she's juggling boyfriends who come over at all hours, and I'm uncomfortable with that."

"How many men are we talking about?" Ella pressed.

"Two—that I know about. One is supersecretive. He comes over late, always after dark, and leaves early. I've heard his voice a few times. It's deep and it mostly sounds like a rumble since he's at least considerate enough to speak softly."

"Is he Hispanic, Anglo, Native American? . . ."

"I'm not sure. I only saw him once, at night, and he was walking away at the time. Very confident step, but in a hurry."

"What kind of car or truck does he drive?"

"Can't say for sure. I was just coming back from the laundry room and had a basket load of clothes, so I didn't stay around long enough to look. But there weren't any pickups in the parking lot, so it must have been a car. Nobody walks around here."

"What about the other man?"

"He only comes over when Mr. Secretive's not around. He spends most of the time, if not all of it, drinking with her and doing whatever else. I met Betsy at the Dumpster in the morning after one of his visits, and she threw out a whole bag full of bottles and three six-pack cardboard thingies. It's sad because she doesn't need any encouragement to drink. She puts away at least a six-pack a day on her own. Betsy's always half-drunk by the time it gets dark, judging from the times I've met her in the laundry room. She's either really unhappy or stressed out major league."

"What can you tell me about the second man? Size, description, race, age, stuff like that."

"Well, I saw him getting into his SUV once, so I know he has dark hair, and is maybe a little shorter than you but weighs more. He struck me as quite a bit younger than the first guy, but I'm not sure why. Maybe it was his walk—more of a lazy killing-time, dragging-your-feet step you see a lot in young people. I was getting into my car at the time, and I didn't want to make eye contact. The last thing I need is to attract a guy who spends all his free time drinking, you know?"

"I hear you. What kind of SUV did he have?" Ella asked.

Margo considered it for a long time. "It was a dark color, black or blue, but other than that I just don't recall."

"Okay. Thanks for your help, and please remember to keep my visit confidential for now."

"I will, but I should tell you, I'd been thinking of moving out and this just cinches it. This place is already getting noisy, and there are drunks all around. Now with the police asking questions about my neighbors—that's just too much. What if I overhear the wrong conversation? I'll end up as a chalk outline out on the sidewalk."

"So you *do* overhear some of their conversations?" Ella said picking up on it quickly.

"Pieces sometimes. But then I usually turn up my music. I listen to classical music so I can study without being distracted."

"Have you ever heard either of the men being mentioned by name?"

Margo thought for a while, her face furrowed in concentration. "No, sorry. I can't say I have. In fact, the only conversation I ever really overheard completely was one time when I was in my kitchen fixing breakfast. Betsy was with the second guy—the beer guy—and I heard him say something that really bugged me—that there was nothing like the living dead." Margo shuddered. "But then I realized that he was probably just a George Romero fan."

Ella gave her a puzzled look.

"Don't you watch old movies? He directed some real funny classic horror flicks, like *Night of the Living Dead*, and *Dawn of the Dead*. One's been remade recently."

Ella gave her a blank look.

"You can rent them. They're really a lot of fun, though I'm not sure if they were meant to be that way or not." Margo checked her watch. "Is there anything else? I need to grab a bite to eat, then it's back to school. I've still got another class today."

"That's all I have for you right now. Thanks for your help," Ella said. Just as Margo opened the door, her cell phone started vibrating.

Ella brought the phone to her ear, and looked outside casually to make sure nobody was near Betsy's apartment. If at all possible she still wanted to avoid being seen.

"Betsy Weaver is the renter's name and she works at the county coroner's office," Justine said. "She's a data-entry operator and she's at work right now. Oh, and I checked and the details have been added to the warrant already."

"Good, let me know when it's ready." Ella nodded to Margo, then headed to her unit as Margo closed the door.

"The warrant has been approved. We'll pick it up at the station later," Justine said as Ella reached the vehicle.

"Good."

Ella slipped into the passenger's seat, grabbed some latex gloves from a box attached to her sun visor, and stuffed them into her jacket pocket as she filled Justine in on what she'd learned from Margo.

"So *Betsy's* the one who has been changing the names," Justine concluded.

"I'd bet money on it. Now I'm going to check her apartment. Based on what Margo told me, I don't think Agent Thomas is in there. She would have probably heard something if they'd been keeping someone prisoner and there are no basements in this building. But I still want to look inside the place for anything that might give us a lead. Margo said she's leaving soon, and, when she does, I'm going to see if I can find a way in."

"It's four now, and Betsy will probably get off work at five. Allow fifteen minutes' travel time from the county offices. . . . If you get caught inside, Betsy will know what's going on, and we'll be screwed."

"I know," Ella said calmly.

"You'll pick the lock?"

"No, I don't think so. I'll check the windows first and look under that big flower pot that's just to the left of her door. People hide keys in case of emergencies, and if she's a heavy drinker, she would want a backup in case she misplaced hers. Or maybe she's very hospitable and leaves one in case a boyfriend drops by."

Margo left less than five minutes later, books and keys in her hands. As soon as the young woman drove away, Ella strolled around the side of the building, checking quickly for an open window. Finding none, she went back to the door and searched beneath the planter. There was no key hidden there or within an inch depth in the soil.

Ella brought out her small pocketknife, which had a lock-pick-type blade, as she continued glancing around for a spare key and making sure she wasn't being watched. Then she spotted a small rock by itself in the dirt just off the concrete walkway about five feet from the door. Ella lifted the rock and saw a piece of flat aluminum foil beneath. When she picked up the foil, she immediately felt the outline of a key nestled inside it.

Ella unwrapped it, and was inside the apartment less than fifteen seconds later. The place was small, about the same size as Margo's, and it was easy to search. The complex was relatively new, and offered few cracks, joints, and cubbyholes to hide things. Ella first looked around for photos but only found one. It featured an elderly couple on either side of a slightly overweight, pretty, dark-haired, blue-eyed woman in her early thirties. Betsy and her parents, Ella concluded, studying the image of the youngest person for a moment before moving on.

Next she went through the desk in the living room. There were no locks on the inexpensive piece of furniture. Among the usual stack of bills that had piled up she found a cell phone bill that listed at least two dozen calls made to the same number. She jotted it down, intending to cross-reference it later.

Seeing some bank statements, Ella took a look at the opened envelopes. A fast glance revealed that Betsy had three separate accounts, all in different banks. There was a modest savings account, and regular checking with direct deposits every two weeks that Ella figured came from Betsy's job for the county. The third account showed larger monthly deposits totally out of line with the modest earnings of a data-entry clerk.

Ella placed the two nondescript statements back in their envelopes, but instead of placing the third with the other two, she slipped it beneath the large TV armoire. Maybe later, once she'd gathered hard evidence from the leads she'd picked up here today, she'd be able to return with a standard search warrant listing specifics. Even if Betsy managed to destroy the rest of the evidence, this one statement would hopefully remain hidden, and go unnoticed.

Ella went to the bathroom and looked inside the cabinet. There were two sticks of deodorant, one new and unopened, the other nearly depleted. Following a burst of inspiration, she took the old canister of deodorant she found there and placed it into a plastic evidence pouch and then in her pocket. Maybe she could lift prints from it. Then she opened the new one, wiped it on her arm to make it look as if it had been used, then placed it where the old one had been.

Her guess was that Betsy's primary boyfriend, the one Margo had called secretive, was Simmons. He was well trained when it came to finding—or leaving—evidence, so he'd know how to avoid the latter. The other, based on the description of the dark SUV, might turn out to be Krause, though the described walk didn't fit the funeral director, unless it was deliberately done to mislead anyone who might be watching. After all, Rainwater had followed him here. Krause and the agent had probably chosen to meet at Betsy's so they could let her know which death certificates would need to be altered.

Each man had his own relationship with Betsy and Ella suspected that they were both using Betsy, to one degree or another, as an informant in an effort to keep an eye on each other. Betsy, of course, was quite possibly using both of the men, too, playing them for all she could get.

Ella made one last stop, peering into the hall closet. Inside, along with a few jackets and a coat, was a straw cowboy hat and a smaller red cap. The most interesting discovery, however, was a round mirror about eighteen inches in diameter. The near-fatal accident with Herman Cloud came to mind instantly. But if Betsy had been the one with the cap and mirror, who'd been at the wheel, Krause or Melvin? Unfortunately, this evidence would have to remain behind for now or Betsy would know someone had been in her apartment.

Ella opened the door slightly, peered outside, then moving fast, locked the door behind her. She then wrapped the key in the foil again and placed it under the rock.

Ella and Justine were soon on their way back to the reservation. After Ella described her search, the items in the hall closet, and the photo she'd seen of Betsy, she brought the bag containing the deodorant out of her pocket. "I really need you to try and lift prints off this deodorant canister. I also want you to check the number I picked up from her cell phone bill and find out who Betsy's been calling."

"It's the mortuary's number. I recognize it," Justine said.

Ella nodded. "I had a feeling I'd seen it before. Now I'm anxious to see what the prints tell us. I wish I'd had time to dust for latents in the apartment."

"If we're really lucky we'll be able to ID both men," Justine said, looking at the deodorant.

"I doubt we'd be *that* lucky," Ella answered. "Betsy might have smudged the other prints even if both men have used the stuff. The one Margo called Mr. Secretive could be Simmons, and I doubt he'd leave personal items behind, which explains the absence of obvious 'men's' items—not even a second toothbrush. And the other guy wouldn't leave anything because it would give him away to Simmons. But then again, you never know. Neither man wore latex gloves while inside, I'm sure."

"One of the things you're really hoping to do is rule out Blalock once and for all. Am I right?"

Ella sighed. "Yeah, but just the absence of his prints on the deodorant won't do that. I know in my head that he's innocent, but I need proof that either clears him or incriminates another FBI agent."

When they reached the station, Justine got out, holding the pouch containing the canister of deodorant. "You're not coming in?" she asked, seeing Ella slip behind the wheel.

"No, I've got some more things to check out," Ella said. "I'll be back later. Pick up the warrant and put it on my desk, okay? I'll sign it later and send it on to Sheriff Taylor's office."

Justine nodded. "Shall I call you on the cell if I get some prints other than Betsy's?"

"Absolutely."

As Ella drove out of the parking lot, she picked up her cell phone and called Teeny. "Anything yet?"

"No, he's been laying low. I think he's scared and trying to figure out how to ditch me. Even though he can't see me at the moment, he probably suspects I'm around."

"Where's he now?"

"Same place—the house in Fruitland."

"I'll be there in twenty. I have a plan."

"I'm not going anywhere."

SEVENTEEN
✖ ✖ ✖

Ella arrived at Teeny's truck thirty minutes later. The simple truth was that she had to start rattling some people real hard or Agent Thomas was as good as dead.

Ella briefed Teeny quickly, then they went up to the porch together, ready to set her plan into motion. Teeny knocked, and his fist reminded her of a battering ram. The door actually shook under the impact.

"Open up, Melvin, or we'll break the door down," Teeny called out cheerfully.

Melvin came to the door a second later, opening it wide enough for even the big man to enter. "Jeez, man. It takes a few seconds to cross the room, you know."

Ella strolled in and made herself comfortable on the sofa, and Rainwater forced himself down uneasily onto a recliner. Teeny remained standing, taking a position close enough to grab their suspect if he made a sudden move. "Relax. I'm here to give you some *good* news, Melvin. You're going to be off the hook, finally, at least concerning Special Agent Thomas."

"Yeah?" His expression brightened considerably and he leaned forward.

She waited, taking her time before enlightening him. Seeing Melvin almost squirming, she finally continued. "We received a very short phone call from Agent Thomas the day all this began.

We kept that piece of information under wraps until now because his cell phone lost battery power during his call and the information we had was sketchy. But now, through Homeland Security channels, we've managed to borrow some special equipment. It's the same stuff they use to track cell phone conversations and locations of terrorist groups in the Middle East and Asia. This state-of-the-art hardware is able to electronically activate the GPS chip in his cell phone and get a return signal despite the fact that the battery has run down. We'll be able to triangulate Thomas's location—that of his phone, actually—and track him down within an hour or so."

Melvin leaned back, trying to look casual but having a hard time of it. "The Rez is a large place and cell phone signals get blocked all the time. How did the techno-geeks get around that?"

Ella shook her head. "I can't go into details—that's classified—and I'd probably screw up the technical explanation anyway. But I can tell you that they're using satellites and the whole nine yards, so no mountains or canyons will be in the way. Not from a hundred miles or whatever overhead."

"So since you know that he's still alive, I'm officially off the hook?" Melvin actually stretched and managed a bored yawn.

"Not exactly. Providing Agent Thomas is still alive when we find him, he'll be able to tell us exactly what happened, and that should clear you—if you've played it straight with us. If that's the case, you won't be facing kidnapping charges."

Melvin sat up again. "Then find him fast, will you? I want you two out of my hair permanently."

"Aw, gee, Melvin, you disappoint me," Ella said. "And here I thought you liked us."

Teeny and Ella left the house and as soon as she was sure they were out of earshot, Ella spoke. "He's such a bad actor, pretending his innocence. I saw my pen sitting on his desk. Keep monitoring him, Teeny."

When they reached the van, Teeny glanced at the small recorder he had attached to the pen monitoring receiver. The device was sound activated, and a white light indicated that it was recording. Currently only the green light was on.

"You think he'll alert the others and lead you to Agent Thomas?" Teeny asked.

"That's what I'm hoping," Ella said.

"He bought your techno-speak, and you did a pretty good job of tying together fiction and reality. The intelligence community is pretty close to doing just what you described. There are chips in just about everything these days, including FBI cell phones. The only problem is that the chips run on battery power, and if the battery *is* dead, or the cell phone is shielded or underground . . ."

"I get it. Well, let's see what he does next," Ella said.

Her cell phone rang, and Ella picked it up. Her heart almost stopped when she recognized Greg Simmons's voice. "Clah, it's me, Simmons. I'm driving through from Flagstaff, and should be in Shiprock by midnight. Any news from your end?"

Ella thought about it for a moment. She had to make sure nothing was said that would disrupt Simmons's plans. She had to catch him with his hands dirty—before he got to Andy Thomas.

"You deaf, Clah?" Simmons's grumbled.

"No, sorry, I was going to tell you that the body of the red-haired man we found—minus his head—isn't Agent Thomas. We're still checking out the people from the Sing he interrupted. That's our best lead right now."

"Sounds like you and your tribal cops are still chasing smoke. Listen, Clah, if you don't find our agent or his body by daylight tomorrow, I'm calling in the calvary. By noon, every back road in the Four Corners will have a carful of feds. Pass that on to Big Ed Atcitty for me." He hung up.

"Jackass," Ella mumbled, then looked up to see Teeny's curious expression. Holding up her hand to assure him she'd fill him in soon, she called Justine immediately.

"Simmons is driving back from Arizona, but doesn't expect to arrive here before midnight. He says he's going to give us another eight hours to find Simmons before the feds take over." Ella glanced at Teeny, who nodded.

"What do you want me to do?" Justine asked.

"Get to Farmington and stake out Betsy Weaver's place. My guess is Simmons will go there. Krause knows he's under suspicion and probably has advised his partner to avoid being seen with him, and Simmons has to know we're onto Melvin. Just keep your distance, cuz, we don't want to tip anyone off or Andy Thomas will lose big-time. Use the cell phone to contact me or our people. Simmons, once he's within range, will have access to their radio frequencies. And let me know if you spot any of our players." Ella ended the call.

After bringing Teeny up to speed on what he hadn't managed to infer, Ella said good-bye and got into her unit. Justine whizzed by in her car, heading east, and Ella waved. She, in turn, headed west, toward Shiprock.

Fifteen minutes later, while stopped for gas in downtown Shiprock, Ella's cell phone rang. She stepped away from the pumps to take the call.

"He's here!" Justine whispered.

"Simmons? In Farmington already?" Ella whispered back.

"Yeah. He lied to you, boss. Not five minutes after I arrived at Betsy Weaver's apartment complex Simmons pulled up. He parked his car right in front of her door. Betsy, or a person who fits the description you gave me, let him in. She's got shorter hair now, though, and may have put on a few more pounds. And Simmons had a purposeful walk, not one of those 'I'm bad' shuffles—if that matters."

"It might. Stay low but keep an eye on the place and don't let him slip away. I'll be there in twenty minutes."

Knowing she was still out of her jurisdiction, and things would get really complicated if she had to make a move, Ella called Sheriff Taylor again as she sped back east toward Farmington.

"I've got a sticky situation here, Paul," she explained, "and I need your help." She gave him a brief rundown. "If I'm right and Simmons is dirty, the fact that he's running the show puts us at a clear disadvantage. We just don't know for sure who else might be in on his operation, or if he has any snitches that could blow the whistle on us."

"So what's your plan, Ella?"

"For now, I'm waiting at the Weaver apartment to see what course of action he takes. I'll call you the second something happens."

"Do that. I have a feeling we're going to be up to our necks in feds, regulations, and recriminations before this is over. I just hope we can find Agent Thomas alive, or we're all going to make the national news."

Waiting was the most difficult thing to do, knowing that every hour placed Andy Thomas even closer to death—from injuries, thirst, or a half dozen other possibilities a fertile mind could generate.

Ella had parked down the street from Betsy Weaver's apartment, not wanting to have two police units, even unmarked ones, that close to their quarry. She'd contacted Big Ed and briefed him, and been able to continue directing some of the logistics of the field search via telephone, but Simmons and Betsy seemed to be the key. Rainwater and Krause were covered and the only thing required from Ella now was patience. It was going to be hell—patience was highly overrated, but at least she had time to switch to a fresh cell phone battery.

It was after dark when Justine finally called her with the news. "Something's finally going down. Simmons is still inside the apartment but Betsy's pulling out now in a blue four-door sedan. She had a briefcase with her and was acting as jumpy as you can get. Something tells me she's going to make a delivery."

"Okay. Stay with Simmons, Justine, I'll pick Betsy up after she goes by. Just in case I have to tail her on foot, what's she wearing?"

"A dark blue jacket, slacks, and a red blouse."

Staying well behind the woman's car, but keeping the taillights in sight, Ella followed while she got Sheriff Taylor on the phone. "I want to bring this woman in for questioning *after* we see what she's up to with that briefcase. But I need to keep Simmons

212 * AIMÉE & DAVID THURLO

in the dark. I'd like Betsy to just disappear for a while and let Simmons worry about it."

"Where's the Weaver woman headed now?" Taylor asked.

Ella followed her vehicle a while longer, giving general directions as the woman drove west down a major Farmington street. "She's slowing and getting into the left lane. The west-side mall is just ahead."

She paused, waited a minute and watched, then confirmed it to Taylor. "Yeah, I was right. She just pulled into the mall parking area and is cruising through the east lot. I'll park close enough to be able to follow her on foot when she gets out and I'll stay on the line. Every other person around here is on their cell phone anyway, so it shouldn't attract any attention."

"Give me a description of the woman," he asked, then listened as Ella gave him the details that Justine had reported, including the clothing and short hair. "Okay. I'll back you up," Taylor added. "I'll be there in five. I'll go into the mall from the north side."

Betsy parked, then took the brown leather briefcase out of the passenger's seat, glanced around nervously like an amateur spy, then headed for the closest mall entrance. Ella gave her plenty of room, hanging back and blending into the gathering of early evening shoppers. The mall didn't close until nine and there were plenty of people around.

Ella updated Sheriff Taylor as she stopped and pretended to be window shopping, telling him what Betsy was doing and where she was at. "Paul, I want to stay with the briefcase, so I'd like you to focus on Betsy. As soon as she makes the drop, take her into custody."

"Sounds like a plan."

Ella stayed as far back as she could, but always kept Betsy in sight, then Betsy stepped into the elevator. Since it only went up one floor, it was used mainly by handicapped people, the elderly, moms with strollers, and the extremely lazy. Not knowing if Simmons had given Betsy her description, Ella decided to avoid the elevator altogether. Instead, she raced up the stairs and caught up with the woman on the second floor.

Betsy stepped out between two men in business suits. A pregnant woman who'd also come out of the elevator stepped around Betsy, blocking Ella's view momentarily. Ella moved aside quickly and saw Betsy leave the briefcase on top of a *banco* provided for shoppers needing a seat, then walk away quickly.

Seeing Sheriff Taylor coming toward her in the center aisle, Ella pointed to Betsy, then hurried to get the briefcase. Ella opened it carefully in case it was booby-trapped, but when she looked inside all she saw were old copies of the *Denver Post*, the *Albuquerque Journal*, and the local newspaper. Her stomach plummeted.

"We've been had," she warned Taylor over the open line. "Keep Ms. Weaver in custody. I need to question her." Ella checked the elevator for another briefcase, then remembered the businessmen who'd stepped out with Betsy. One had been carrying a briefcase, and she tried to remember what color it was.

She glanced around, but neither businessman was in sight. Quickly she called Justine and apprised her of what had just happened.

"Simmons is leaving now," Justine interrupted. "I'll stay with him."

"Good. I'm going to join Sheriff Taylor and see what we can get out of Betsy. Maybe he got a look at the businessmen that were on that elevator. I was so intent on Betsy, I never even checked out their faces."

At the county lockup, Ella and Sheriff Taylor tried for a half hour to get Betsy to reveal something that would lead them to Agent Thomas or incriminate the mortuary but Betsy was sullen and refused to cooperate. She wouldn't even answer their questions about the elevator ride. Despite the outward bravado, Ella could sense that she was really scared.

Leaving her alone to brood for a while and bumping up the room temperature by cutting off the air conditioning, Ella stood with Sheriff Taylor just outside the two-way mirror, waiting for the room to get uncomfortably stuffy. Ordinarily this interview room was pleasant, with a soothing light blue paint scheme and curtains on the window. The table and chairs matched. It was all designed to put a witness at ease.

Another interview room across the hall was stark—only a table, one uncomfortable and two comfortable chairs, and an institutional puke green paint scheme on four bare walls. That room was intended to set an entirely different mood, and now Ella was regretting not having gone with it—the bad-cop environment.

"I think she's terrified of Simmons," Ella said. "I suspected as much and that's why I picked this room over the other one. But, even so, whenever we brought up his name, she still freezes on us."

"She won't even admit she knows him, though we already know that he visited her apartment. And no explanation at all why she was carrying around a briefcase full of old newspapers. She must have made a switch, there's no other answer."

"It's not just that she's stonewalling us, Paul. Betsy actually locks up. That's either paralyzing fear or experience under questioning."

"She has a record for embezzlement and two prior convictions for credit card fraud in Arizona. She left those off her résumé with the county. So much for background checks. I can't wait to see what her supervisor over in Records has to say."

"The weird thing is that she just sat there expressionless when we confronted her with the rap sheet Phoenix sent us. Most suspects who've been in the system would have started screaming for an attorney from the get-go. But she didn't—in fact, she waived her rights. That makes absolutely no sense to me," Ella said, shaking her head.

"Nor does her silence about changing the names on those death certificates. Most people would have at least tried to defend themselves," Taylor said, "or played dumb."

"Maybe she believes that even if she spills everything, the courts will take the word of an FBI agent over hers. Could be that Betsy thinks she's safer in jail than on the outside." Ella remained silent for several moments. "I've got an idea," she said at last. "Let's use her fear against her," she said, then led the way back into the interrogation room.

Betsy's short dark hair was damp with perspiration by now. "Can I have some water, please?"

"Certainly." Ella nodded to Sheriff Taylor, who stepped out into the hall, called out to a deputy, then returned with a bottle of water. "Betsy, you know you're in way over your head, don't you?" Ella asked, then without waiting for an answer, continued. "If we let you walk now, how long do you think it'll be before your partners—maybe you-know-who from the elevator—will make sure you die in a car accident? Maybe he'll shine a mirror in your eyes and blind you in heavy traffic, or something like that?"

Betsy inhaled sharply, then quickly looked down at her hands, composing herself again.

"Or maybe they'll make it look like you took your own life in some horrible, excruciatingly painful way."

"I don't know where any of this is leading," Betsy said flatly. "And I don't know any man from the elevator either."

"Of course you do," Ella answered. "But just to make your life interesting, maybe we'll let you go *after* exercising our own freedom of speech and telling all our snitches that you decided to cut a deal."

"If you do that, I'm as good as dead. Don't you get it?" Betsy demanded, her eyes filling up with tears.

"We *can* protect you. But we'll need a really good reason. You help us, we'll help you."

"I—" Betsy shook her head, then leaned back in her chair. "I don't know anything. Arrest me for carrying concealed newspapers. That's about the only thing you'll be able to prove."

Ella nodded to Sheriff Taylor, and the two of them stepped back out of the interview room together. "She's not going to crack."

"If we let her go now, she'll either contact Simmons or Krause and blow the whole thing, or skip town. I say we keep her for the maximum time allowed—twenty-four hours."

Ella considered it, then agreed. "Okay. After that, cut her loose and put a tail on her. Use the best you've got on this assignment. I'm betting she'll do her level best to avoid being anywhere near Simmons or Krause. But she'll need an ally, so she may lead us to other players we don't even know about yet."

"Okay, I'll delay her for as long as I can, then get my people in position before we release her. Let's see where she takes us."

"You might have a deputy check on the possibility of a mall security camera picking up the occupants of that elevator. Maybe they'll have video that'll give us a hit on who might have made the briefcase switch with Betsy," Ella said.

"Good idea, Ella. I'll put someone on it."

Ella was on her way back to her unit when Blalock called. "I just got back to my Shiprock office, and I want in on the investigation. How close are you to finding Agent Thomas?"

"Closer than I've ever been, but not close enough," Ella said, then told him about his supervisor, Simmons, and what she'd set into motion with Melvin Rainwater and Betsy Weaver.

"Damn Simmons. I never could stand him and now I know why. If one of the Bureau's own is dirty, I have to be part of the operation that takes him down. The Bureau cleans up its own messes."

"I hear you, but right now we have a problem. All we've really got against Simmons is circumstantial, and he could worm his way out by insisting he was working the case undercover on his own. He might have even left a fake paper trail just for this eventuality," she said. "And we have another problem. Strictly speaking, you're not off the suspect list—not conclusively."

"That's a load of crap and you know it."

"Yes, as a matter of fact, I do. But I need something solid that will establish your innocence. . . ."

"*When* was Agent Thomas last seen?"

"Three days ago," Ella replied, "after sunset."

"I can prove I was in Colorado at that time."

"A relative that can vouch for you?" Ella said, not bothering to hide her disappointment.

"Yes, that, but there's also the coffee shop owner near Lake Granby who can verify I came in at around six-thirty and stayed for at least an hour. That's northwest of Boulder. I couldn't have possibly made it here and back in time. And you can check out my credit card records. I'll give the department permission."

"You could have loaned your credit card to someone. We need to rely on people who actually saw you and remember."

"There are witnesses who can identify me, people I've known for years who were at that coffee shop and the lodge where I was staying. There's my signature on the charge slips for every gas station and motel I stopped at coming and going, and perhaps a security camera or two at the lodge's front desk up near the lake. You can check my phone records too. I've had no contact with the mortuary or any of the key players other than Simmons at his Albuquerque office. Put it all together and I think it'll stack up."

"This will all have to be checked out, unless we nail Simmons solidly before then. You know how it works."

"Put it all in motion now, Ella. I need a clean bill of health if I'm going after my supervisor."

"While I'm making the calls, look around for the case file you said you gave Agent Thomas. We haven't been able to find it."

Ella walked back into the station a short time later and began to check out Blalock's accounts. He'd already called the bank and the phone company, paving the way for her inquiries.

Ella called Colorado's Grand County Sheriff's Department next, asking them to verify Blalock's alibi for her. The sheriff knew Blalock, who'd been a resident agent in Boulder years ago, and a deputy was being sent to the coffee shop, and to the lodge where Blalock had been staying.

By the time the Grand County sheriff called back a half hour later to confirm Blalock's statement, Ella had made up her mind to include Blalock in the operation even before he could be checked out completely. The simple truth was that the evidence pointed to

Simmons, not Blalock, and right now Blalock's assistance would be invaluable. He understood the current protocols at the local Bureau offices, knew how to get around Simmons, and was in a position to give her the tactical and technical support she needed.

She was about to leave the office when the phone rang again. Ella picked it up and identified herself. "It's Carolyn, working for my best customer." The ME's familiar voice came through clearly. "I've got some news on the body you found. The description—estimated height, weight, coloring, and even the scar on his left leg—matches that of an accident victim that was taken to Mesa Vista a few days ago, according to the Farmington PD officer I spoke to. I'll be filing a full report within the hour."

"Thanks, Carolyn. I don't know what we'd do without you."

"Save the sweet talk. Just remember this next week during lunch."

Ella chuckled. "Okay. We're due for a lunch date anyway."

Ella placed the phone down, satisfaction and excitement pounding through her. This was the first piece of hard evidence linking the mortuary to their investigation—and the body. She had them now. She'd wanted leverage and this, at long last, was it.

EIGHTEEN
——— ✖ ✖ ✖ ———

There was no time to indulge the feeling of victory. Before she could even take a breath, the phone rang again. It was Justine.

"Bad news—big-time. Simmons left the main highway and went into Kirtland, then made some turns and stops designed to make sure no one was following him. I was overly cautious and hung back more than I should have—and lost sight of him in the dark," she said, frustration evident in her voice. "But he has to come back to the main road eventually if he's going on to Shiprock."

"Where were you when you lost him?"

"At the turnoff opposite the old El Paso Gas site with the flare tower," she replied. "He stopped at Nakai's Feed Store and bought a big coil of rope, so maybe he's going after Agent Thomas. If Thomas is trapped inside a mine or well, he's going to need that rope to get to him. What do you think—logic or reaching?"

"It's a good theory. Simmons doesn't seem the macrame type, so let's get people we trust in on this and find him. But stay off the law-enforcement frequencies. Simmons is bound to be listening in."

"I've already asked Neskahi, Tache, and the Cloud brothers to join us. They're converging on the area right now."

"Good choices." Ella trusted Philip and Michael Cloud with

her life, and she knew they weren't dirty. "Once we find him we'll see what kind of Bureau support Blalock can bring in when forced to bypass his supervisor. In the meantime, we need someone to stick to Krause, too," Ella said. "Let me see what I can work out with Sheriff Taylor."

Ella telephoned Paul Taylor next, and the sheriff quickly agreed. "Not a problem. We'll put a deputy on the mortuary and one on Krause's home, with backup standing by. Once the officers are all in position I'll let you know. After that, if Krause goes on the move or we learn anything new, you'll be notified immediately."

Ella hurried down the highway toward Shiprock. If Simmons was on his way to find Agent Thomas, and the missing agent was still in the general area south of Shiprock where he'd disappeared, the best chance she had of catching up to Simmons was to wait south of the intersection of Highway 64 and old 666, now re-named 491. If her guess was on target, he'd have to pass that way and, with luck, she'd be right there waiting. But it would be tricky. In the dark, she'd have to be close enough to the road to recognize him, or at least get a look at his vehicle tag. Yet if she did that, he'd be likely to spot her too.

She'd have to disguise herself somehow—and that meant a trip home. Ella drove quickly, sirens on, calling Justine so they could implement a stop-gap plan. Ella wanted to make sure both intersections—the eastern one in downtown Shiprock and the western one across the river—were covered by plainclothes officers until she could get into position.

Fifteen minutes later as she passed through the area she'd targeted, she saw officers already there, one pretending to be working on a stalled pickup, the other "changing" a flat tire. Both of them saw her, but neither gave any sign of recognition—which was exactly as it should have been.

After a quick acceleration, now south of Shiprock, Ella turned off the sirens and drove west up the road leading to her mother's house. It was seven-thirty now, and Dawn was miles away at her father's, probably curled up on Kevin's sofa, reading, or watching a children's or nature video he'd rented for both of them. Kevin thoroughly enjoyed any chance he got to spend time with their daughter.

Ella thought about calling Dawn just to tell her she loved her, but knew she'd then have to explain why she couldn't take time to stop by even though she was in the neighborhood. Dawn understood her mother was a police officer, but it still didn't make their long hours apart any easier for Ella. The good thing was that Dawn was becoming more and more independent. But as a mom, that wasn't a trend she really welcomed wholeheartedly.

Ella pulled up to the house a few minutes later. It was encased in darkness, except for the small lamp in the living room. Ella tiptoed inside through the kitchen. Everything was still and she could hear the soft rumble of Rose's snoring.

Ella tiptoed past her mother, who was leaning back in her comfortable chair, eyes closed and head turned away from the reading lamp. A mystery novel was on Rose's lap, still open.

Two, their mutt, was lying down in the hall and seeing her, stood up and followed Ella into her room. Two liked to sleep at the foot of her bed, and was undeniably the best foot warmer around.

Ella gave him a quick pat on the head, then got down to business. First, she took an old long skirt from the closet and pulled it up over her slacks. A dark long-sleeved tunic slipped over her own lighter top easily. Going to the bathroom mirror, she covered her shoulders with a towel and shook talcum powder liberally over her hair until it was mostly gray, then pulled it back into a bun at the nape of her neck. A pair of reading glasses grabbed from her mother's knitting basket, slipped down upon her nose, would also help.

Pushing the small, folding grocery cart she'd grabbed from the kitchen, Ella was sure she'd be indistinguishable from many of the elderly Navajos who still walked for miles on the reservation. She also had a paper sack from a local store to put in the cart, to complete the illusion.

Ella walked back through the house noiselessly. Her mother had shifted her head slightly, still sleeping peacefully despite the fact that she'd stopped snoring.

Once she reached her vehicle, carrying the items picked up from the kitchen, Ella put everything in the back and focused solely on the case. A quick call confirmed that Simmons hadn't passed either checkpoint, which meant that he was probably taking his time, making sure he wasn't being followed. She wondered briefly where Melvin Rainwater was right now, and what he was doing to cover his trail.

Rushing back north down the highway, she arrived at the turnoff to a tribal industry warehouse. As she pulled up, Ella released the officer who'd been faking the car problem, instructing him to return to the station and await her call for backup.

Making sure her unit was parked out of sight from the road, she hurried back on foot to the intersection of the highway and the secondary road. There she set up her mother's grocery cart, placing her jacket inside the empty paper bag to fill it up. Ella then waited, sitting down on the ground, and watching in the direction Simmons would have to take to approach. She'd be able to see headlights coming miles away.

Time passed slowly. Three or four sets of headlights had traveled south in her direction, but then had taken a turn west on Highway 64. With nothing to do until Simmons passed by, Ella let her thoughts wander.

Although her priority on this case had been clear from the start—she had to find Agent Thomas—she'd known in her heart that it would be a no-win situation for her and for the department. First, Agent Thomas had interrupted a Sing, and trying to rescue him would be seen by traditionalists as proof that the tribal police was nothing more than a servant of Anglo law.

Second, although the tribal police was doing its best to track down a missing Bureau agent, there would be a long list of feds who'd resent them for taking point on the investigation. Making that situation even worse was the fact that the tribal police had been the ones to discover that an FBI supervisor had gone bad. When that news hit the media, and it would, relations between the Bureau and the tribe would plummet.

An incoming call on her cell phone reminded her with a start that she'd forgotten to turn the ringer off. "We've got Jack Krause under surveillance, Ella," Sheriff Taylor said. "So far, so good. That big SUV is hard to miss, even at night. But he's on the reservation now. Our deputy called Sergeant Joseph Neskahi in for backup, and both officers are working the tail. Krause made a turn to the west on Shiprock's southwest side, and is now on Highway Sixty-four."

The news surprised her. "I saw some vehicles north of here making that turn just a few minutes ago. That must have been them." Ella knew the area west of Shiprock well. Over in the mountains west of Beclabito and south of Teec Nos Pos, Arizona, were more undocumented mines. But they hadn't searched there at all, figuring that Agent Thomas couldn't have made it that far on foot in the time between when he was last seen and his phone call to them.

Of course it was entirely possible that Agent Thomas had been transported in a vehicle along the back dirt roads before he'd escaped . . . or maybe Krause was trying to mislead them while Simmons went to the real target, south where most of the mines were located.

"I'm staying put," Ella said firmly. "But thanks for the heads-up. I'll stay in touch with Joe Neskahi from here on."

Ella hung up, and contacted Joe immediately. "I was about to call you, Ella," he said. "I'm about six miles east of Beclabito, off the side of the road, looking down on Krause, who's at the bottom of a hill. He pulled off the road, too, and is just sitting there in his SUV, as far as I can tell. He's either waiting for someone or it's possible he suspects he picked up a tail and has decided to cool his heels for a while. It's pretty empty out here, so he may have seen my headlights."

"What if he decides to double back?"

"No problem, I'm parked behind that old closed-down Texaco gas station. He won't spot me, I'm hidden by some trees. Wait a sec. Here comes another car—a sedan."

He paused, and another two minutes went by as Ella waited impatiently.

"It's Simmons," he said finally. "I can see him clearly through my binoculars. He's transferring some ropes into Krause's vehicle."

"Stay with them, just don't get seen. I'm on my way."

Ella ran back to her unit, carrying her mom's grocery cart in order to make good speed, then stepped out of the cumbersome clothes in a flash. A minute later, wearing her original clothes and her jacket, she was on her way north.

"They're on the move," Neskahi said, reporting. "Going south on a dirt road that leads up into the foothills."

"Hubert Eltsosie lives out that way, doesn't he?" Ella asked, turning west on Highway 64 as she sped through the western out-skirts of Shiprock. She was still over twenty miles away and needed to cover ground quickly.

"Yeah, I think so."

"I remember my mother saying that he's deaf as a stone, but even with that disability, he refused to move when the uranium mining companies came. There are old shafts everywhere you turn out there, but he still lives in his hogan with a dozen or so churro sheep. He has to buy or trade for hay for them, or watch them outside their pen because it's dangerous to let them graze unattended."

"I've met Hubert a few times," Joseph replied. "He's a real tra-ditionalist, even compared to your mother and the Plant Watchers. Some of the local officials tried to get him to move into Shiprock to the low-income housing. They even asked me to drop by during one of my patrols and try to convince him that he'd be safer there. I paid a visit, but he wouldn't budge. Not that I blame him. As he told me, he stays because that's where his memories are. If he moves he'll lose the only connection he's got left to his past."

Ella thought of her mother, then quickly focused back on the case. "We'll want to keep an eye on Eltsosie and any other locals who may be in the area so they don't show up at the wrong place at the wrong time," Ella said, quickly reaching for the cell phone's headset, and then loosening her hair so it would stop tugging at her scalp. "We'll have to use Simmons and Krause to lead us to where Agent Thomas is, but once that's done, we'll need to take them into custody ASAP. We can't allow them to reach Thomas. They might consider using him as a hostage rather than risk prison."

Leaving Neskahi to shadow the two Anglos, Ella continued her high-speed race west while she called Blalock.

"I've got a team of agents in my office now. We can be in the Beclabito area in less than fifteen minutes," Blalock said.

"Do it. I have a feeling this is the end of the road."

As soon as she ended the call, her cell phone rang again.

"I've got bad news," Teeny grumbled, "and I've put off calling you until now, hoping I'd catch up to him again."

"Rainwater?" The pieces were starting to make sense again.

"Yeah. That dirtbag gave me the slip. He left his house just before dark in what I'm sure he thought was a great disguise. His hair was slicked back nice, and he had a phony mustache and was wearing a business suit."

"And he had a briefcase?"

"How'd you know?"

"Lucky guess. What happened next?"

"It sounds like you already know, but, to make a long story short, I followed his blue-green Chevy Blazer to that west-side Farmington mall. He got out, walked a short distance in that lazy stride of his, then stopped, shifted gears, and stepped off like a businessman late for a big meeting. Unfortunately, I lost him when he slipped through a coffee shop."

Ella realized she'd never seen Melvin walk more than a few steps. He'd either been basically still or running every time she was around him up to now. She quickly explained what had happened with Betsy, then asked Teeny to keep searching for Melvin.

She was less than three minutes from Neskahi's position when she got a call from him. "They continued south after turning onto a dirt road just past highway marker twenty. Right now they've stopped about fifty yards east of Eltsosie's hogan behind some junipers. They're probably out of sight from his place, but I can see them clearly. There's just enough moonlight for me to use my binoculars. They're getting out that rope, it looks like. And a big lantern."

"Is Eltsosie home?"

"I think so," he said. "There's no vehicle, but his horse is in the corral and he's got a fire going. I can see a puff of smoke and an occasional glowing ember shoot up from the smoke hole in the center of the hogan roof."

Ella took the turnoff Neskahi had indicated, cut her lights, then proceeded slowly down the dirt road, hoping to avoid any noise that would alert Krause and Simmons. Spotting Neskahi's unit, she parked beside it and cut the engine. The two vehicles effectively blocked the road at the point where it crossed an arroyo. Even the big Expedition would be unable to deal with the eight-foot vertical drop off.

Reaching for the shotgun clipped to a bracket behind the seat, she slipped out of her vehicle silently and joined Neskahi, who was crouched low between two big clumps of brush, north of the hogan. The Anglo men he was watching were about sixty yards farther out, looking down at a big piece of corrugated aluminum on the ground. The ten-foot-long piece of metal had rocks placed atop it in several places, obviously intended to keep a strong wind from blowing the thin sheet away.

"They're arguing about something," Neskahi whispered, handing her his binoculars. "They're easier to see now that they've turned on one of those big electric lanterns. And we're going to be nearly impossible to spot because they've lost their night vision."

"I wonder why the old man's staying inside? He's deaf, not blind. Unless he's asleep, he couldn't help but notice that big lamp. It lights up the whole area."

"I was just going to get to that," Neskahi whispered. "After we spoke last time, Simmons went up to Eltsosie's hogan. Eltsosie came out, they talked—or gestured a lot—then Simmons wrote something on a piece of paper and showed it to the old man. After reading the note, the old man went back inside and hasn't been back out since. No telling what Simmons told him."

"That sheet metal on the ground. You wanna bet it's covering one of those mine openings?" Ella noticed the two men were re-moving the rocks now, tossing them to one side.

Hearing a faint sound behind them, Ella and Neskahi both whirled, aiming their weapons. Seeing Blalock and three other armed men approaching, crouched low, they both relaxed.

"Is that any way to greet the cavalry, Clah?" Blalock hissed with a grin.

"We're Indians. Get used to it." Neskahi snickered, putting his pistol back into the holster as FB-Eyes and three men carrying assault rifles and a shotgun joined them.

"I'll keep watch, Ella," Neskahi whispered.

"Here, take this," she said, handing Joseph her shotgun. He nodded and turned to watch Krause and Simmons.

As the four Bureau men gathered around her, Blalock intro-duced them quickly.

The agents—one a short, young-looking Hispanic man and the others seasoned-looking Anglos six feet or taller, nodded matter-of-factly with grim expressions. Ella figured that they were all probably pretty pissed off because Simmons, one of their own, had crossed the line and was maybe responsible for the in-jury and possible death of Andy Thomas.

"Where's Simmons?" Blalock asked next, his hand curled around a bolt-action Winchester with a nightscope.

Ella pursed her lips and gestured toward the SUV. Blalock motioned to his men, who formed a loose skirmish line behind cover, giving each other room. Blalock then moved in for a closer look with Ella. The rogue agent was tying a length of rope to the tow ring of the vehicle while Krause dragged away the corrugated metal, revealing a dark hole about five feet in diameter.

"When do you want to make a move?" Blalock whispered.

"We'll have to box them in, but I don't want to risk a cross-fire," Ella said. "Have two of your men go around to the west and use the hogan for cover. Joseph can circle left with your other man and take a position northeast of the perps. You and I will provide cover for them while they get into position. Once everyone is in place, I'll move in."

"I'll go with you."

Ella shook her head. "I can move faster and more silently. You cover my back with your rifle."

He scowled but nodded, knowing she was right.

"With everyone in place, the perps will have nowhere to run except south, away from their vehicle, and if they're stupid enough to draw weapons, we'll all have a clear field of fire. But we want to take them alive if we can."

Blalock nodded. "Less paperwork." Moving away, he spoke quickly to the others, then came up beside her again as she took over Neskahi's position. "I'll watch out for you. With this rifle I can hole a quarter at a hundred yards."

Krause and Simmons continued their preparations, arguing back and forth as, first, Simmons, then Krause looked down into the mine shaft, aiming a powerful flashlight. Finally Simmons took the rope and began to fasten it around his waist in a bowline.

After getting verification from Blalock, who could see the others were in position by using his night scope, Ella moved forward quietly. When she reached the outside of the illuminated zone, she slowed, staying low.

Simmons, at the edge of the mine shaft and about to step down, suddenly decided to take one more quick look around, and spotted her as she moved forward. Reaching down to his waist, he pulled out his pistol and snapped off two quick shots. One whizzed by her ear, the other over her head as she hit the dirt.

Ella fired back and, at nearly the same moment, heard a rifle crack from behind her. Simmons's body jerked and fell back, disappearing into the mine shaft. Krause, apparently unarmed, turned to run south. Bullets impacted on the ground around him, and Neskahi and one of the FBI agents yelled "Halt!" at the same time.

Krause flattened. "Don't shoot, don't shoot! I'm unarmed."

Ella got to her feet and ran forward, ignoring Krause. The rope leading from the SUV to Simmons was taut but she had no idea how far had Simmons had fallen into the mine shaft. She edged forward carefully, then circled around to the other side of the hole to look in. It was too dark to see much of anything, but somewhere below Simmons was groaning and cursing.

Pulling a flashlight from her jacket pocket, she held the light well away from her body and inched toward the edge, circling in case Simmons had somehow managed to hang on to his weapon and was aiming up. He was about fifteen feet down, hanging on to the rope with one hand, his body against the cut sandstone wall of the mine shaft, a blood-soaked hand pressed against his chest. The rope, which was still looped around his body, had saved him from falling any farther.

"Clah! What the hell is going on? You just shot a federal officer," Simmons challenged angrily. "Get me out of here and call an ambulance."

As Blalock and the other agents moved in, Krause suddenly scrambled to his feet and took off running, brushing past Ella before she could grab him.

"I'll get him. Don't shoot," Ella called out, then added, "Let Simmons dangle, and look for Andy Thomas down there."

Ella raced after the mortician, glad that she'd avoided looking directly into the lantern on the ground, so her eyes were at least as well adjusted to the darkness as Krause's. Alternating between watching the ground before her and the area ahead, she kept a steady pace, following the man from the sound of his heavy footsteps. Suddenly, as she went past a large boulder, she saw Krause ahead, frozen to the spot.

"Stay where you are!" she ordered, closing in on him.

"I'm not moving," he called back softly without even turning his head. "There're snakes everywhere. I just stepped on one, and there's another coiled in front of me."

NINETEEN
✖ ✖ ✖

Ella turned on her flashlight again and aimed the beam of light at the ground. "There's only one snake. You must have stepped on that branch instead." She studied the timber rattler coiled just in front of Krause, half sheltered by a low sandstone outcropping. The rattling of his tail reminded her of the sound made when shaking a hollow gourd half full of rice.

"Back away from it slowly," Ella instructed quietly. The snake was obviously out hunting for rodents, not undertakers, but Krause's presence had put the creature in defensive mode.

"Just shoot the damn thing!" he whispered harshly.

"It's not ready to strike—not yet, anyway," she said, noticing the swelled area several inches past the rattler's jaws. It had swallowed prey not long ago and was still sluggish. "Back up."

"Dammit, shoot it!" he hissed.

"No," she said flatly. Navajo ways taught that to kill a snake would drive away the life-giving rains. Snakes were linked to Thunders and the Lightning People. Although she wasn't superstitious, she found it repulsive to kill an animal or any other living creature unless there was no other choice. And, at the moment, Krause was in no immediate danger, despite what he believed. "What do you say we talk about Agent Thomas, *then* I rescue you."

"That's blackmail," he said.

"You're warning *me* not to break the law?" Ella said, and chuckled. "Just step back slowly and carefully. I'll cover you, if it'll make you happy."

Krause moved out of range, one step at a time. As soon as he cleared the snake's strike zone, Krause turned, and as he looked at her, his face contorted with anger. "Where's your gun? I thought you were protecting me."

"Oh, yeah." Ella brought out her pistol. "Turn around, I need to handcuff you."

Ella read him his rights as she patted him down. After verifying that he didn't have a weapon, she led him back toward the hogan. "If I were you, Krause, I'd start talking. When I left, Simmons was already starting to sing. He said he was working undercover to get evidence on you and Rainwater."

Privately, Ella wondered if Simmons was still hanging by the rope or if he was out and in a talkative mood. Somehow, she doubted that. But a bluff could be useful.

"I'm not saying another word without my attorney," Krause said flatly.

"You and Simmons know Andy Thomas is probably still alive, otherwise you wouldn't be here. I'm sure Andy will have a lot to say once we pull him up. But since Simmons is the only man outside my department who knew Thomas had phoned us, that fact will put his butt in a sling. Simmons has enough legal background to know how smart it is to make the first deal. Think a former FBI agent wants to go to prison—all by himself and unarmed? If he cuts a deal before you do, *you're* the one who's going to be screwed, that's a guarantee."

Ella knew there was a chance that Andy Thomas had died since his desperate phone call about three days ago. But Krause would be on the defensive and not likely to talk if he even suspected that he'd be facing murder charges. A softer approach was the most logical option.

"You said Simmons is blaming all this on me?" Krause asked, turning to look at her. He stumbled on a rock and nearly fell.

Ella nodded, then yawned as if slightly bored by the whole

232 × AIMÉE & DAVID THURLO

thing. "Watch your step." She aimed the flashlight in front of him so he could see a little better.

"This scam was *his* idea and if Simmons had pulled Thomas off our backs like he was supposed to none of this would have happened. When Simmons found out that Thomas was going after Rainwater, he came up with the idea of coldcocking Thomas, then hauling him away from the Navajos so we could work on him and find out what he knew. We were even wearing masks so Thomas couldn't make a positive ID. But things got fouled up. Thomas wasn't out cold. He was faking, waiting for a chance to get away. He grabbed his cell phone from where I'd set it after emptying his pockets, then dove out the door.

"We tried to track him, but there were open mine shafts everywhere around here. I almost fell into one of them myself. I went back to the SUV to get a flashlight, but when I returned, Simmons said he'd heard a yell, like someone falling."

"So you gave up the search?"

"No, we kept looking around for hours, but couldn't find a thing. When it started getting light outside, we saw the hogan and the old man. He'd come out to take care of his sheep, I guess, or else he heard us walking around. He had a rifle, so we decided to leave before he spotted us. But I'm telling you, *Simmons* jumped Thomas and clobbered him, not me. I'm not to blame for what happened to that FBI guy."

As they returned to the lighted area beside the mine shaft, Ella turned Krause over to one of Blalock's men. Seeing FB-Eyes standing beside the hole, aiming a flashlight down, she went to join him. "Simmons still down there?"

"No. I had my guys give him first aid, then haul him away to the hospital. He's lucky he's alive. He was wearing a vest, or my shot would have killed him for sure."

"The bullet from the rifle should have penetrated anyway. He must have been wearing body armor."

"More like body armament. My bullet hit the cylinder of a backup revolver he had in a shoulder holster. Gonna leave an imprint for sure." Blalock looked anxiously down at Neskahi who was climbing up the rope from inside the mine shaft.

"No Agent Thomas," Ella observed, seeing Neskahi alone and, as she glanced at Blalock, noted that he looked as discouraged as she felt.

They both took hold of the rope and pulled Neskahi up the rest of the way. "Is Thomas dead?" she asked, her voice taut.

Neskahi shook his head as they grabbed hold of him and helped the chunky officer to solid footing. "All I can tell you for sure is that he's not there now. But he *was* in there earlier today. The shaft goes straight down, then at the bottom angles off in a steep slope for another twenty feet before ending with a solid wall. Down there, out of sight from above, Thomas scratched the date and some names into the sandstone. I also found his cell phone. Someone stomped it into pieces. I was hoping to get a camera so I could go back down and take photos."

"You're sure he's not buried down there somewhere? A lot of these mines are unstable," Ella said, remembering her own experience in one. Even the memory left a bitter taste in her mouth.

"Nope, the ground is intact and there are footprints everywhere. And judging from the fact that I saw two different size and type shoes, somebody was down there with him. But even the climb up the lower slope to the bottom of the main shaft would be difficult without a rope. He didn't get out on his own, that's for sure."

Ella glanced at Blalock. "Maybe the old man knows more than he told Simmons," she said, gesturing toward Eltsosie's hogan.

"Sounds like it to me," Blalock nodded. "But you or Neskahi should interview him. I've got a feeling an old traditionalist would be more comfortable speaking his own language, or at least to another Navajo."

"I'll do it," Ella said, then motioned to Neskahi, who was examining some marks on the ground. "Joe, take a look around for any sign of Agent Thomas or any previous visitor, then start processing the aboveground site."

Bringing out her cell phone, she got Justine on the line and explained the situation. "I need you and Tache here with the crime-scene van, and bring climbing gear. Also, do you know any of the tribal mining engineers? We need someone who's very familiar with mines of this era."

"I'll call my uncle Ernie. He worked as a mining engineer in the late '60s. He's retired now, but he's sharp as a tack and knows his field."

"Get him here ASAP, then," Ella said.

"I'm going to the hospital to question Simmons," Blalock said as she hung up. "I've already made a call to Big Ed, and he said he'd meet me there. Are you going to follow after you talk to the man in the hogan, or will you be staying here with your people?"

"I'm staying. Simmons may or may not give us any answers that'll help us find Agent Thomas, but Eltsosie or the evidence may tell us what we need to know."

"You plan on searching the area?" Blalock asked. "If so, I can send my guys back within the hour."

"Hang on until I speak to the old man. If there's a chance Thomas is still around, I can use your people."

"If we get anything at my end, I'll let you know immediately," Blalock said.

"Thanks. Same here."

Neskahi came back to where she was standing. "No sign of any footprints that match those I saw down in the mine, except at this one spot." He pointed to the east side of the hole, away from the hogan. "I think you'll find what's there real interesting."

Ella walked over, and, using her flashlight, examined the marks. There were three sets of footprints and an indention at the rim of the mine opening that looked as if it had come from a rope.

"One person was using a rope here," Ella observed, "probably anchored to a vehicle, like Simmons did. Then there's this long, connected trail, like a person was being pulled or dragged. I also see a set of footprints I'm guessing belong to Eltsosie. They're small and look like they came from moccasins. Since they're superimposed over the other two, that tells us he was here last."

"That's the way I read this, too. A man hauled Thomas out, and carried or dragged him to a vehicle. Then Eltsosie came out to take a look," Neskahi said.

"So Thomas was rescued . . . but by whom, and what did they do with him?" Ella mused. "Looks like I need to talk to Hosteen Eltsosie," she said, using the Navajo word for "mister."

"It's odd that he still hasn't come out," Neskahi said thoughtfully.

"Seeing Anglos on our land is often not a good sign, particularly to someone like him," she reminded. "First, strangers disrupted his land when they came in with their mining equipment and pretty much did away with his chances to live a traditional life," she explained. "And we don't know if Simmons threatened to kill his animals or him if he didn't stay away. The words 'Trust me, I'm from the government' are normally enough to make most people run away screaming—and it's worse here on the Rez."

Ella saw him nodding as she walked away.

Ella skirted the mine shaft and came up in a direct line to the hogan so she could be seen. She knew Eltsosie had been watching. She'd seen the blanket doorway moving the few times she'd looked over. But no one had come out.

Fighting the temptation to simply walk up, she stopped, squatted down and studied the ground. Two sets of prints led to the entrance—one from new-looking shoes obviously belonging to Simmons. The other, close together, indicating small steps, came from soft-soled moccasins and were probably Eltsosie's.

Finally, an elderly man who must have been close to ninety came out, holding an ancient-looking thirty-thirty rifle. Though his face was weathered and lined deeply, his hand was steady and his eyes were clear. "What do you want?" he asked in a very loud voice.

Right to the point. She couldn't fault him for that. She held up her badge. "You haven't come out, sir, so I was curious. Are you all right?"

He held his hand cupped over one ear. "What?"

236 ✗ AIMÉE & DAVID THURLO

Ella drew closer, and shouted the question again.

"Yes, but the Anglo with the government badge said that there was a dead man in that old mine. He said he'd be getting the body out so I wanted to make sure I stayed away until it was gone," he shouted back, unaware of the loudness of his own voice.

She shook her head. "That wasn't true," she said, hoping to put him at ease. "But now I need to ask you a few questions."

Eltsosie nodded. "Come in." He gestured to the doorway. As soon as they went inside, he went clockwise to the south side as was proper and she to the north of the roundish interior of the hogan. A small lantern hanging from a wire attached to a ceiling log provided a cozy glow, though the smell of kerosene was a bit distracting.

Eltsosie walked over to a large plank shelf attached to one of the pine logs that comprised the walls and retrieved a hearing aid from atop an unopened can of sliced peaches.

Ella looked at him with raised eyebrows and the old man grinned as he inserted it in his ear.

"Sometimes I don't want to hear," he said, this time in a normal voice. "When I go to Shiprock, I make everyone shout, and they all hate it, except for the children and the really old Navajos. They just laugh. But I especially like to upset big shots like that Anglo with the gold badge. He thought I was stupid and didn't know English, so I had fun with that. When he started shouting his face turned as red as cactus fruit," he said, laughing.

Ella smiled, then heard a vehicle outside that she recognized from the engine noise. Justine and Ralph Tache had arrived. "So tell me. Have you seen anything unusual happening around here?"

"A few hours ago, after sunset, someone came up in a dark blue carry-all with a tribal Forest Service sign on the door. He parked out there in the area of that hole for about a half hour. I thought it was just one of those engineers who are trying to do something to get the mines sealed up. When he tied a rope to his bumper and climbed down, I quit watching and had supper."

"Did he take anything out of the mine?"

"I guess so, from all that's happened after he drove off."

"When the guy in the Forest Service vehicle left, did you go out and take a look around?"

"I sure did. He left his rope. It was still lying there next to the hole." He reached behind a pile of blankets on the ground and handed it to her. "I looked down into the mine shaft with a lantern, wondering if he'd left anything else behind, but all I saw were some footprints at the bottom. After that I carried that piece of roofing over to cover the hole so people from the tribe wouldn't file a complaint against me for having a hazard out here. But everyone sure seems to like that old mine now, don't they?"

"Thank you for telling me all this," Ella said. "One more thing. I know it may sound strange, but the man in the vehicle with the Forest Service sign—did you notice if he walked like an old man or a young man."

"If you ask me, he walked like one of the punks you see in town sometimes—a kid who walks like he has all the time in the world. You know what I mean?"

Ella nodded. "I think so. That's a big help, thank you."

"Can I keep the rope? It's perfectly good and the guy didn't want it."

"After the case is over, I'm sure no one would mind. But for now, it's evidence."

"That guy really wasn't working for the Forest Service, was he?"

Ella shook her head. The vehicle he'd described sounded like Melvin Rainwater's too, except for the Forest Service sign, but that wouldn't have been hard to fake. The fact that Thomas's phone had been destroyed also pointed to Rainwater, considering the line she'd given him about the tracking signal.

"Are you going to tell me what really happened here?"

"No, not now, but I'll come back as soon as I can."

He nodded once. "I'll hold you to that."

Ella joined Justine at the mine shaft a moment later. Seeing the line leading down into the shaft, Ella surmised Tache was already down at the bottom, taking photos. The floodlights below, powered by a portable generator, radiated outward from the black hole casting an unearthly light into the trees, and eerie shadows across the piñon and juniper forest.

"Anything new?" Ella asked her.

"Joe had it pegged. Agent Thomas was definitely down there at one point, and the evidence that he was removed from here by one person is right on the money, too. Tache took close-up photos of the three names that Thomas had scratched into the sandstone while he was trapped, along with the words 'dirty, SS fraud,' and 'Yellowhorse.' Thomas also scratched his own name and the date. There's one name on the list that has been rubbed out with a piece of metal, like a key or something, but from the length of it, I'd bet it's Rainwater's."

"Not a surprise. It just further confirms, in a backhanded way, that Melvin was here. Thomas was obviously trying to tell us about the social security scam in case he didn't survive. Let me guess, the two names still there are Simmons and Krause."

Justine nodded. "Bingo. There are some chemicals I can use to try and restore the missing name. Hopefully that'll work, because we'd have a heck of a time cutting out the rock face and bringing it to a lab. I also found a few hairs and drops of blood, so we'll have DNA evidence too."

"Keep working." Ella said, then stepping away, called Blalock. "I need your help. I believe I'm going to get a call very soon from Melvin Rainwater. I'm positive he snatched Agent Thomas before Simmons and Krause showed up. My guess is that he took the agent as leverage, hoping to cut a deal. Can you set up a trace?"

"Sure thing. I've been able to pull in some real handy state-of-the-art hardware Homeland Security has made available for field testing. Even with cell phones, we'll be able to get a fix inside sixty seconds. Uses satellite technology, GPS software, and maybe a little voodoo on the side. Much better than current Bureau issue."

"Great," she said with a chuckle. As Teeny had indicated, the story she'd concocted for Rainwater was turning out to be dead on. "Get busy, 'cause I expect he'll call as soon as he figures we've discovered that Agent Thomas was moved."

"On it now. If it's not up and running in fifteen, I'll call you."

"Will it kick in immediately, or do I have to let you know he's on the line?"

"You don't have to do a thing. Once it's set, the monitoring is automatic," Blalock said, then disconnected.

TWENTY

✖ ✖ ✖

Ella was helping Justine load up equipment thirty minutes later when her cell phone rang.

"You know who this is?" he asked.

Ella recognized Melvin's voice immediately. "You've been a busy boy, Melvin," she answered, "but did you know we can still read your name from the spot on the sandstone where you tried to scratch it off? The wonders of modern forensic science are amazing." Uncertain whether the trace was working already, she wanted to stall to make sure they'd get a fix. At the same time she was hoping to undermine whatever confidence Melvin had in his own bargaining position.

"Are you ready to deal? I've got something you want—the FBI agent—and you've got something I want—Betsy. I want her out of jail and a guarantee that we'll both avoid prosecution. Let's talk."

His words verified it. He'd seen Sheriff Taylor take Betsy into custody. "We already know that you removed Agent Thomas from the mine. But how do I know he's still alive?"

"You have to take my word for it. I rescued him, that's enough. But he might get lost again unless you act quickly."

"Sorry. I need proof he's alive and in your care before we cut a deal. And if he ends up dead not only will the deal be off, you'll also have every law enforcement officer, local and federal, out looking for you. Your life—as you know it—will cease to exist. You get what I'm saying?"

"Yeah? Well, talk fast. Thomas is running out of time."

"What's that supposed to mean?"

"Whatever you want to believe. It doesn't matter. Do we have a deal or not?"

"What do you want? Reduced sentence for testimony against Simmons and Krause? A window in your cell?"

"Immunity from all charges in exchange for delivering Thomas—for Betsy and me both. Otherwise I'm hanging up."

"I'm not the district attorney. I don't have the authority to grant something like that. I'll have to check this out and get back to you."

"You've got fifteen minutes. I'll call back."

"No, wait. Make it thirty. It's late now and I don't know the DA's private number. It'll take me at least one additional call to get it."

"I'll give you twenty. That's my final offer."

He hung up before Ella could say anything else. Without skipping a beat, Ella ran to her vehicle, waving good-bye to Justine. Once she was rolling, she switched to her headset so she could have both hands on the wheel, then called Blalock immediately. "Did you get his location?"

"Not exactly, but it's within a half-mile range of a particular cell tower in Shiprock, one on the east side and south of the highway."

Ella told him about the pen she'd had Justine rig up using the small microphone he'd loaned them a few months ago. "We can drive around that neighborhood and see if the equipment can pick up Melvin's voice. My guess is that he's kept the pen as a trophy."

"Good thought. What's the frequency?"

Ella told him, then added, "Where can we meet? We should work as a team when this goes down." She was back on the main highway again, making good time. Nobody was on the road this time of night and she could fly.

"How about the parking lot of the convenience store at the western junction of Sixty-four and Four-ninety-one? It's across town so Rainwater won't be likely to spot us."

Ella called Big Ed next, filled him in quickly, then with his permission called the district attorney. Time was running out, but after a three-minute delay, she finally got the sleepy counselor on the phone and explained what was going on.

"I'll agree to those terms only on two conditions. Agent Thomas must be found alive and healthy, and Mr. Rainwater's testimony has to be sufficient to convict the others of the charges filed. Miss Weaver is on her own."

"I'll pass that along. Thanks, Counselor."

By now, she was close to Shiprock, so Ella cut her speed to fifty. To her right stood the high school, and beyond, the convenience store where Blalock would be waiting.

Tires squealing, she braked, then pulled up next to a blue van and hopped out quickly. Three men were standing beside the Bureau vehicle, one of them Blalock, the other two, agents she'd seen earlier with FB-Eyes.

"When this goes down, *we'll* make the actual arrest," Blalock said as everyone scrambled inside the vehicle.

"Actually, that works just fine for us, too. No matter how you slice it, my department isn't going to get any brownie points for rescuing a man who interrupted a Sing. Better that the FBI should take point on that," Ella said.

"Glad we're on the same page." Blalock was seated in the backseat beside her, and gave her the once-over as the van hurried east across the bridge. "You look like hell, Ella. Had any sleep?"

"Yesterday, or maybe the day before. I'm okay."

"Running on adrenaline?"

"Coffee, actually. Got a cup?"

The younger agent in front on the passenger side handed her a foam cup with a plastic lid. "Here you go," he said, giving her a lopsided grin. "My name is Newberry. Ken Newberry."

"Bless you, Agent Newberry."

"Your chauffeur tonight will be Agent Martinez," Newberry added.

"Detective Clah." Martinez nodded.

"No need to get up, Agent Martinez," Ella joked, then took a sip of coffee.

Just then Ella's cell phone rang again, and she handed Blalock the cup so she could grab the device. Seeing the number register on the caller ID, Ella nodded to Blalock, who tapped the shoulder of the passenger up front. He put on a headphone set, then pointed back at Ella.

Signal given, she touched the button that made the connection. "Clah here."

"So tell me, does Agent Thomas get to go home today?" Melvin asked.

Ella ignored the implied threat. "The district attorney says you have your deal on two conditions. First, Agent Thomas must be turned over in good shape, and second, your testimony in court has to lead to the conviction of Simmons and Krause."

"And Betsy Weaver?"

"She's on her own."

"That's not good enough. Without Betsy, the deal is off. You have ten more minutes to convince the DA."

"Melvin, it's the best you're going to—"

Rainwater ended the call. Ella looked at Blalock as she took her coffee. "Did you get anything?"

"Newberry?" Blalock looked toward the passenger in the front seat.

Newberry was watching a small LED display on his lap. From where Ella was sitting, it looked like a street map of Shiprock. "We narrowed the area down by half, but still no exact location. There just wasn't enough time," the agent replied, looking at Blalock, then at her. "At least we know he's not in a moving vehicle."

"The transmitter inside that pen is our best chance of pinpointing his exact location now." Blalock reached behind the seat and brought out a hard plastic box with a small monitor and headphone set. He passed it up to Newberry, who set his other equipment aside for the moment.

As Ella watched, the young tech switched on the unit, then put on the headset and set it to the frequency she'd given Blalock earlier. Again she could see a small grid with street names.

Blalock looked toward Martinez. "Go ahead and enter the neighborhood. Everyone needs to keep a sharp eye out for Rainwater's vehicle or anyone watching out their window like they're paranoid."

Less than two minutes later, Newberry looked up again. "I've got something," he said, then switched on a speaker so they could all hear.

Melvin Rainwater's voice came through clearly a second later. "Andy, you still with me?"

There was a muffled sound.

"I'll take that as a yes, Red. Hey, your friends are still tossing a coin, trying to decide if they really want you back. Looks like it's going to be close. You hang in there, okay? I'll be right back." Melvin chuckled, then there was the sound of a door closing.

Ella watched through the gap between the seats as Newberry studied the screen. There was a red dot in the center of the display now, and a green dot, which was moving and getting closer to the red dot. Ella assumed the green spot represented their van, or more precisely, the receiver the tech was holding.

"It's got to be right ahead." Newberry looked up, then pointed out the window to his left as they passed a stucco house with a single light on in one of the rooms. "In there."

"And that's his vehicle," Ella pointed out the Chevy in the driveway. The phony tribal Forest Service sticker was still attached to the door.

On Blalock's instructions, they circled the block, checking out the layout, then parked one street over, more or less even with the house where Rainwater was keeping his hostage. All the homes, four to a block with large backyards separated by wire fences, were dark except for a few porch lights. No dogs were barking and everything was quiet.

Blalock handed Ella a ballistic vest—all the agents were wearing them already. Nodding silently, she took it and studied the taut expressions on the faces of the three agents with her in the van.

To the two young agents Blalock had brought in, she guessed that this was a welcome opportunity to go to the aid of one of their own. But to Blalock, it was much more than that. This was one way of dealing with his guilt. Deep down he'd known that Agent Thomas hadn't been prepared to handle a case on the Rez, but he'd still allowed it to happen.

"When you've been with the Bureau as long as I have, nothing surprises you anymore," Blalock told Ella as he picked up a shotgun and checked the magazine. "But this took me completely off guard. I figured the kid would get himself into a scrape or two, like I did when I first came to the Rez, but I never expected a complete disaster."

"We'll set things right soon enough," Ella said, totally focused on the job now.

"Agent Martinez," Blalock told their driver, "make sure the paramedics are available and on stand-by."

Martinez nodded and picked up his cell phone.

Ella adjusted her vest. "You're calling it, Agent Blalock. What now?"

Blalock brought out a flash-bang grenade, inspected it for a moment, then stuffed it back into his pocket. "Martinez, you and Newberry cover the rear. Clah and I will take the front. When everyone's in place, I'll identify us, and toss the flash-bang into the house via the door or the window."

Everyone nodded.

"If Rainwater is armed and makes a move to resist, take him out, but don't risk shooting the hostage." Blalock was looking at his own people now. He and Ella had worked together enough that they trusted each other's reactions and instincts without question.

Martinez and Newberry started out first, circling together, sticking to the street until they could see the back of the target house. Once they disappeared from view down the alley, Ella and

Blalock moved in from the front. There were no trees, just low clumps of weeds and native grasses, but the night was their ally. With the moon hiding behind the clouds and no streetlights, the darkness seemed like a yawning void that shrouded them as they made their advance.

They reached the front door unimpeded, then Blalock tested the screen door. It was unlatched and moved freely. He took a look at the entry door next. Ella noted that it was cheap laminate, probably hollow core and easily defeated.

Looking back, he nodded to Ella, who was doing her best to watch the windows and the corners of the house at the same time. Then he brought out the flash-bang and pulled the pin. "FBI!" he shouted, kicking the door open and tossing in the grenade. They both turned their heads away to avoid being blinded.

The building shook from the blast, and the flash illuminated the entire yard like daylight for just a second. Blalock went in an instant later, followed by Ella.

It was dark inside, the flash-bang must have shattered a bulb, but they could see well enough to find Rainwater. He was lying on the floor moaning, his hands over his ears. A pump shotgun was on the carpet three feet away.

Blalock pointed his weapon at Rainwater, at the same time shoving Rainwater's shotgun away with his boot. "Find a light, Ella."

Ella turned, felt around the door trim, and located the switch. An overhead fixture came on.

"Clear!" Blalock yelled. A few seconds later they heard the back door being forced open and a light came on in the kitchen to their right.

"Clear!" Newberry and Martinez yelled almost together, then they entered the room.

"Don't shoot," Rainwater yelled, trying to get to his knees, his arms raised over his head.

Ella kept her weapon trained on Melvin as Blalock applied the cuffs, none too gently, then removed the pen/transmitter from Rainwater's shirt pocket. "Where's Agent Thomas?" he demanded.

"Find him yourself," Rainwater spat out.

"You're out of options, Melvin," Ella said quietly, stepping up close to their sullen prisoner. "Help us out and I can mention it to the DA. It might get you a better cell."

"He's in the hall closet," Melvin said dejectedly, gesturing with a tilt of his head.

Hearing Melvin, Blalock strode to the closet Melvin had indicated and jerked open the door. A skinned-up young man with short red hair and filthy clothes was curled up in the corner, blindfolded and gagged and tied hand to foot with a length of nylon rope.

"Agent Thomas," Blalock said softly, "you're safe. Just don't move until I check you over for injuries."

As soon as Blalock took off his blindfold and gag, Thomas began to cough. Martinez, who'd been watching, went to the kitchen, returned with a glass of water, and held it to his mouth.

"Sip it carefully," Blalock said, noting the young man's parched lips as he cut the ropes binding him. Thomas's arm had apparently been broken. It lay limply against his body, swollen between the wrist and elbow.

Thomas reached for the glass with his good hand and finished drinking. "My arm . . ."

"I see it," Blalock said. "We'll have the EMTs here soon."

Ella looked over at Agent Martinez and noted that he was calling the paramedics.

"Did you catch Agent Simmons? He's in this up to his ass. He thinks he destroyed all my files, but I have backups of everything," Thomas managed, his voice a little less raspy now. "I had them—Krause, that Weaver woman at county records, and Rainwater. He was even stealing an old lady's mail because she'd figured out she was being ripped off. All I needed was a little more time to put everything together—and a break. That's why I decided to go for it and stake out Melvin's Sing."

Thomas shifted and groaned but continued, his voice gaining strength. "That's when it really hit the fan. Two Navajos with a rifle chased me off before I could talk to Rainwater. Then Simmons showed up. Before I realized Rainwater had already tipped him off, he reamed me out for antagonizing the tribe, then ordered me into my unit. When I turned my back, the bastard coldcocked me."

"That supports everything we've gathered so far. Just keep it fresh in your mind and we'll talk about it later," Blalock said, stepping aside for the paramedics, who'd made the trip in just a few minutes.

Blalock stood with Ella near the door. "He has a badly fractured arm, I think, but Andy's in surprisingly good shape considering all he's been through." He paused, then added, "But once this is over, he and I are going to have a *long* talk about what never to do on the Rez."

Ella chuckled. "Somehow I don't think that'll be necessary. He's learned his lesson the hard way." Hearing a commotion outside, Ella moved to the door and saw Rainwater struggling and yelling at Newberry and Martinez as they hauled him toward the street. His swagger was gone, she noticed.

Ella shook her head. "Rainwater might have gotten away with a lot more if he'd just left Agent Thomas down in that mine shaft. I wonder if Melvin grabbed Thomas for himself or just to take a little pressure off Betsy? I'm certain now that he was the second man coming to her apartment, not Krause. Judging from his efforts to get Betsy's charges reduced, they're obviously in love."

"How sweet."

"Gee, Blalock, you're a real cynic. You know that?"

"I've been called *much* worse, Clah." He looked through the open doorway at Thomas, who was being helped into the ambulance. "I better ride with the kid to the hospital and get his statement before they zone him out with painkillers. Then I'll meet you back at your station."

Ella glanced at her watch. It was well past midnight now, but she wasn't tired anymore. "I love it when all the pieces of the puzzle come together. You can almost feel it in the air when harmony has been restored."

"It's one heckuva rush, even for an old *bilagáana* like me."

Ella watched the senior agent go. Despite Blalock's many

years on the Rez she was sure that he still didn't really get the whole concept of harmony and balance. But that was okay. Accepting the differences between them was also part of walking in beauty.

TWENTY-ONE
—— ✖ ✖ ✖ ——

Big Ed stood beside Ella, watching through the one-way glass into the interrogation room as Agent Blalock questioned Betsy Weaver. They were at the city jail in Farmington, out of Navajo jurisdiction, but their presence had been required because of the on-reservation investigation and arrests made.

"You were right about the woman. She won't even acknowledge Rainwater," Big Ed said. "Not that it matters much. The feds will still get Melvin for kidnapping a federal officer. The DA said Melvin's attorney is trying to see if he can try Rainwater on the Rez for the other charges. But considering what Melvin did for a living and the scam he was part of, I doubt he'll get any sympathy from the Dineh. The tribal newspaper will show him no mercy, that's for sure."

"At least Betsy is testifying against Simmons and Krause," Ella answered. "The feds really want to nail them, and her testimony will go a long ways with a jury, especially because she knows all the names and dates. She and Melvin kept good records, obviously to prevent Simmons from turning on them later if the authorities got close. The briefcase found in Rainwater's vehicle ended up being a gold mine, according to Blalock."

"This case has really taken a high toll on everyone—and I'm not just talking lack of sleep. Compromises had to be made and some of us came dangerously close to crossing the line," he said slowly.

Ella looked over at Big Ed and wondered if he knew or suspected that she'd been in Krause's garage. "We all did what was necessary to save a life, Chief. Sometimes in a crisis there's just not enough time to make sure it's all by the book."

Big Ed gave her a long searching look but said nothing. He didn't have to, Ella already knew what he was thinking. The rules of police work and their adherence to them was what defined them as law-enforcement officers. But, all things considered, she had no regrets.

"I've left the preliminary paperwork on your desk, boss, but I'm beat. If you don't need me anymore, I think I'll go home and catch up on my sleep."

"Go ahead. Our part's pretty much done. This is now the FBI's mess."

Ella looked back through the glass one more time at Blalock, who was still pressing Betsy Weaver for every piece of incriminating evidence he could get on Simmons. Ella knew FB-Eyes was proud of the gold badge he carried and of the Bureau itself. He saw what his fellow agent had done as the ultimate betrayal, and she agreed wholeheartedly with that assessment. She'd experienced those feelings herself several years ago with the tribal police leadership—before Big Ed—and knew exactly how he felt.

Ella walked down the hall and saw Justine coming out of a meeting with other federal officers. Their department had signed over all the evidence that had been legally collected on the Rez during their search for Andy Thomas.

Seeing Ella, Justine smiled. "You look as tired as I feel."

"My body's tired—exhausted, really—but my mind's still wide awake. Sometimes after a case like this one it's hard for me to wind down. But when it finally hits me, I'll be out like a light," she said.

"I've got a routine. I go home, fix myself a hot cup of herbal tea, strip down to a T-shirt, and put on my favorite slippers. That usually does it for me. What about you?"

"The usual. I'll tiptoe into the house and try not to wake anyone," she said with a wry smile. "Then I'll sneak into my daughter's room and sit with her while she sleeps. When I look at Dawn, the love I feel for her just fills me to bursting. She's all the good things we fight for. People do all kinds of things for money, but to little kids like her, it's just green paper. Being with Dawn puts everything back into perspective for me after working a tough case and makes me feel less . . . dirty."

Justine nodded slowly. "It's like what my dad told me when I said I wanted to join the department. 'If you play in the ditch all day, you can't expect to come out smelling like a rose.'"

"True," Ella admitted quietly. "But someone has to keep the ditches clean so that the good water can fill the fields and help crops grow."

Justine smiled. "That's pretty close to what I said. Besides, it can be fun to play in the mud sometimes."

Ella laughed. "See you tomorrow . . . well, in a few hours, I guess. It won't be long till the sun comes up again."

On the dark, lonely drive home, with the adrenaline rush starting to settle, Ella's thoughts drifted. Despite all the drawbacks, police work could be addictive, and somewhere along the way, being a detective had become a vital part of her. She couldn't imagine doing anything else for a living.

Suddenly remembering that Dawn was still at Kevin's, she decided to go there first instead. Dawn would be asleep, and Kevin too, but Ella had a key and could let herself in. Kevin wouldn't mind if she peeked in on her daughter. Then again, maybe she *should* call first and let him know she was coming. Sneaking in quietly was a bad idea. He had a gun and was very protective, as was she, after their daughter had nearly been kidnapped a few years ago.

Ella arrived at Kevin's modern house twenty minutes later, and parked beside his new pickup. She knocked twice, then unlocked the door and stepped inside. A night-light in a wall plug, placed there for Dawn, no doubt, enabled her to see well enough to locate Dawn and Kevin immediately.

Her daughter was sleeping peacefully on the sofa bed, a tiny smile on her face. The raggedy stuffed horse she claimed not to play with anymore was underneath the covers too, tucked tightly in her arms. Of course it was only a substitute for Wind. If Dawn could have brought her pony with her she would have, in an instant.

Kevin, in a T-shirt and slacks, was obviously half-asleep, sitting in a big leather recliner a few feet away from where their daughter was sleeping. He'd watched Ella come in, and smiled but didn't speak.

Ella sat down on the edge of the sofa bed and brushed Dawn's soft black hair away from her face and kissed her forehead gently. Her child was, at times, her only point of sanity in an otherwise crazy world.

Ella looked over at Kevin, who nodded, then closed his eyes and stretched out on the recliner as she lay down beside her daughter. Dawn instinctively snuggled up against her, still fast asleep. Feeling her daughter's strong and steady heartbeat against her, Ella closed her eyes and drifted away.